Vanishing DREAMS

By Nicole Edwards

The Alluring Indulgence Series
Kaleb
Zane
Travis
Holidays with the Walker Brothers
Ethan
Braydon
Sawyer
Brendon

The Austin Arrows Series
Rush
Kaufman

The Bad Boys of Sports Series
Bad Reputation
Bad Business

The Caine Cousins Series
Hard to Hold
Hard to Handle

The Club Destiny Series
Conviction
Temptation
Addicted
Seduction
Infatuation
Captivated
Devotion
Perception
Entrusted
Adored
Distraction

The Coyote Ridge Series
Curtis
Jared

The Dead Heat Ranch Series
Boots Optional
Betting on Grace
Overnight Love

By Nicole Edwards (cont.)

The Devil's Bend Series

Chasing Dreams
Vanishing Dreams

The Devil's Playground Series

Without Regret
Without Restraint

The Office Intrigue Series

Office Intrigue
Intrigued Out of the Office
Their Rebellious Submissive

The Pier 70 Series

Reckless
Fearless
Speechless
Harmless

The Sniper 1 Security Series

Wait for Morning
Never Say Never
Tomorrow's Too Late

The Southern Boy Mafia Series

Beautifully Brutal
Beautifully Loyal

Standalone Novels

A Million Tiny Pieces
Inked on Paper

Writing as Timberlyn Scott

Unhinged
Unraveling
Chaos

Naughty Holiday Editions

2015
2016

Vanishing DREAMS

DEVIL'S BEND
Book 2

NICOLE EDWARDS

Nicole Edwards Limited
PO Box 806
Hutto, Texas 78634
www.NicoleEdwardsLimited.com

VANISHING DREAMS – A Devil's Bend novel is a work of fiction. Names, characters, businesses, places, events and incidents either are the products of the author's imagination or used in a fictitious manner. Any resemblance to actual persons, living or dead, business establishments, events, or locales is entirely coincidental.

Cover Image: ©Sergejs Rahunoks | 123rf.com

Cover Design: © Nicole Edwards Limited
Editing: Blue Otter Editing | www.BlueOtterEditing.com

ISBN (ebook): 978-1-939786-34-0
ISBN (print): 978-1-939786-29-6

Romance
Mature Audiences

DEDICATION

Chancy, Katie and Tonya.
This one is for you.

PROLOGUE

October

Sitting on Cooper Krenshaw's back porch, his girl by his side, Dalton Calhoun wasn't sure anything could knock him from his perch on top of the world. This beat the best nights up on that stage that he loved so much. And that was saying something.

Not that he would call Katie *his girl* to her face. Knowing her, she'd adamantly deny anything serious between them.

Dalton would argue right back, but that was a moot point.

"Topless, I'm not kiddin'," Eric said with a chuckle.

"Are you serious? What'd Tessa do?" Dalton asked the Rusty Nail's bartender, who had befriended him in recent weeks.

"Oh, you know Tessa," Eric said facetiously. "She was a good sport."

Izzy's sweet full-belly laugh echoed out into the twilight. "Right. Tessa. Good sport. Yeah, if you consider throwing an apron at the woman before hustling her out of the bar a good sport."

"Where was Jack?" Dalton asked, referring to Tessa's younger brother who helped manage The Rusty Nail, the small town bar in Devil's Bend that was owned by Tessa herself.

"He pretended not to notice," Eric added, grinning. "But yeah, Tessa tossed the woman out of the bar and told her not to come back."

"All because of Coop, huh?" Dalton glanced over at his good friend. The man who'd wandered from Tennessee to Texas on a whim and found himself caught up in the middle of what appeared to be a rocky little love fest.

"Don't act like you don't have women tossin' their panties at you on a nightly basis," Izzy accused Dalton directly.

"I don't know what you're talkin' 'bout, ma'am," Dalton said deadpan.

The small group erupted in a fit of laughter.

There was no telling what would come flying at him on the nights he took the stage. He'd pretty much seen it all.

When Dalton's good buddy, Coop, a fellow country musician, had mentioned they'd be having an impromptu cookout at his house in the small town he recently moved to, Dalton hadn't been all that surprised. Even back in Nashville, Cooper was always putting together spur-of-the-moment meals just so he could get his friends together. And it looked like Coop had acquired a close little group of friends in the short time he'd been in town.

Since Dalton was staying in Coop's guest room, he had inquired as to whether he could bring someone, namely the woman sitting beside him – Katie Clarren, a waitress at The Rusty Nail, who, from what Dalton could tell, Tessa considered a friend. As it would seem, Cooper wasn't the only one who was a little smitten over a woman. However, Dalton wasn't looking to announce that to anyone at the moment. Despite his lack of interest in a serious relationship, he'd found himself a little hung up on the black-haired beauty who'd caught his eye almost instantly.

Luckily for him, Katie had agreed to join him at tonight's little soiree with relatively minimal coaxing, which these days was somewhat iffy as to whether she was going to want to hang out. The woman seemed to be busy all the time, or at least that was the excuse she gave him whenever he tried to get her to go out with him.

But not tonight.

Tonight they were sitting on Cooper's back porch, watching Tessa's huskies Havoc and Harmony chase one another around the yard, yapping and growling as they fought over a tennis ball. The sun had recently settled beyond the horizon and a string of white lights hanging haphazardly from one edge of the patio cover offered enough light to see by, but not too much to attract the bugs. At least not yet.

Not that Dalton would've noticed. He was too busy trying to keep from staring at Katie in that little white sundress that accentuated all of her luscious curves along with the golden gleam of her tan skin. The woman stole his breath without even trying and it took a tremendous amount of self-control to keep from making his intense interest known.

Dinner was finished and partially cleaned up, and now the beer was flowing, as was the conversation. Along with his notorious bar stories, Eric Lancaster, one of Tessa's friends since childhood, was telling them about growing up in the small town of Devil's Bend, Texas.

Every now and then Katie would chime in; her soft, reserved voice slid right along Dalton's much too sensitive skin, making his hair prickle with awareness. Much to his dismay, Katie wasn't speaking nearly as much as Dalton would've preferred. But damn he loved to listen to her talk. Although she seemed engrossed in the conversation, she wasn't making a lot of reference to herself, which was something Dalton had grown accustomed to since the very first time she agreed to go out with him. But he was incredibly curious about what made the woman tick, yet he never seemed to get much out of her.

His attention turned to Tessa, who was sitting on one of the steps that led down to the yard while everyone else sat up on the porch behind her. She seemed a little retrospective at the moment, and Dalton wondered what she was thinking about. Whatever it was, she clearly felt as though she needed to keep her distance because of it.

Cooper, on the other hand, was brimming with pride, not to mention, slightly oblivious to Tessa's distance-keeping maneuver. Regardless, it was good to see the man so damned happy these days. What with all the shit he'd endured recently with his crazy-fuck of a manager, Marcus Evergreen, Dalton was hoping the guy would get a moment's peace. Took running off to Texas to find it, but from the looks of it, Cooper had found it.

Dalton thought Texas looked good on Cooper. So much so, that he was personally thinking about making the move as well. When Cooper had presented his plan of opening up an equestrian center in the backwoods town, Dalton had been on board almost from the beginning. Now that he was here, he couldn't see any reason not to follow through with it.

It wasn't that his music career wasn't in full swing, but this was the sort of peace he had been searching for, one he couldn't seem to find in the bright lights of the stage. The sweet smell of the country was the yin to the country music yang, something that would balance him and offer him a little downtime from all the chaos.

Speaking of chaos, Dalton knew there were three news vans sitting out front; probably full of reporters chomping at the bit to figure out just what Cooper was doing down here. Dalton knew it hadn't helped when he'd stepped into the picture, drawing even more attention to the situation, and because of that, he'd kept his mouth shut. They damn sure weren't getting any juicy details from him. What Cooper did with his life was his own business. On a good day, Dalton avoided them like the plague and in the event he was cornered by one of them, he merely graced them with a smile and a nod. No comment, no sir.

This was the life; that was for damned sure.

"How long have you two been married?" Dalton asked Eric and Izzy when there was a lag in Eric's latest story.

"Almost six years," Eric answered easily. "We got married a few months after Tessa and… Oomph!"

Izzy's well-placed elbow to Eric's ribs effectively shut the man up, but Dalton wanted to know just where he had been going with that statement. Before he could inquire, or before Izzy could offer an apology, Tessa spoke up.

"It's ok, Izzy," Tessa called out, her focus still on the two dogs trampling across the yard.

"Sorry, Tess," Eric said, his tone chock full of sincerity.

Tessa seemed to wave him off before she said, "Eric and Izzy got married two months after Richie and I did. The only reason they waited was because high maintenance over there insisted on this huge wedding."

Dalton laughed, looking over at Izzy who was blushing profusely. *Richie?* As he watched the pretty young woman turn beet red, he attempted to tie the pieces of Tessa's statement together. It took him a second, but then he remembered. Katie had mentioned Richie, Tessa's late husband. The guy was killed in the line of duty from what he recalled.

"So not true," Izzy stated a little defensively, her wide eyes turning to her husband. "He's the one who wanted a big wedding."

"Okay, so that was mostly true," Tessa added with a laugh.

"Do you guys have kids?" Dalton asked, watching the two of them as they sat side by side, their arms and knees touching, almost as though they couldn't stand to be too far away from one another. Clearly in love.

Dalton admired the pair. At thirty-one, he'd hit a point in his life when he wished he could find what they had; although he truly wasn't quite to that permanent, happily ever after place just yet. But he was getting there. The thought had him glancing sideways at Katie. She was smiling, but she didn't seem all that engaged in the conversation.

"No kids. Not yet. We've been talking about it though."

Dalton saw Tessa flinch, and the way she jerked her head back, looking up at Izzy had probably hurt. Her mouth opened, then closed, and if he wasn't mistaken, the maneuver had effectively cut off something she had wanted to say before she settled with, "It's about time. I've wondered if you two would ever get with the program."

That clearly didn't sound like what she'd originally intended to say, at least not based on her facial expression.

Dalton continued to watch the interaction, noticing the way Izzy's face fell. There was a story there; even he could figure that out. "Do you want to try to have kids again?" Dalton asked, the inquiry directed at Tessa this time.

A slight elbow from Katie was a subtle hint that he'd gone and done it now. Aww, hell. That clearly wasn't the right question to ask and Dalton felt as though he'd been punched in the gut the moment Tessa pushed to her feet and took off around the side of the house, disappearing from sight.

"Shit, man, I'm…" He was sorry, but right then, the man he was trying to apologize to obviously wasn't interested in hearing it because Cooper was on his feet and flying down the stairs in quick pursuit of Tessa.

Way to go, Calhoun!

CHAPTER ONE

Two months later

Katie Clarren was walking on a cloud, the big, puffy white kind that dotted a brilliant blue sky on a beautiful summer day. Or at least that's what it felt like as she floated across the rustic, hardwood floors in what had become her favorite bar, taking drink orders and chatting it up with the customers. They were unusually busy tonight, but she knew who to thank for that.

Unlike her mood, the weather outside was dreary, the sky a dull gray, and the dark, heavy clouds were threatening to open up at any time. But that hadn't stopped anyone from coming out to The Rusty Nail, even on a Monday night. They were here to see *him* and she certainly couldn't blame them.

Up on stage, Dalton Calhoun was gearing up to play for the small gathering, laughing with a group crowded by the edge of the stage while he set up, his wondrous smile making him even that much more attractive. And that was saying something. The way he moved reflected his excitement and stirred the energy in the room, and yes, even Katie was infused with it. Yeah, the guy certainly loved to entertain a crowd which was a good thing considering he was so freaking good at it.

Dalton was exactly as he appeared on television and in magazines, his picture probably hanging on the walls of teenage girl's rooms everywhere. Having gotten to know him on another level, Katie had learned early on that there wasn't anything fake about him. He was a country music phenom, one who had garnered the attention of women of every age. From his sexy dark hair usually hidden by his signature, black Stetson, to his drool-worthy ass, there was no question as to why everyone loved him. Including her.

However, Katie's love was a little deeper than theirs was. Or at least she liked to think so.

Not only was she drawn to all six foot two inches of him, and his intense, dark brown eyes, Katie had managed to establish a friendship with the man known for his quick smile and charming drawl. Aside from a few make out sessions, it hadn't gone much farther than that. Yet.

And each night that she watched him up on that stage was a little different from the last time Katie had watched him play. He was more at ease with every performance, befriending the locals and becoming an integrated part of the town. However, she still recalled the first night she saw him walk into The Rusty Nail. Not to sound like a bad cliché, but that night had been the night that had changed her life.

Well, maybe not entirely, but from the moment she'd been introduced to Dalton by an incredibly enthusiastic Izzy, Katie had been pretty certain the world had taken on an entirely different hue, a little brighter than before he arrived in their small town.

As though Cooper Krenshaw hadn't ratcheted up the pulse of their tiny little town enough, they went and added Dalton Calhoun to the mix, and Devil's Bend was now at risk for high blood pressure.

The testosterone had hit astronomical levels that first night, and Katie was pretty sure it had only intensified ever since. Dalton was sex personified, all wrapped up in an extremely attractive, good ol' boy package. And when he was up on that stage, all eyes went to him.

Including hers.

Not that she wanted him to know that, which was why she tried to play it cool. Katie would admit that she was good at quite a few things, but remaining calm and collected around Dalton wasn't one of them. She hoped she was succeeding somewhat because having to turn him down time and again for dates was getting a little troublesome. Mostly, because she didn't *want* to turn him down.

If Katie had her way, she would've long ago pursued something with Dalton. Perhaps a relationship, even something exclusive. If she hadn't misread Dalton's intentions, then it was safe to say that was the direction he'd been leading them for the last couple of months.

Unfortunately, her current life wasn't at the appropriate stage for a relationship with the likes of Dalton Calhoun, or anyone for that matter. She had too much going on to entertain the idea of having a man in her life, no matter how much she enjoyed Dalton's company. And that was why she had pushed back on him so much, limiting their time together as often as she could. Sure, they'd gone out a few times, but she'd insisted that they kept things on a more platonic level. Not that she'd succeeded because when Dalton kissed her, all good intentions took a flying leap. The only way she managed to keep her distance was by insisting she was too busy to date. Which wasn't exactly untrue. Between school and two part time jobs, along with all of her personal responsibilities, Katie rarely found time to sleep, much less date.

Not that she was convincing Dalton of that.

Most of the time he managed to corner her at closing time, inviting her to breakfast, sometimes alone, other times with Tessa and Cooper. Katie found that she enjoyed her time with him, but she knew that it wasn't going to last. It couldn't. However, if she wasn't careful, she'd find herself actually dating the man, and that wasn't in her plan. Not at the moment anyway.

It was the nights he waited for her *after* the bar closed that were the hardest times to try to wrangle out of a commitment because he was offering to take her to breakfast and by that time of the morning, she was usually starving. Dalton was rather persuasive, and she found it difficult to refuse the man, especially when he turned those sexy, chocolate brown eyes on her.

It sure beat going home to her tiny apartment and tiptoeing around to keep from making any noise so that she didn't wake her roommate, who was a shockingly light sleeper. In order to do that, she usually had to avoid food altogether.

"Howdy, y'all! How's it hangin'?" Dalton's smile-laced voice echoed through the speakers in the ceiling, riling up the crowd who was still filing in through the front door, bringing with them the chilly evening air.

A round of whistles and cheers erupted, making Katie smile in response to his obvious good mood. She had to admit, it was quite heady the enthusiasm that Dalton inspired in the people he came into contact with. Then again, being female and all, Katie couldn't deny her intense attraction to the dark haired, dark eyed cowboy. When he smiled, there was a small dimple that formed in his left cheek, giving his ruggedly handsome face a somewhat boyish look. But his smile... his smile was potent enough to make her limbs turn to jelly.

"What're y'all doin' tonight?" Dalton asked casually. "Like now, I mean. Not later. We'll talk about that in a minute."

Katie tried to listen to the crowd's fervent response. Not that any of the answers were distinguishable because it was as though everyone in the bar spoke up at the same time, vying for an opportunity to chat with the handsome superstar.

Dalton's sexy, rough chuckle vibrated through the speakers.

"Alrighty then," Dalton crooned. "How 'bout we get this party started? What d'ya say? Then we'll chat s'more."

Another ruckus burst within the thin walls of The Rusty Nail as Katie eased her way back to the bar. Within seconds, Dalton's lyrical voice was resonating through the place, the steady strum of his guitar competing with the thunderous boom of his silky drawl.

"Whatcha got for me?" Eric asked when Katie approached the far side of the bar.

She pulled out her notepad and listed off the orders. "Two Buds, a shot of Cuervo, and a glass of white wine."

Eric's nose scrunched at the mention of wine as usual, or maybe it was the mention of tequila, she didn't know. Either way, he started working with the skill and precision of an experienced bartender as he moved about getting the order ready. While she waited, Katie took a moment to sneak a peek at Dalton up on stage.

Damn.

That's the only word that came to mind as she watched him move around that stage, leaning forward and then back, nodding and grinning at the crowd gathered on the small dance floor. He was energy and light, never sitting still, and most importantly, always smiling.

What it came down to was the fact that she loved watching him.

Sometimes she wondered whether it was that air of celebrity that made her knees weak, but other times Katie got the sense it was something much more than that. It was the whole package. It was hard to describe the way he made her feel just by being in the same room. Kind of like trying to wrangle the moon, an impossible feat, but one that still seemed attainable.

Of course, there was that glimmer of heat she noticed in his eyes every time he looked at her and that only made her want to accomplish the impossible at every turn. Sometimes she thought it was surreal to have that sort of intensity turned on her, but for the life of her, she couldn't find it in herself to dislike the feeling.

When the song came to an end, the crowd went crazy, hooting and hollering their approval. Katie offered a round of applause as she watched Dalton, secretly wishing he'd send a glance her way.

Yeah, well, okay. Holy crap.

Dalton looked right at her from across the room, and the wink he offered made her breath hitch in her chest.

"See that pretty little thang over there?" Dalton asked the crowd, and Katie's face felt like it was on fire as several heads turned in her direction, the same direction Dalton was looking.

"Yeah, her. That's my girl. Did y'all know that?"

His girl?

Instinctively, Katie shook her head. She wasn't his girl. No way.

No one seemed to be paying her any attention, or they weren't accepting her denial anyway. Applause and whistles made her head roar. Or maybe that was her blood pressure, skyrocketing thanks to Dalton's acknowledgement.

"See, I kinda need y'all's help," Dalton continued, his eyes locked with hers. "I've been tryin' to get another date with her, but she keeps turnin' me down."

The crowd clearly didn't approve of that if their boos and hisses were anything to go by.

Katie was tempted to run upstairs to the office and hide out for the rest of the night. One, because she didn't care to have the attention of so many of these people on her, and two, because she might've needed time to comprehend just what Dalton was saying.

"Hold up," Dalton said sternly, addressing the crowd. "It ain't like that. You know how it is. We're all busy, right? Well, she is too, but I have to say, I'm dyin' to get her to go out with me again. That's where y'all come in. This next song, I'm dedicatin' it to her, and I could sure use your help. If you know the words, sing along."

Dalton shot her another wink, and the amount of oxygen in the room decreased by at least half. Was he really doing this? And to think, just a moment ago she'd been caught up in his enthusiasm, now she just wanted to…

Holy hell. She didn't know what she wanted to do.

The room erupted in a chorus of song with Dalton leading the pack. Some folks were still focused on her, others were back to watching him. She wished they'd all turn around and look at him, but since she didn't have any superpowers, Katie tried to pretend that this man – the one who had called her *his girl* – was not serenading her with an entire bar full of people helping him.

What she figured was a four-minute song seemed to go on forever. At least that's what it felt like, but finally it was over, and only then did Katie retrieve the drinks that Eric had set in front of her. Grabbing the tray, she scurried off to deliver them, doing her best to ignore all of the good wishes from the people around her. Seriously, what were they congratulating her for? Nothing had happened.

"Make sure you tip your waitresses tonight," she heard Dalton say as she squeezed between the bodies packed on the crowded floor. "And if y'all don't mind, I'm gonna take a short break so I can go hang out with my favorite waitress."

Yes, Katie blushed, even as she kept her eyes down and her focus on not dropping her tray of drinks. She couldn't help herself. Not only had Dalton just laid on the charm, but he had also directed it at her. Of course, the curious folks in the bar were once again looking in her direction, which made her even more uncomfortable. Not that she had long to think about it before Dalton was making his way to her side, smiling down at her.

"Hey, beautiful," he greeted. "Care to have breakfast with me when this is over?"

And just like that, all of her mortification took a back seat to this man's incredible smile. Katie couldn't speak. As she stared up – way up, considering there was an entire foot difference in their heights – into Dalton's glimmering brown eyes, she thought of all of the things she wanted to do to him and having breakfast with him was the least of her concerns at the moment.

"Okay," she agreed, and the smile that gleamed back at her confirmed what she feared. It'd been a long, long time since she'd had any sort of reaction to a man, and certainly never anything of this magnitude. But the more time she spent with Dalton, the more she realized she was headed for a heartache.

No matter how much she fought it.

CHAPTER TWO

The chickens were close to waking by the time the crew had finished closing up the bar around three o'clock in the morning. Dalton had pitched in, unable to sit still while everyone around him worked diligently. He'd actually been grateful for the distraction because had he been waiting for Katie to finish up, he would've gone mad just staring after her, desperately wanting to get his hands on her.

He knew that she hadn't worn that particular dress with the short frilly skirt and breast hugging sweater just for him, but every time he took in the sight of her in that cream colored fabric and those brown cowgirl boots… Yeah, *damn* was about the gist of it.

Thank God, they'd managed to close the place up. And not a moment too soon. Now Dalton and Katie were heading out of The Rusty Nail, Eric following them to the door and locking up behind them. While they trekked across the parking lot, Dalton had to make a conscious effort to keep from dragging Katie to the truck rather than walking like a man who possessed at least a minimal amount of decorum.

"Still up for breakfast?" he asked, taking her hand and leading her around to the passenger side of his truck.

"Depends. Are we talking taquitos to go?"

"Taquitos?" he asked, grinning. "As in Whataburger on the run?"

"That's what I was thinkin'. I was kinda hopin' to get some time away from people," Katie told him, looking up at him, a sexy little glimmer in her charcoal gray eyes.

Ok, so Dalton hadn't expected that. Nor did he anticipate the promise he saw reflecting back at him. They'd been dating – for lack of a better term – for the last couple of months, but just when Dalton thought they were making a little progress, Katie was always the first to put the brakes on. He couldn't say he was disappointed in the possibilities the night still had to offer.

"Whataburger it is. Any thoughts on where to go after?"

"I'll let you choose," she said sweetly.

"I know a place," he informed her, willing his body not to overreact too quickly. It was bad enough that his jeans had been getting increasingly tighter every time he looked at her. The woman had a penchant for making his dick hard. Then again, he was the one responsible for putting himself in that position, so the case of blue balls he'd been sporting for the last couple of months was solely his fault. His current streak of celibacy had started the day he met her.

Taking her hand, he led Katie to his truck and after helping her in, closing the door behind her, he was damn near bow-legged as he made his way around to the driver's side. Yeah, it'd been a while since he'd been laid, and although he had no intention of going that far with Katie tonight, his dick didn't seem to realize that. For the first time in his life, Dalton was trying patience on for size. Not that he was all that happy with the fit, but he was working on it.

Good things come to those who wait, right? At least, he hoped like hell that that was the case.

Once they were out on the main road, leaving Cooper and the rest of the gang back at the bar, along with a handful of reporters still hanging out in the parking lot, desperate to get a glimpse at Cooper's new life, Dalton tried to think of something other than sex.

It wasn't easy.

They ventured into the small neighboring town to get taquitos, but at that time of morning, they made good time. Since they'd made that particular food run a couple of times recently, the overnight crew at the fast food restaurant knew exactly who he was when he pulled up to the window. He laughed when they all vied to get to him through the small opening, everyone speaking at once. Thankfully, they weren't pushy, probably because they knew he'd be back, so several minutes later they were pulling out.

With food sitting in a bag between them, Dalton turned the truck back toward Devil's Bend.

Night had fallen hours ago, blanketing the chilly Texas day in darkness. The temperatures were hovering in the forties, significantly warmer than Dalton was used to, but still cold enough to warrant a jacket. Thankfully, the wind had died down after the clouds had been blown out, and now the night was clear, the threat of rain a distant thought. The only reason Dalton had the heater on was for Katie's benefit. Had he been alone, he would've had the windows down to offset the warmth from the vents, but he wasn't looking to freeze her out.

But he was hot. And he wasn't sure it had anything to do with the heater either. That or he was as nervous as a teenage boy was on prom night.

"Where are we goin'?" Katie asked as she stared out the window when they crossed the county line.

"I thought we'd head to the lake," he answered, glancing over at her briefly, wiping his hands on the leather covering the steering wheel.

"Okay."

"No arguments?" he teased, his voice rough with anticipation.

"Nope," she said softly. "Not tonight."

Dalton heard a world of innuendo in those two words and he started to fear he was thinking with the wrong part of his anatomy. It wasn't all that difficult to succumb to his little head's curiosity though, especially with Katie sitting beside him, the tops of her trim, tan thighs on display beneath that skirt. That and boots.

Lord help him, if he made it through tonight he was going to be inducted into sainthood.

"Did you enjoy the show?" he asked, trying to make small talk.

"It was decent," she said, causing Dalton to dart a look her way. The adorable smile that tipped her full lips made his dick harden that much more.

"Decent? Well, I'm not sure I've ever heard that said about my shows."

"Yeah, well…"

Dalton knew she was joking and he enjoyed her banter. The fact that things could be so easy between them was one of the reasons he enjoyed being around Katie so much. She wasn't like most of the women he met, who were constantly competing for his attention or trying to keep it if he even looked their way.

Nope, not since he'd made it in the country music world had he met a woman like Katie. One who just wanted to be friends and nothing more.

Katie reached for the bag and rummaged through it noisily. She chuckled and he looked over at her, noticing she was holding something up for him to see.

"They gave you an apple pie," she said with a grin.

Dalton laughed. Sometimes being famous did have its perks. It was the little things.

Katie continued to pull items out of the bag, before handing him one of the breakfast burritos. Egg, potatoes and cheese wrapped in a flour tortilla should've been enough to bring him out of the lust-induced haze, but even that was making his dick hard. No, wait, it wasn't the taquito, it was the brush of Katie's hand against his that did it.

Come on, Calhoun. You're not fifteen.

"Since we're havin' breakfast on the run, maybe we should get the traditional part of the date over with as well," Dalton said, willing his body back under control. Katie's curious glance didn't help.

"First of all, Calhoun," Katie told him as she held her burrito to her mouth, "this is *not* a date."

"You see, it kinda is," he replied, darting his eyes over to meet hers briefly before turning his attention back to the darkened road in front of him.

"No. It's not," she said more insistently.

"Fine. It's not," he replied with a chuckle. Whatever she wanted to tell herself. But to him, this was a date. "However, I still think we should get the pleasantries out of the way."

"Pleasantries?"

"Yeah. You know. Routine date questions, the whole gettin' to know you part."

"We already know each other. And as far as I'm concerned, you've asked enough questions," Katie told him, her voice a little harder than before.

Dalton knew Katie wasn't much for his queries, but considering he wanted to know everything there was to know about her and she wasn't very forthcoming in sharing pieces of herself, he wasn't left with much choice. So he pretended not to notice her affront.

"So, this is like our tenth non-date," he told her for her benefit, "and I still don't know much about you other than you work at the bar and you're in school. Tell me somethin' else."

"Nothin' to tell," Katie said a little too fast for his peace of mind.

It wasn't the first time he'd gotten the sense she was hiding something. What, he had no idea, but he did notice that as soon as he tried to get to know her better, she tended to shut down.

Luckily, Dalton didn't scare easily. He knew with a little encouragement, Katie would open up. Eventually.

"Nothin'?" he asked, smiling and trying to keep the subject light.

"Nope," she added, her tone less strained than a moment ago, but he could still detect her hesitancy.

Well, shit, this wasn't going quite the way he had planned.

"Do your parents live in Devil's Bend?" he asked, going for polite conversation now. Although the two of them had gone out quite a few times, anytime Dalton moved the subject to Katie, she always managed to deflect.

"Nope. What about yours? Do they live in Nashville?"

This time clearly wasn't going to be any different. Going with the flow, Dalton said, "Georgia."

Damn the woman was a dichotomy. He never knew what to expect from her, but he did know that she wasn't keen on talking about herself. That was only a small problem where Dalton was concerned because he had this overwhelming inquisitiveness when it came to her. Had since the moment he laid eyes on her at The Rusty Nail just a few short months ago.

It was a wonder he didn't know much about her by this point, but that was only proof that she had succeeded in shutting him out whenever he tried to get closer.

The conversation had hit a lull by the time they were pulling down one of the dirt roads that led to a secluded section of the lake he'd recently located when he was looking for a place to hide out from everyone. The good news was that breakfast was out of the way, thanks to Katie encouraging him to eat rather than talk.

Bless her. The woman thought she could get by without sharing more of herself with him. He'd just have to see about that.

As though she suspected he wasn't about to let go of the questions, Katie shocked him by speaking up as he navigated the truck down the narrow road.

"So, you didn't grow up in Tennessee?" Katie asked as he pulled the truck into a small alcove, doing a K-turn and then backing the truck closer to the water.

"Nuh-uh," he told her, putting the truck in park. "Come on, let's sit on the tailgate."

"Seriously?" she asked as he leaned between the seats to retrieve the blankets he had stashed in the back seat. The ones he'd put there for specifically this purpose.

"Yep. Come on."

Katie met his gaze across the dimly lit truck. For a brief moment, he thought he saw concern on her pretty face. What did she think he was going to do? Jump her bones right there at the lake? Hell, they'd had more than their fair share of chances for him to make a move and he'd held back all this time. It wasn't as if he was going to push her to do something she wasn't ready for.

Dalton happened to like that about Katie. She wasn't the type of woman he was used to meeting these days. Most of them were more than willing to get naked and horizontal before he even knew their last name. He knew it was more due to his fame than his incredible personality, which was why he welcomed a chance to spend time with this woman.

Katie Clarren seemed to care less that he was one of the biggest names in country music at the moment. And Dalton's ego wasn't involved in the latter part of that statement. It was a fact. The Billboard charts didn't lie. Nor did his bank account.

Exiting the truck, Dalton made his way to the back, lowered the tailgate and spread one of the blankets on the cold metal bed before moving around to the passenger side to help Katie. The ground was soft beneath his feet and he didn't want her to fall – or at least that was his excuse. What he really wanted to do was to touch her, to feel her soft skin beneath his palms.

When she allowed him to slide his arm around her waist and help her down the slope, he took the opportunity to breathe her in.

Damn this woman did something crazy to him and he had no idea why that was. It wasn't as if she was all that easy to get to know. In fact, quite the opposite.

Helping her onto the tailgate by placing his hands on her waist and lifting her up, he took a seat beside her, taking her hand in his and linking their fingers. It was that or stand between her legs and he knew good and damn well that wasn't the appropriate way to start what he would consider their eleventh official date.

Yes, he was counting.

"You grew up here?" he asked, staring out into the inky black night, catching a glimpse of the gentle waves backlit by the bright moon, crashing against the bank just a few yards away from where they sat.

"I did," she said hesitantly. "Hey, Dalton."

"Yeah?" he asked, turning his head to peer over at her.

Katie's long black hair was pulled back in a ponytail, she had tiny little diamond studs in her ears that twinkled every now and again when the moon hit them just right, but what kept drawing his attention was the smooth, sleek column of her neck. He just wanted to press his lips to the soft skin there, to breathe her in, taste her. He wanted to see if she was as sweet as he suspected she was.

Sweet. That was always the first word that came to mind whenever he looked at her. She looked like the typical girl next door with her thin sweater, short flowing skirt, her tan skin quite the contrast against the off-white color.

"Are you gonna kiss me?"

Dalton kept his jaw hinged, not wanting to show his surprise. As much as he'd wanted to kiss her, he tended to keep his desire to himself. Sure, there were the few times he'd given in when the temptation had been too great, but he still tried to keep himself in check. He never seemed to know just what Katie expected from him. But right now, right here, with her posing a question like that, his body was roaring to life once again.

"Kiss you?" he asked stupidly.

Katie smiled and her white teeth shone in the darkness. "Yeah. You know, what a boy does to a girl when he likes her."

"Is that how it goes?" he joked, all the blood in his body flowing to one particular region, leaving him a little light headed.

"That's what I hear."

Innocent.

That's another thing he loved about this woman. She spoke her mind, as long as it didn't have anything to do with her personally, but she was seemingly innocent when it came to so many things.

She just asked you to kiss her.

Yeah, well, there was that. Maybe innocent wasn't the correct turn of phrase.

Twisting just enough to face her, Dalton released her hand and slid it up behind her neck, his eyes boring into hers as he studied her. He wasn't sure when the last time was that he'd catalogued when his lips touched a woman's.

Maybe this was the first time.

Leaning forward, Dalton went slow. There was an inferno building deep inside him, one that threatened to consume them both, but he managed to keep it under control.

Barely.

However, when Katie's lips touched his, he lost his grasp on his common sense as well as his self-restraint. And when her arms came up and wrapped around his neck, he damn near lost his mind.

This was unlike any of their previous kisses. Their lips brushed one another's briefly, but when he expected her to draw away, leaving him to savor the brief taste of her, Katie surprised him. It wasn't long before the heat was turned up. The next thing Dalton knew, Katie was straddling his lap, the blanket wrapped around her shoulders, her knees on either side of his hips, his hands on her waist and his tongue delving into her sweet mouth.

He growled, unable to help himself.

Lord, have mercy.

This woman…

Fucking hell, Katie's tongue plunged against his and that's about when all thoughts fled.

CHAPTER THREE

Katie had no idea what came over her or why she was now straddling Dalton's lap, eager to slide her fingers into the soft hair at the nape of his neck or slip her tongue into his mouth, but here she was.

And wow! She wasn't sure she ever wanted to stop kissing this man.

His body was hard as steel pressed up against hers, his thighs rock solid beneath her, the chiseled planes of his chest a wall against her aching breasts. And she couldn't seem to get close enough, although she was practically climbing his body.

When his big, warm hands gripped her hips, her body caught fire, soaring several hundred degrees and it single-handedly warded off the chill in the December night air. By the time they came up for oxygen, she was coated in a thin layer of perspiration thanks to her body heat and the blanket, but she didn't care. If she had her way, she'd lose the skirt and Dalton would lose his clothes, right there on the tailgate of his truck.

Too bad it wasn't warmer because skinny-dipping would be good, too. At this point, she just needed something to quench the incredible thirst she'd acquired for this man.

"Katie," Dalton growled, his hand palming the back of her head as he stared back at her. "Damn, darlin'. You sure about this? Keep this up and you're gonna kill me."

"Can't think of a better way to go," she whispered breathlessly.

Katie didn't want him to stop touching her, didn't want him to stop kissing her. She was primed and ready, and even though he seemed to have a little more self-restraint than she possessed, she wasn't willing to let him lead the way.

"Kiss me again, Dalton. Kiss me again, and please don't ever stop," she pleaded, needing that human connection. It'd been too damn long since she'd felt close to anyone like this. And never to this degree.

"Fuck," he growled hungrily before crushing his mouth to hers, pulling her closer until she was grinding against the hard ridge of his erection.

She knew she shouldn't be doing this, shouldn't be so aggressive, but shit; she was so damned tired of the good girl routine. So tired of people believing only what they saw. Katie knew she was so far from good that she couldn't even see it with binoculars, but no one else did. And she wanted this.

More than her next breath.

Katie slid her hands around to Dalton's back, pushing them beneath his jacket and then under the cotton T-shirt he wore, her palms gliding over the hard ridge of muscles she found there. She moaned into his mouth, her fingernails raking across his skin as though that might possibly bring them closer.

"Katie," Dalton said, pulling back.

"Please don't," she whispered. "Don't warn me that this isn't the right thing to do. That it isn't the right time. That it isn't the right place. You and I both know those are just social niceties and I'm so far passed that—"

"Are you sure?" he asked again, cutting her off midsentence.

"More than sure. I don't want anything else," she answered, pulling him closer, pressing her breasts firmly against his rock hard chest while she nipped his lower lip.

"Oh, hell," Dalton mumbled before surprising her when he launched to his feet, his hands cupping her ass and holding her astride him.

Wrapping her legs around his waist and her arms around his neck, Katie held on to the blanket and to him for dear life, not wanting him to drop her.

"I've got you, baby," he muttered, his lips pressed to hers.

God, if he only knew how much she wished that were true. And she wasn't just talking about right here and now.

Dalton carried her to the passenger side of the truck, but he didn't deposit her in the front seat as she expected. Instead, he opened the back door of the truck and set her on the edge of the backseat. Not willing to let him go, Katie pulled him, forcing him to climb in the truck with her.

Only when he said he had to start the truck or they were going to freeze did she let him go. But even as he reached over the front seat to twist the keys in the ignition, Katie worked to release the button and the zipper on his jeans, easing her hand inside before he joined her again.

"Darlin'," he crooned.

"I love when you call me that," Katie told him as she wrapped her hands around the silky smooth length of him. Even in the darkness, she could see the pure ecstasy on his face as he stared down at her, his hips thrusting forward ever so slightly as she stroked him.

"Oh, damn. That feels good."

No, what felt good was when he pressed his knee between her legs, grinding against her aching sex. She moaned, unable to control the gentle rumble that started in her chest, but he quickly swallowed the sound when his mouth came down and met hers.

Katie whimpered, the burning desire to have him right here in the backseat of his truck overwhelmed her, stole her breath. She was sure she'd regret this tomorrow, but right now, getting her hands on him was the only thing that mattered.

It would seem that they were on the same page because Dalton managed to shove his jeans down over his hips, freeing his thick cock. Katie gripped him with both hands, stroking slowly, firmly, loving the rumble that erupted in his chest as she continued.

Dalton's forehead came to rest against hers as they both fought to suck in air. "This wasn't exactly my intention for tonight."

"Are you sayin' you don't want this?" she teased.

"Oh, darlin', I want this more than anything. But when I fantasized about this, it wasn't in the backseat of my truck."

Katie met his dark gaze in the shadows. "I can't think of anywhere I'd rather be," she told him.

"Me either."

Katie felt the emotion that was behind those two words and her heart actually trembled.

"I want to feel you, Dalton," she whispered, releasing him from her grasp and sliding her hands beneath his shirt, pushing it higher as she went.

"Then this ain't the position to be in," he said, and she heard the smile in his voice.

Before she knew what was happening, Dalton had resituated them so that he was sitting on the seat, his jeans pushed down to his ankles while she sat astride him.

"Hold on," he instructed as he reached around her, searching the floor for... "Condom."

Katie smiled at that. Her mind had been elsewhere, so she loved the fact that he'd been thinking about their safety.

That was like the third or fourth time she'd referenced loving something about him in the last few minutes and part of her was beginning to worry. As much as she wanted to keep herself distanced from him, she knew she wasn't built that way.

This might've just been sex to him, but to her it was... everything.

"Work with me, darlin'," Dalton murmured, easing his hands between them.

Katie laughed and then shifted so that he could roll the condom over himself.

"How much do you like these panties?" he asked her, his face serious.

"I don't know, why?"

The heart-stopping grin he gave her should've eliminated the panty issue altogether, but it was then that she realized what he was saying.

"They're not my favorite," she tacked on.

"Just what I wanted to hear."

And then her panties were no longer an issue because Dalton had torn them off her and... "Oh, my God," she groaned as he guided himself inside her without preamble.

"Fuck."

Burying her face in his neck, Katie bit her lip, fearful that she would draw blood. The pain was... excruciating, but she didn't want him to know.

After all, she was pretty sure Dalton Calhoun wouldn't have touched her if he knew she was a twenty-three year old virgin. Needing a distraction as her body adjusted to his size, she trailed kisses along his neck until she reached his mouth. Plunging her tongue inside, she whimpered as he eased deeper inside her.

"Katie," Dalton moaned, his hands moving up to cup her face and pull her head back.

A tear trickled down her cheek as he stared at her. She prayed he thought she was just emotional because that was the lesser of two evils.

His voice lowered. "Have you…"

Katie was grateful that he'd cut the sentence off. She didn't want to lie to him, but she didn't want to tell him the truth either. Instead, she crushed her lips to his once more as she lowered herself onto his thick erection.

It wasn't long before the pain subsided, replaced by an overwhelming, intense pleasure.

While Katie's body adjusted to his size, she explored his mouth with her tongue and Dalton slid his hands beneath her sweater, forcing it higher until he was pulling it over her head. His fingers fumbled with her bra, but it didn't take him long to release the hook, freeing her breasts. He once again broke the kiss, forcing her to look at him. Their eyes met, held briefly.

He knew.

It was right there in his beautiful brown eyes. He knew what had just transpired between them. Thankfully, he didn't say anything. Instead, he leaned forward and wrapped his lips around one painfully hard nipple. Katie cried out, instinctively latching on to the back of his head and holding him to her.

"Yes," she moaned over and over, as she began rocking her hips. Between the intense friction of him inside her and the wondrous suction of his mouth on her nipple, Katie wasn't sure she was going to actually last long enough to call this sex.

∞ ∞ ∞ ∞ ∞

"Katie." Dalton released Katie's nipple from between his lips and slipped his hands beneath her ass, pulling her closer, forcing him deeper inside of her. "You feel so good."

Too good. He had to do elementary math problems in his head just to keep from coming too soon.

But she was fire in his arms, and honest to God, he hadn't expected this. Not tonight.

Sure, he'd fantasized about it plenty, but to have her wrapped around him, her pussy milking his cock… It was more than he imagined.

And he never wanted it to end.

For a brief moment there, he'd nearly panicked. When he had first slid into her slick heat, he'd been met with resistance. She was so fucking tight, almost painfully so. And that's when a single thought crossed his mind. Was she a virgin?

Was he the first man she'd given herself to?

The idea of being her first nearly leveled him.

Using his arms, he rocked her forward and back, his cock sliding deeper and then withdrawing only a fraction before he was once again thrusting into her. He was still trying to be gentle, not wanting to hurt her. The tear that had leaked from her eyes had his heart skipping a beat, the thought of hurting her enough to deflate any hardon. But then she began to move, thrusting her hips forward, sending him deeper.

She was so wet, so warm. So very, very tight.

He would've much preferred a bed, some place he could have her sprawled out beneath him so he could have had his way with her, made this last for hours, if not days. But he wasn't going to complain because the heat of her was threatening to send him over the edge as it was.

"Faster," she pleaded, and Dalton thought his head might explode.

"If we go faster, this is gonna be over, darlin'," he admitted honestly.

"Whatever it takes," she said with a sweet chuckle. "Just please fuck me."

Oh, mother fucking hell. Katie Clarren just dropped the F-bomb. Dalton knew he wasn't supposed to find that so fucking hot, but he did. Sweet, little innocent Katie had a dirty mouth, and he wanted to ask her to talk some more, to tell him just what she wanted, but he didn't.

Instead, Dalton eased down into the seat just a little, holding her ass up off his legs, her knees resting on the seat on each side of his hips. "Don't move from right there," he instructed, meeting her eyes in the dark.

"Okay," she said and he could see her grin.

Without much room to gain traction, Dalton had to make do with what he had so he began to thrust up inside her while digging his fingers into her hips. He didn't hold back, fucking her hard and fast as she moaned and whimpered, her head falling back.

She was the sexiest woman he'd ever met in his entire fucking life and taking her here in the backseat of his truck was the hottest thing he'd ever done. Only because he was with her.

"Dalton, yes. Oh, yes! Fuck me!"

Dalton nearly exploded. Seriously.

Those words from her lips nearly launched him into the ether, but somehow he managed to keep himself grounded, unwilling to come until she did.

"Come for me, Katie. Come on my cock, darlin'." He was testing the waters; unsure how she would take him talking to her like that, but he didn't worry when she dug her fingernails into his shoulders, meeting his upward thrusts with her own.

"Oh, yes! Dalton! You're gonna make me come. Oh, yes! Please make me come."

He found her clit with this thumb, making small circles over the little nub until she was whimpering again.

"Come for me, darlin'."

And then she did, her scream would've been heard for miles around had they not been inside his truck. That, mixed with the sight of her straddling him, her beautiful breasts bobbing in front of his face and the way her pussy clamped down on him sent him right over the edge.

As his dick pulsed inside her, Dalton wrapped his arms around her waist and pulled her flush against him, never wanting to let her go. They were both struggling to breathe, their rapid pants causing the windows to fog up. Or maybe that was from the heat they generated.

Fuck. He didn't know, and he didn't care.

"Please tell me we can do that again," Katie whispered against his ear.

"I hope you don't mean now," he said lightly.

"Ten minutes?" she asked and he could hear the teasing in her voice.

"Thirty and you have a deal."

Katie laughed and the soft, sultry sound made his heart swell.

Yeah, this woman had wrapped him around her little finger, and he doubted she even realized it. Tenth date or fiftieth, Dalton knew it was inevitable… He was falling for her. And he was falling hard and fast.

And for the first time in his life, he didn't care. He wasn't scared of what might happen; he was just ready to experience it.

One incredible day at a time.

CHAPTER FOUR

Two hours later and still no regret.

Huh.

Interesting.

Katie was sitting in the front seat of Dalton's truck, leaning against him while he sat behind the wheel. They were once again in the parking lot of The Rusty Nail and the sun was just beginning to turn the sky a resplendent shade of orange as it made its ascent.

They had spent the entire night together, making love – in Dalton's truck no less – and then holding one another in the aftermath. The former should've been the reason for her regrets or at least the reason she was questioning her sanity. But she wasn't worried about either.

Instead, she was just wishing she didn't have to leave him, but she really did have to get home. She'd shucked her responsibilities for the first time in as long as she could remember, and Katie knew she would pay the price later.

"I wish you didn't have to go," Dalton said.

Katie wished the same. She also wished she could've invited him back to her place, but there were a plethora of reasons why that wasn't in the cards. Dalton wouldn't be going back to her apartment. Not today, not tomorrow. Probably not ever.

But she wasn't going to ruin their time together by telling him that or by thinking about the repercussions of her actions tonight.

Rather than dwell on all the things she had to do when she left him, Katie decided to blow them off for just a few more minutes because kissing him had become her new favorite pastime and their time together was slowly coming to an end.

Looking up at him, she smiled and his beautiful brown eyes returned the smile without his lips even moving. Then she was kissing him, turning so she could get closer. His tongue plunged into her mouth and she wished they were naked and somewhere a little more private one again.

Preferably, somewhere they could have more space as well. Having sex in his truck hadn't been the most comfortable place to be, but her orgasms hadn't been all that particular. He'd made her body burn on more than one occasion and she had the feeling she was going to crave him the instant they were apart.

She'd have to think on that a little later too because as much as she enjoyed being with him, Katie knew their time together was limited. But that was something she'd considered before this all began and for what it was worth, she was going to ride it out for as long as possible.

Her body craved him. Needed him. And she didn't want to fight it anymore.

"I really need to go," Katie said, mumbling against his lips.

"Me too," he told her. "I'm heading back to Nashville in a few hours."

"Really?" There was no way to hide her surprise at his admission. "I didn't know you were goin' back."

"Won't be for long. A week at most. I'll be back."

Katie forced a small smile. It wasn't that she wasn't happy to hear he was coming back, she was just sad for the time they would have to be apart. But maybe that was a good thing. More time to think.

Great. Just what she didn't need.

"Will you call me while you're gone?" she asked, feeling a little needy.

"Every day."

This time her smile was genuine and she pressed her lips to his. "Well, in that case, what am I wastin' my time here for?" she teased.

When she tried to move away, Dalton caught her, his heavy arms wrapping around her, solidly holding her in place against him. He pressed his lips to her forehead, and she fought the urge to sigh in complete contentment. She hadn't felt this safe, this cherished in… far too long.

"Can I tell you somethin'?" she asked before she thought better of it.

"Sure."

"This has been the best night ever."

Dalton turned her in his arms and their eyes met. There were no shadows to hide behind now because the sun had breached the horizon and the brilliant orange glow was lighting up the world around them.

"I agree," Dalton admitted, his eyes seemingly looking for something in hers.

"No regrets?" she asked.

His chuckle made her insides sing. "Not a one."

"Good." A quick glance at the clock and Katie knew she was pushing her luck at this point. "I really do need to go."

Dalton nodded, his lips finding hers once again. The kiss lingered for longer than she intended, but she had a hard time pulling herself away from him.

"I'm building a house here," Dalton said, his statement taking her by surprise.

"That's what I heard," she replied, her anxiety level ratcheting up a notch. It wasn't that she didn't like the idea of him being there in Devil's Bend, but that presented a problem on several levels. Problems that she didn't want to face.

"Yep. When the equestrian center is up and runnin', I'll need to be close."

Equestrian center. Right.

Cooper was building an equestrian center, and Dalton had mentioned that they were going into business together. Which meant he'd be there for extended periods of time. "What about your music career?"

"It's still in full swing," he said easily. "That won't change. But I'll be here when I'm not on the road."

Katie nodded, doing her best not to start worrying about what that meant. A few hours ago, when this had been just a fun little fling, she'd been fine. Now that she knew he was intending to be around more often, her fears were starting to flood her mind.

"When will you be back?" she asked, trying to force her thoughts back to the present. Tomorrow didn't matter. What mattered was right this minute. Before the day was out, Dalton would be gone again and she'd have plenty of time to figure it all out.

She hoped.

"Next Monday at the latest."

That was a solid week away. Plenty of time.

Katie leaned forward and kissed him, keeping it playful this time. She would not ruin this moment. "Good. Well, I'm expectin' a phone call," she said softly.

"Yes, ma'am."

Katie could see the exhaustion in Dalton's eyes. She'd kept him up all night and although she was used to being up until the wee hours of the morning, sometimes making it on just a couple of hours of sleep, she wasn't sure he was.

"Bye, Dalton," she finally said after staring at him for longer than was probably appropriate.

"Bye, darlin'."

She really did love when he called her that. She'd heard Cooper call Tessa that and she figured it was one of those country things, but regardless, it gave her a sense of comfort that she hadn't known before.

Reaching for the door handle, she forced herself to look away from him. Grabbing her purse from the floorboard, she slipped out of the truck, offering him one last smile before she shut the door and walked away.

That was the moment she realized just how much trouble she was in.

And it wasn't only due to the fact that she was pretty sure she'd fallen in love with a man she knew she couldn't keep.

∞ ∞ ∞ ∞ ∞

Dalton tried to be quiet when he snuck in the front door of Cooper's house at dawn. The last thing he wanted to do was either interrupt or wake Tessa and Coop. The first would result in him getting a stern "be quiet" from his buddy, which in turn would make him laugh; the second might require him to have an actual conversation with one or both of them.

He much preferred a quick shower and then hopefully a solid two hours of sleep before he had to get on the road. Or hell, maybe he'd just sleep in, catch a good four or five hours of shuteye and then be on his way.

That was if he could sleep at all.

His brain was still trying to break down the events of the night. Or more accurately, the early morning hours.

Katie.

Holy fuck. The woman had blown his mind in every way imaginable.

Truthfully, he wished he were at her place, falling into bed with her so he could hold her for the rest of the day. Having to drop her off at her car had felt oddly like they were teenagers sneaking around.

He didn't like the feeling either.

But he couldn't very well change the outcome. Considering everything else that had happened tonight, he could easily overlook that minor detail. Since his brain was more interested in reliving the moments when Katie was riding his cock, it was easy to forget the way she'd looked when she slipped out of his truck anyway.

"No more," he told his dick as he made his way to the bathroom in the hall.

Cooper would just have to deal with the water running and he knew from experience that the pipes in Coop's old house were loud enough to rouse the dead. In an effort not to piss off his host too much, he shed his clothes before turning on the water and then hopped into the tub – *slash* – shower before the water even heated.

Not that the cold splash bothered him. He'd sweated off at least three pounds from the incredible sex and the warmth from the heater flooding his truck, but he wasn't complaining.

It didn't take long for him to soap up and rinse off and then he was traipsing into the guest room he'd commandeered with a towel wrapped around his hips. The door had barely clicked shut before he was flat on his face, giving in to sleep.

Unfortunately, two hours of sleep only left Dalton with scratchy eyes and an oncoming headache.

Forcing himself out of bed, he was met by the alluring smell of bacon and eggs. Cooper was at it again. The man loved being in the kitchen, which was amusing, although somewhat satisfying when you woke up hungry in the man's house.

Dalton pulled on his jeans and a T-shirt, not wanting to stumble into the living room undressed. Cooper was rather protective of Tessa, and Dalton couldn't very well blame the guy.

Scratching his five o'clock shadow, which actually was more of a two-day beard, Dalton padded to the kitchen in search of food and coffee.

"Thought you were headin' back to Nashville today?" Cooper said by way of greeting.

"Mornin' to you, too," Dalton grumbled as he headed right for the coffee pot. Caffeine would go a long way to clearing the fog, and if he was lucky, driving the throbbing in his temples away.

"Nashville?" Cooper asked with a chuckle, reminding Dalton of his question.

"Headin' back in a bit."

"You were out late last night, huh?"

Who was he, his mother?

Okay, so the pissy mood had set in early. Dalton purposely thought of Katie as he poured coffee into a glass mug, one of the newer things in Cooper's recently renovated kitchen. And as the memories from last night made a reappearance, he forced them into slow motion as he took the first sip of caffeine heaven.

"That good, huh?" Cooper asked.

At first, Dalton thought the man was referring to the coffee, but then he realized he'd plastered a smile on his face, so either the coffee was the best he'd ever had, or those memories were the cause. Dalton would have to go with the memories.

Katie.

Damn.

He wished he could stop by her place on his way out, but he didn't even know where she lived.

At that moment, Tessa came waltzing into the kitchen, a smile on her face. She looked as though she'd been thinking, too, which was probably the reason her smile looked a little forced.

"Hey, do you know where Katie lives?" Dalton asked before he could think better of it.

Tessa glanced at Dalton then to Cooper and back again. "Me?"

"Well, I'd hope he didn't know where she lived," Dalton said, nodding his head in Coop's direction.

"Sorry, no," Tessa said, shaking her head and pushing her way past Dalton.

Clearly, coffee was the breakfast of champions these days.

Dalton stepped out of her way, moving a foot or so down and then leaning against the counter as he studied the pair in the kitchen. Cooper had busied himself at the stove and Tessa appeared to be trying to avoid him.

Interesting.

These two had overcome some major issues, but really, that was none of his business. He'd thought they had worked things out, considering Cooper had proposed, but truth was, Dalton wasn't privy to a lot that went on between them. Not to mention, it was too damned early in the morning to try to psychoanalyze his buddy's love life.

With her coffee poured, Tessa turned to look at him.

"She uses a post office box as her official address."

A post office box? Really?

That seemed a little odd.

"You've never been to her house?"

"Not a house, an apartment. At least that's what I've gathered when I've talked to her. And to answer your question, no, I haven't been there. We're friends, just not that close," Tessa explained, both of her hands wrapped around her mug as though it was the only source of warmth in the world and she was trying to wring out every last bit.

Dalton shot a look at Cooper.

All right then. Time to get going.

"I've gotta head out," Dalton said to no one in particular. "I'm plannin' to be back in a week. Think you can keep it together while I'm gone?"

Cooper shot him the finger, accompanied by a grin.

"Remember that benefit concert we talked about?" Dalton asked before he headed toward the guest bedroom.

"Yep."

"I wanna do it."

"I'm in," Cooper added.

Returning his thoughts to the woman who'd sent his world spinning in crazy directions last night, Dalton decided it was time to get back to Nashville.

And the sooner the better. Because, quite frankly, he wasn't sure his mind was actually going to leave Devil's Bend.

CHAPTER FIVE

Saturday morning

Katie had just slipped into bed when her cell phone chirped, notifying her of an incoming text. She knew without looking who it was. At four o'clock in the morning, it could only be one person these days.

Reaching for her phone, Katie rolled over to her back and slid her finger across the screen to bring it to life.

Mornin' darlin'

Katie smiled to herself, tempted to hug her phone to her chest, just to bring Dalton that much closer to her heart. She missed him.

Although she'd talked to him every day since he left town on Tuesday, she still longed to hear from him. In fact, she thought of little else besides him when she wasn't buy doing other things.

She quickly typed up a return message: *Hey cowboy*

Waiting to see if he would respond, Katie stared at the ceiling. Her room was dark, just enough light coming in through the slats in the blinds from the yellow street lamp in the parking lot to see the outline of her furniture, but not much else.

The phone chirped again and she smiled as she looked at the phone.

Miss me yet?
Very much.
How was your day?

Katie smiled at the phone before she typed in her reply: *Better now.*

For the entire first day he'd been gone, Katie had told herself that she needed to break things off with Dalton, let him go on with his business so she could go on with hers. But that had lasted until he called her later that night from his house in Nashville.

Somehow, she had managed to convince herself that being with him for a short time wasn't going to hurt. Not her and not him. They could give in to this fling and no one would be the wiser.

Strange how her feelings for him had intensified over the course of a few days and she hadn't been able to see him. Now, she feared she was getting in too deep, but she had come to enjoy hearing his voice and she worried she may not be able to give that up as easily as she had originally hoped.

Can I call?

Katie glanced at her bedroom door. It was closed, as it usually was when she went to bed. Knowing her roommate Sarah wouldn't hear her from her room, she sent another text letting Dalton know that he could call.

Less than a minute later, her phone was ringing. She'd held it under her blanket to reduce the sound and hit the talk button as quickly as she could.

"Hey," she greeted, keeping her voice low.

"Hey, beautiful."

"What are you doin' up so late?" she asked him as she rolled over to her side.

"Thinkin' 'bout you," he replied.

Katie's heart swelled. She had no idea where things were leading with her and Dalton, but the way he talked to her, the sincerity she heard in his tone, it was filling her with hope. A hope she had no business giving in to.

Not that she cared to think about that at the moment.

"What about me?"

"I'm thinkin' about what it would be like if you were here in my bed. Naked."

"Mmmm," Katie replied, pretending to be thinking about the same thing. The fact of the matter was that exact scenario had been on her mind for a few days now. After the night in the truck, she had replayed the incident over and over in her mind, wishing the opportunity to do that again would present itself. "And if I was naked, what would you do to me?" she asked, shocked by how bold she was being.

Dalton cleared his throat, his reaction reflecting his own surprise.

"Do you really wanna know?" he asked, his voice gruff.

Holding her cell phone to her ear, Katie swallowed hard, realizing exactly what she was asking him to tell her. As crazy as it was, she wanted this man. Any way that she could get him and if that meant having phone sex while he was hundreds of miles away, so be it.

"Tell me," she whispered, her tummy fluttering.

She had no idea why she was so nervous; it wasn't as if he could see her.

"First, I need you to do something for me," Dalton said.

"What's that?"

"Get naked."

Katie swallowed hard.

Naked?

Wow.

"Okay. Hold on," she told him, tossing the phone onto her pillow while she quickly pulled off her T-shirt and panties. She took a deep breath and then grabbed the phone, falling back onto her pillow. "Okay. I'm naked."

Dalton's rumbling growl sent a bolt of heat through her.

"I need you to do something else for me, darlin'," Dalton stated.

Katie noticed his voice was rough, gravelly. As though he were just as affected by their little encounter as she was. And to think, they hadn't even done anything yet.

"What?" she questioned. She was pretty sure she knew where this was heading, but she wanted him to say it anyway.

"I want you to slide your hand down the front of your body. Go slow. Start at your right breast. Tease your nipple with your finger and thumb."

Katie sucked in air, her hand sliding to her breast as though it was taking direction without her brain being any part of the decision making process.

"Are you doin' it, Katie?"

"Yeah," she said on a soft sigh.

"Good girl. Now, I want you to slide your hand farther down your body."

"Okay," she replied as she did as he instructed.

"When you get to your pussy, I want you to slide your middle finger through your folds."

Katie did just as he said. She was wet, just from the sound of his voice.

"Talk to me, Katie. Tell me what it feels like."

Shoring up her nerve, Katie tightened her grip on her cell phone and then said, "I'm wet. I wish you were here."

"What would you want me to do if I was there?" he asked.

She had no idea how he had managed to turn this around so that she was the one having to talk, but Katie did her best to go along with it. At this point, her body had ignited and not following through would just leave her frustrated.

"I'd want you to lick me," she admitted, surprised she could get the words out. She felt her cheeks heat from her embarrassment, but she reminded herself that he couldn't see her.

"Where?"

"Everywhere," she answered.

"I'd start between your thighs," Dalton explained. "I'd slide my tongue against your clit, teasing you for hours."

"Hours?" Her voice was a mere whisper.

"Yep," he confirmed. "I'd lick your pussy until you were begging me to let you come. Then I'd tease you some more."

"Oh, God," Katie groaned, sliding her finger inside slowly. It was nothing compared to the feel of Dalton inside her, but it was something.

"Are you fucking yourself?" he asked.

"Yes," she said breathlessly.

"Keep fucking yourself, Katie. Slide two fingers inside your pussy, baby."

Katie did, but she couldn't talk. The pleasure assaulted her, compounded by the rough rumble of his voice in her ear.

"I'm strokin' my cock right now," he said.

Katie imagined him lying in his bed, his cock in his hands while he stroked himself faster.

She began thrusting her fingers in deeper, faster, trying to focus on the phone at her ear, but the only thing that mattered was driving herself higher, reaching that pinnacle that was just out of reach.

"I want to bury my cock in your pussy, Katie. I want to fuck you until you scream my name. God, I miss you so fucking much."

Well, that did it.

Katie bit her bottom lip to keep from crying out as her orgasm consumed her. Her fingers stilled, her chest rising and falling as she tried to suck in air. She could hear Dalton breathing hard into the phone and she listened, wishing she were there to see him, wanting to watch as he jacked off. The thought had an aftershock of pleasure ripping through her.

"Katie."

"Come for me, Dalton," she urged, keeping her voice as quiet as she could.

"Oh, damn, baby. I wish you were here. I just wanna... Oh, fuck, Katie."

She knew by the growl that followed that he'd come. He was silent for a moment, but then his breaths began to slow somewhat.

"That was... unexpected," she told him.

"I do miss you, Katie," Dalton stated, his tone serious. "I'll be back in town tonight. I wanna see you."

Katie glanced at the clock. It was nearing four in the morning, which meant he would be getting on the road soon if he intended to be back by then. She thought about what he'd said. He wanted to see her. She wasn't sure how she could make that happen with everything that was going on, but she decided that she had no choice. She needed to see him, needed to spend some time with him.

"Okay."

"I wanna cook you dinner," he explained. "My house isn't completely finished, but it's far enough along that I can stay there. Will you have dinner with me, Katie?"

"Yes," she said, answering faster than she should have.

"I'll let you go so you can get some sleep. And I'll see you tonight. Think about me."

"I will," she assured him. "Good night, Dalton."

"Good night, darlin'."

With that, the phone disconnected and Katie held it close to her chest.

She would have dinner with him tonight. She'd figure something out so that she could at least do that much. But after that, she really needed to get her head on straight. What she was beginning to want from this man wasn't something she could afford to have. Not right now.

How she was going to tell him that though... that was what she had to figure out.

NICOLE EDWARDS

CHAPTER SIX

Dalton rolled into Devil's Bend around seven-thirty. The sun had already gone down and darkness had taken the place of the light. He'd called Katie and hour ago to let her know when he expected to arrive, not wanting to spend any more time away from her than he had to.

He'd made good time, but only because he'd hit the road as soon as he ended his call with her that morning. In fact, he'd set his alarm to wake him at four so he could do just that before he set out. She had made his day when she agreed to meet him at his house at eight. He still had a few minutes to spare, but without any food at the house, he had to make a stop.

As much as he wanted to cook for her, knowing that the house wasn't set up, he opted to stop by Charlie's and pick up an order to go. It was either that or he would have to go to the grocery store, which he didn't have the patience for at the moment.

He just wanted to get to his house, take a quick shower and then have dinner with Katie.

He'd been looking forward to seeing her again since the moment she climbed out of his truck at The Rusty Nail just a week ago. It'd been too damn long.

For the last week, he'd immersed himself in work. Cutting a new album required a lot of time and effort, but he had managed to keep himself engaged long enough to keep everyone happy. But he'd told his agent that morning that he needed a break. He informed him he'd be heading back to Devil's Bend to take care of a few things that needed his immediate attention.

It hadn't been a lie.

His house was close to being finished and he wanted to make sure everything was in order. But more importantly, he needed to see Katie. He needed to wrap his arms around her, hold her for just a little while. He wasn't sure what had gotten into him, or why he couldn't stand being away from her, but it was what it was. And Dalton had no intention of fighting it.

Ten minutes later, Dalton was walking into his house carrying a six-pack of beer and another of water, along with the paper sack with their to-go containers from Charlie's. The house smelled like fresh paint, but it looked like it was completed. He knew that wasn't the case because there were a few additional things that had to be done to the upstairs rooms, but for the most part, the downstairs was complete. And that was all that really mattered tonight.

Hoping to air out the place, he propped the front door and the back door open to allow a cross breeze through the house. He tapped the screen on the thermostat to turn up the heater a couple of degrees, wanting the house to be comfortable when Katie arrived.

He had just placed the food on the table when he heard a light tap against the front door. He turned to see Katie standing there, backlit by the front porch light.

"Hey," he greeted, making his way to her without hesitation.

As though he'd been gone for months and not just days, Dalton scooped her up, melding his mouth to hers, holding her flush against him.

"Hey yourself," she replied long seconds later when he finally released her lips.

She was smiling.

"Damn I've missed you," he told her, setting her back on her feet. "You hungry?"

"Starving," she told him, taking his hand when he held it out to her.

"Sorry, we don't have much in here right now, but I figured we could make do." And Dalton wasn't exaggerating when he said there wasn't much there. He had a small dining table with four chairs, a new recliner for the living room and a complete bedroom suit in his room. Other than that, his stuff hadn't been moved from Nashville and probably wouldn't for at least another month. He had just put his house on the market and it was getting good traffic, but no offers yet. Not that he cared. He could sit on the house for a while, that wasn't a problem.

Dalton led Katie to the table and pulled out a chair for her. "Beer or water?"

"Water, please," she said, placing her purse on the chair beside her before lowering herself into her seat.

After retrieving one beer and one water, he returned to the table, dropping into the seat across from her and sliding her the bottle across the table.

"Are you tired?" she asked after opening the foam container in front of her.

"I was until about two minutes ago," he answered, watching her face.

The smile that crinkled the corners of her eyes pulled an answering one from him. God, he was so glad she was there.

"Did you drive straight through?"

"Left Nashville at five this mornin'," he told her. "Right after I hung up the phone with you. I showered and then headed out. Already had my stuff packed."

"Please tell me you slept at least a little last night."

"I set my alarm for four. I slept like a baby until then." The last part wasn't exactly true, but only because he had dreamed of her, wanting her. And when he woke up alone in his bed, it'd been devastating. But then he'd called and heard her voice, which was the second best thing to seeing her. "How's work?"

Katie's eyes widened briefly as she stared back at him, her fork held halfway to her mouth, her eyebrows cocked in question.

"The Rusty Nail?" he clarified, chuckling.

"It's good," she said, her eyes darting down to her food. "Nothing new. Cooper played one night last week, but other than that, it's been kinda slow."

"How's school?"

"A pain in the ass," she admitted, her smile returning. "Keeps me up late just trying to get my homework done."

"Anything I can do to help?"

"Probably not," she said, lifting her gaze back to his. "This is great, by the way. Charlie's is my favorite."

"I would've cooked for you," Dalton gestured around the room, "but as you can see, I'm not quite set up yet. However, I intend to rectify that in the very near future."

"When do you move in?"

"Plannin' for early January. Gonna spend a couple of weeks at my folks for Christmas, but then I'll be headin' back. Gotta move in and then head off on a three month tour."

"Tour? Really?"

"Yep," he told her, grinning. He was excited about this one. With the help of Cooper's father, better known these days as Coop's manager, they'd put together a kick-ass thirty-stop tour that would end in April, just before Coop's wedding.

"So you'll be gone for three months?" she asked, looking dejected.

"I'll come home for a day or two, here and there." Dalton didn't like the idea of being away from Katie for that long, but his music career was the only thing he had at the moment. With the equestrian center finally getting up and running, he had to do what he needed to do. If he ever expected to settle down in one spot, he had to do the time now.

"Cooper and Tessa are gettin' married in May, right?" Katie questioned, stirring her food around on her plate.

"Yep. He's actually agreed to let Tessa plan his bachelor party. Dumbass. I tried to weigh in, but she insisted. I figure we'll be hangin' out at a bingo hall drinkin' warm beer and puttin' dots on little cards all night."

Katie laughed, the sound the equivalent of coming home. He wasn't sure what it was about her, but Dalton knew one thing for sure… Hell, it was something he'd known for a couple of months now... Katie was the one. She was the woman he could see himself settling down with eventually.

Not that he would tell her that. As closed off as she was, he knew she'd spook easily. But he had vowed that over the course of the next few weeks and months, he would convince her that he could be the man she needed.

And he damn sure didn't intend to give up until she was his. Forever.

Katie's head was spinning from everything Dalton had just told her. He was permanently moving to Devil's Bend in the next few weeks, he was going off on tour for a few months… It was all too much to take in.

The short-term affair she thought they were going to have clearly wasn't going to happen the way she intended. With him in town, she wouldn't be able to avoid him. More importantly, she wouldn't be able to keep him from finding out who she was.

Up to this point, she had managed to keep everyone out, limiting the people she interacted with outside of the bar, choosing a more solitary life so no one found out. But now Dalton was going to be around and if she planned to see him, he was going to find out.

But he couldn't. She didn't want him to know. She didn't want anyone to know.

"You finished?" Dalton interrupted her thoughts, causing her to look up and meet his dark brown eyes.

"Yeah," she told him. She was no longer hungry. In fact, she was tempted to tell him she needed to go, but the thought of walking away from him right now didn't sit well with her.

He'd ruined her. That was all there was to it. He'd made her hope for the impossible and she'd allowed him to get under her skin. What should've been a friendship had quickly morphed into something significantly more than that and she knew it was all her fault.

She had slept with him, wanting her first time to be with a man like Dalton. A kind, gentle man who didn't look at her as though she had secrets.

Then again, if he knew her secrets, Dalton would've probably run far and fast.

Shaking off the thoughts, Katie helped him clear the table, placing the food back in the paper sack it came in so Dalton could toss it out in Cooper's garbage can later.

"So what do we do now?" Katie asked, glancing around the nearly empty house.

"I'd say we sit out on the porch, but it's gettin' colder," Dalton answered, making his way over to her before pulling her against him.

"Well, I know a way to keep warm," she told him, smiling up at him.

At least they had tonight.

"Yeah?" he asked, nuzzling his face into her neck, the warmth of his breath tickling her skin.

"Yeah," she said softly. "Why don't we close the doors and snuggle?"

"Snuggle, huh?" Dalton's chuckle sent a tremor through her.

When he stood, Katie kept her eyes locked on his face. The heat she saw reflected in his warm brown gaze made her body tingle in so many places. She had never met a man who she desired as much as she desired this man. Dalton Calhoun.

He stole her breath.

He made her want things she knew were impossible.

And most importantly, he made her believe that fairy tales might just come true.

Not that she was naïve enough to truly believe that, but for tonight, she was going to pretend.

She watched him move across the room, the muscles in his back flexing as he walked, pulling his gray T-shirt tight, his biceps flexing. The man was solidly built, all muscle and sinew. There was definitely not doubt as to why women tripped over themselves just to get in his line of sight.

Katie had never been that type of woman, but for him, she could see it being a possibility.

Dalton passed her on the way to the back door, sliding her a sexy smirk. That, mixed with the glimmer in his eyes set her body aflame.

Yes, she certainly knew what was coming next.

And she welcomed it.

Oh how she welcomed it.

She stood in the same place where he had left, waiting for him to finish his task. When he approached, she smiled up at him. "Ready to snuggle?"

Dalton's smirk spoke of wicked promises. He surprised a shriek from her when he lifted her in his arms, sweeping her feet out from under her with one arm beneath her knees, the other under her back as he held her against him. Wrapping her arms around his neck, she held on tight, not wanting him to drop her.

"I'm ready for a lot of things, darlin'."

The erotic promise in his tone had Katie ready to strip him naked as soon as she got back on her feet, but he had other plans. When they reached the bedroom, she noticed it was fully furnished. There was a huge king bed, lavishly decorated with a thick, dark comforter and several pillows. Two nightstands flanked the bed, both with a lamp burning, the soft yellow glow flowing over the bed. On the other side of the room, a huge chest and a matching dresser completed the set.

"Nice," she told him when he dropped her unceremoniously onto the bed, making her laugh.

"Like it?" he asked, crawling up on the bed, hovering above her.

"I definitely like," she answered, no longer talking about the furniture.

Dalton was sin in its finest form, a temptation the likes of which women just didn't survive. He was like a lifetime supply of chocolate coupled with around the clock massages. Every woman's fantasy.

And tonight he was all hers.

Katie prayed she could survive the wild ride he was going to take her on because there was no doubt in her mind that he was going to take her to the moon and back.

"I missed you," Dalton whispered, his gaze traveling from her eyes to her mouth.

Instinctively, Katie slid her tongue out over her lips, watching his eyes flare. She kept her gaze locked with his as she reached for him, sliding her hands over his scruffy jaw, rubbing her thumbs over his cheeks. He really was beautiful.

Ever so slowly, Dalton leaned down until their mouths touched. Katie didn't waste any time as she met him, coaxing his lips open with her tongue, slipping inside his mouth. He tasted like beer and masculinity, morphed together in one sinfully delicious concoction.

The kiss ignited instantly, the gentleness she'd expected from him dissipated, leaving a hunger the likes of which she'd never known in its wake. She wanted him, but she feared she would never get enough. Giving in to him was second nature, something she didn't even have to think about. When his hand moved beneath her T-shirt, her skin tingled and the muscles in her belly fluttered. It was too much, but not enough.

Katie pulled him closer, causing him to lose his balance briefly, his big body coming down on top of hers. She held him to her, refusing to let him go, needing to feel every inch of him against every inch of her.

"I need to feel you," she whispered against his mouth. "I need to feel you now."

"Slow, baby," Dalton crooned, his sexy voice caressing her as much as his hand was.

"I can't wait, Dalton," she pleaded. She didn't want to wait. Didn't want to waste one single second in his arms. The few days they'd been apart had been hell. More so than she wanted to admit and now that he was there with her, alone, she felt rushed, desperate to have him.

Dalton managed to ease off her, breaking the kiss and kneeling between her splayed thighs. He pushed her T-shirt up over her stomach, his eyes grazing her exposed skin. She could feel the warmth of his gaze as it touched her, leaving her breathless and needy.

Wanting to speed him along because the aching need that had settled in her core was too much to bear, Katie gripped her shirt, arched her back and pulled it over her head, tossing it to the floor at the end of the bed. And then, when she was lying there in her bra, she reached for his shirt, her fingers grazing the warm skin beneath. She could feel the hard slabs of muscle beneath her fingertips.

Dalton offered her one of his signature smirks and then relieved himself of his T-shirt in one easy move. She looked her fill, taking her time to admire every tanned, toned inch of him, admiring the muscles as they flexed and bunched with every move he made. His stomach was a series of ripples, his chest two smooth, hard planes. "You're…" She couldn't even finish the statement, wasn't sure what she was trying to say but he took her breath away.

The night in his truck held nothing on this moment. That had been fast and dirty, intense. And this… This was so different, yet her hunger for him was still the same.

Thankfully, Dalton must've been on the same page because she hopped off the bed, toeing off his boots as he unbuttoned his jeans, lowering the zipper and then forcing them down his narrow hips. His cock was thick and hard, slightly curved and jutting out from his flat stomach. He was the embodiment of sex, all lean, delicious male.

Unable to resist, Katie forced herself off the bed, coming to stand directly in front of him. While he watched her, he wrangled his socks off his feet, kneeling as he did. And then she was looking down at him, while he was staring up at her. His fingers went to the button on her jeans. Without breaking eye contact, he quickly slid them down her hips, leaving her standing there in her bra and panties. She'd chosen the black lace just for this moment, just for this man.

He crawled closer, leaned forward and pressed his lips to her stomach while his hands slid up the outside of her thighs, coming to rest on her hips. While he lowered her panties down her legs, she reached behind her back and unhooked her bra, allowing it to slide down her arms and drop to the floor beside where they stood.

His tongue laved her belly, dipping into her belly button and sending a shiver racing down her spine. He continued to kiss her, moving down her hip, the outside of her thigh while his hands mirrored his movements on the other leg. As he stood back up, his hand slipped between her legs and she widened her stance just a little to give him better access. His fingers slipped between her folds and she cried out, the touch so intimate, so sweet.

"Dalton."

"Tell me, darlin'," Dalton said. "Tell me how it feels."

He didn't falter, sliding the tip of his finger inside her slowly.

"Oh, God. So good."

"I've been dying to touch you again, love." He nuzzled his face against the crook of her neck, his breath teasing her oversensitive skin while his tongue blazed a trail of fiery heat along her skin.

He continued to finger her, his other hand coming up to cup her head as his lips made their way to her mouth.

Katie reached between them, wrapping her hands around his cock, stroking him slowly, gently. The hunger that urged her to hurry took a backseat to the reverence that she felt. She needed to go slow, to savor the moment. As far as she knew, this was the last time they'd be together and as much as she hated the thought of never being with him again, she wanted to remember this moment for the rest of her life.

"Katie." Dalton groaned her name as he pulled is mouth from hers, his finger stilling inside her. "Baby, that feels so good."

Swallowing hard, Katie lowered herself to her knees in front of him, looking up to meet his eyes as she did.

"Damn, baby. I'm not sure I'll survive your mouth on me."

Well, he was going to have to try because Katie wanted to taste him, to pleasure him in a way that she'd never pleasured another man.

Men had never been part of her plan, which the only reason she'd remained a virgin until the night in Dalton's truck. It wasn't because she hadn't had the desire, she just had refused to lose focus. Her life was a mess without men interrupting the natural course.

But Dalton was her exception to the rule. He was the one man who had caused her to deviate from her well thought out plan.

Curling her fingers around his shaft, Katie licked the head tentatively, using his groans of pleasure to spur her on. When his fingers slipped into her hair, holding her to him, she took him completely in her mouth, sucking him. She tried to keep her urgency at bay, but the more he groaned, the more she wanted to please him, to send him higher, to allow him to feel even a fraction of what he made her feel when he touched her.

"Katie."

Her name on his lips sounded like a warning, but she continued to suck him, taking him deeper, sliding her tongue over and around the engorged shaft. She allowed him to control the movements, loving the way he flexed his hips, thrusting into her mouth, his fingers tangled in her hair as he continued to pant her name.

"Darlin'," Dalton said harshly, "you're gonna have to stop doing that."

Funny how he said that, but he didn't stop thrusting into her mouth. Until he stopped, she wasn't going to.

Not until she sent him over.

CHAPTER SEVEN

Dalton was doing his damnedest to keep from exploding in Katie's lush mouth, but the woman was making it damn hard to focus. The way her tongue laved his dick, sliding underneath, teasing the tip. She was slowly blowing his fucking mind and he wasn't going to be able to control himself if she didn't stop.

Yet he couldn't bring himself to pull away. The warmth of her mouth felt so damn good. Her tentative movements, the hesitancy in the way her tongue caressed his cock… If he had to guess, the woman had never done this before.

It made sense, and it set off something intensely possessive inside of him as well.

"Fuck, darlin'," he growled. "You've gotta stop."

This time he did tighten his hold on her hair, pulling his cock from between her lips. He wanted to be buried deep in her pussy when he came; he wanted to send her soaring long before he found his release which meant he had to rein himself in.

Reaching for her arm, he helped her to her feet, backing her up until her knees touched the mattress.

"My turn, darlin'. Sit down." He wasn't trying to be forceful, but the grip he had on his control was shaky at best.

Urging her onto the bed, Dalton eased between her legs, leaning over her and sucking her nipple into his mouth. He wasn't gentle, unable to control the debilitating hunger that had infused him the instant they stepped into his bedroom.

He wanted to savor this moment, but he knew he wasn't going to make it that far. He wanted her too damn much. She pushed every button he had, and not in a bad way.

Even knowing how inexperienced she was, he didn't seem to care. He wanted to be the one to teach her, to show her just how a man pleasured a woman.

After teasing her nipple with his tongue, he gently nipped it with his teeth, loving the way her back arched and she cried out his name.

While he focused his attention on her breasts, he used his fingers to part her slick folds, using the tip of his finger to flick her clit gently until she was writhing on the bed, her hands grabbing the comforter tightly.

"That's it, baby," he encouraged. "Let it feel good."

He trailed his mouth down her stomach, then over her smooth mound.

Pausing momentarily, he instructed her to move up on the bed while he retrieved a condom from the box he'd placed in the nightstand when he arrived earlier. If he didn't make preparations now, he feared his brain would be too overloaded to worry about it later and that was the last thing he wanted. As much as he wanted to slide his dick into the warm, wet depths of her pussy, feeling her skin to skin, he knew now wasn't the time. They had to work up to that.

Which he fully intended to do, just not tonight.

Tossing the foil package onto the bed beside her, Dalton knelt on the bed, leaning forward and sliding his tongue through her swollen pussy lips, not giving her a chance to stop him. He eased between her thighs, forcing her legs over his shoulders as he ate her like the starving man he was. He devoured her, licking, sucking, using two fingers to penetrate her. He couldn't stop himself. She tasted so fucking good, the musky scent of her sex driving him forward, making him crazy with lust.

"Dalton," Katie cried out. "Oh... Oh, my... Dalton, I'm gonna come."

He wanted to urge her to come, but he didn't remove his mouth from her pussy, flicking her clit relentlessly while thrusting his fingers into her, feeling her muscles clamp down on him. Fuck.

He had no idea how much time passed while he continued to finger fuck her, teasing her clit. Her body went rigid beneath him, her clit pulsing against his tongue as she cried out. He wanted her to scream his name, and he would get there, but at the moment, the way she screamed was enough.

While she came down from her climax, Dalton rolled the condom over his rigid cock, his eyes never leaving her. And when he was suited up, he spread her legs with his knees, aligning their bodies as he came down over her. Using one hand to guide himself, he pushed inside, her tight pussy sheathing him.

Sweat beaded on his forehead as he held himself back, not wanting to hurt her. When he was balls deep, he held himself above her, their eyes linked together.

"You're so tight. Wet. Damn, Katie. You feel so fucking good."

Her hands came up and wreathed his neck, her arms pulling him to her. His lips hovered above hers.

"Lick my lips," he instructed. "Taste yourself."

Katie did as he commanded, her little pink tongue darting out and sliding over his bottom lip, then his top. He met her tongue with his own, before crushing his mouth to hers and thrusting deeper. Deeper than he thought possible.

Her legs came up and wrapped around his hips, holding him to her. His dick throbbed and pulsed, the vicelike grip of her pussy testing his restraint.

Needing air, he pulled back, studying her face.

"I'm gonna fuck you, Katie."

She nodded.

He took that as permission and resituated himself so that he was on his knees. He gripped her hips, pulling her to him until her ass was off the bed as he began tunneling in and out of her. He drove his hips forward, slamming into her and retreating just as quickly. He couldn't help himself. His sole objective was to possess her, making sure she knew just who she belonged to. Because even if she hadn't realized it yet, she did belong to him.

Dalton had never felt like this with a woman. Sure, he'd had rough sex, crazy sex, but never had he wanted to claim a woman. Not the way he wanted to claim Katie.

"Fuck, you feel so good." Lifting her hips higher, he changed the angle, driving into her over and over, faster. "Come for me, Katie."

Katie's fingernails dug into his forearms as she held on. "Yes. Oh, God, Dalton. It feels so good. Don't stop. Please, don't stop."

Every muscle in his body tensed as he tried to hold back, needing to send her over before he lost it. Watching the way her beautiful tits bounced with every jarring thrust, the way her back bowed, her head tilted back as he pounded into her.

He would never forget this moment. Not in a million years.

Letting go of her with one hand, he found her clit with his thumb, circling the little bundle of nerves, pressing firmly until the muscles in her neck tensed.

"Fuck yes," he growled. "Come on my dick, baby. That's it, darlin'. Come for me."

"Make me come," Katie pleaded.

Dalton thrust forward hard, slamming into her as he continued to press his thumb against her clit.

"Say my name, Katie. When you come on my cock, say my name."

He needed to hear it, needed her to acknowledge just who was fucking her. Who owned her.

Driving into her over and over, Dalton felt the telltale tingle erupt in the base of his spine, taking him by surprise. He couldn't hold back. "Come for me, Katie. Oh, God, baby. I can't hold on. You feel too fucking good."

Katie's fingernails dug deeper into his arms as he thrust into her again and again, his body coated in perspiration as he tried to control his release.

"Oh, God, Dalton. Fuck. Yes! I'm coming. Dalton, I'm coming!"

Dalton's hips jerked forward one last time, his release detonating at the sound of his name. He fell forward, trying not to land on her, but the orgasm brutally gripped him.

Katie's arms wrapped around his neck, holding him to her as his cock pulsed.

And when he finally found the strength to move, Dalton pulled out and dropped to his side, wrapping his arms around Katie. He buried his face in her neck, trying to catch his breath.

Several minutes passed before his heart rate returned to normal, his breaths no longer soughing in and out of his lungs.

He looked up at Katie, noticing she was watching him. She pressed her lips to the corner of his mouth, the move so unexpected, he felt a strange swelling in his chest. It was a combination of the feelings the woman invoked in him and something else…

The look in Katie's eyes wasn't one of promise. No, what he saw in the stormy gray depths was something else. Something that scared him on more than one level.

No, Katie wasn't looking at him as though she was looking forward to spending a lifetime with him. She was looking at him as though their time together was about to come to an end.

♥ ♥ ♥ ♥ ♥

Lying in the dark, wrapped in Dalton's arms, Katie couldn't bring herself to give in to sleep. Although her body was completely sated, her brain was working overtime.

She didn't want to leave, but she needed to go.

What she wouldn't give to spend the night in his bed, letting the feeling of safety and security to wrap around her. It was a feeling she'd never felt before. She'd spent her life hoping to one day find it, never truly believing she would, but now that she was here, she was scared.

Scared that the truth would come out.

Scared that Dalton would figure out she was a fraud.

She couldn't be with him. It wasn't in the cards, no matter how much she wished it were.

Her life was too complicated. It also wasn't her own. Whatever control she thought she had over the decisions she made, she knew it was a lie. Every thought, every decision she made was to survive. To survive in a world she hadn't wanted to be a part of but hadn't been able to escape.

And there was someone else who depended on her. Someone whose needs came before her own.

Dalton stirred, his arms tightening around her as though he were trying to make sure she was still there. She was. For now.

But she did have to leave. She had to get back to her life, had to leave this man behind because the secrets she kept would only hurt him. And that was the last thing she wanted to do.

Dalton made her feel special, he made her feel whole for the first time in her entire life yet she knew it was too good to be true.

"Don't leave me, Katie," Dalton whispered, his voice rough from sleep.

She wished she could tell him that she wouldn't, but that would just be another lie. And up to this point, she hadn't lied to him. She'd merely kept him in the dark. Where she needed him to stay.

"Stay with me, darlin'."

"I wish I could," she told him. "You don't know how much I wish I could."

Dalton's lips pressed against the back of her neck, gentle and warm. She categorized the feeling, tucking it away with all the others because even when she wasn't with him, she would always remember.

No. There was no way Katie would ever forget the only man she had ever loved.

And that was what this was. The feeling that filled her chest. Love.

It was overwhelming with its intensity and she wished she could spend the rest of her life with him. But it wasn't in the cards.

"Tonight," Dalton whispered. "Just stay with me tonight. Please."

A tear slipped from the corner of her eye, sliding down her cheek and falling onto the pillow. Another followed and then another. "Tonight," she agreed.

Just for tonight.

That was all they could have, so she'd stay.

And tomorrow she would go back to her version of normal.

Unfortunately, there was no room for him in her life.

No matter how much she wished there was.

When Dalton's breathing evened out again, his arms relaxing around her, Katie swallowed hard, fighting the tears. And as exhaustion finally took her, Katie closed her eyes, snuggled against Dalton and whispered into the darkness, "I love you, Dalton."

CHAPTER EIGHT

Dalton woke with the sun shining through the windows, no blinds or curtains to stop the cruel intrusion. He was warm beneath the blankets, pressed up against the sweet woman still in his bed.

Honestly, he had expected to wake up alone. But he wasn't.

Katie was sleeping beside him. He was spooned up to her back, his erection pressing against her, eager to find its way into the warmth he remembered from the night before. She must've felt it too because she moved, sliding her smooth backside against him, making him moan.

Without thinking, Dalton lifted her leg and eased between her thighs, pressing against her entrance and slowly sliding inside.

Her soft moan had his breath hitching. God, she felt good.

And yes, he knew what was missing. There was no latex barrier separating them. Just skin to skin. Her soft heat enveloped him, her pussy tightening around him as he pulled her against him, pushing his hips forward slightly until he was buried to the hilt.

"Katie." God, she felt so damn good. Too good.

He knew he should've pulled out, shouldn't have started something that he couldn't finish, but heaven help him, he didn't want to. He wanted to stay right there, connected to her.

When she rolled over onto her stomach, he followed, refusing to pull out of her. And when he was kneeling behind her, he ground his hips against her ass, pushing himself deeper as he held himself up with his arms. He kept his movements slow, unhurried, enjoying the silky grasp of her body, the way his cock tunneled in and out of her.

So good.

He wasn't sure anything felt better than being inside her.

Pressing gentle kisses to her shoulder, he continued to screw into her, rotating his hips, relishing her soft moans. And when she linked her fingers with his, he felt that same overwhelming emotion bubble up in his chest.

Then the memory of the night before came to him. What she'd told him, obviously when she thought he was asleep. She loved him.

He tightened his grip on her fingers, pumping into her and retreating slowly, fucking into her from behind. "Oh, God, Katie," he whispered, his voice rough with the emotion that had consumed him.

"Make love to me, Dalton," she urged softly, her voice raspy.

"I never wanna stop, darlin'," he told her, his lips traveling up to her neck. She smelled sweet, a scent he would never have enough of.

God, he loved this woman.

The feeling should've scared him to death, but it didn't. What he felt for her was so right, so real. Something he'd never felt before and he had no idea how they'd gotten this far. This fast.

But it was the truth. He loved her.

What had started out as friendship had morphed into something so great, he was shocked by how much he felt for her.

"Dalton." Katie drawled out his name, her soft sigh making his cock harden more than he thought possible. "Oh, God, Dalton. I'm gonna come."

Dalton knew he should've pulled out of her, but he couldn't. He didn't want to. He wanted to spend the rest of his life right there, making love to her first thing in the morning. It was the greatest feeling in the world.

When her pussy clamped around his dick, he sucked in a breath. He tried to do the right thing, tried to pull out, but he couldn't. Or maybe he just refused to. Either way, his release took him, and he came deep in her body, the sensation unlike anything he'd ever felt before.

He'd never had sex with a woman without a condom and yet he'd just come inside Katie without one. He had no idea whether she was on the pill or if what they'd done could possibly have other repercussions.

The strangest part of all… He just didn't care.

If they made a baby, then that was what was supposed to happen.

He only prayed she felt the same.

Two hours later, Dalton was climbing into his truck. Katie had left a short time before, kissing him goodbye on his front porch before walking away from him. He'd felt an odd pang in his chest as he watched her leave, but he chalked it up to his need to possess her. As much as he wanted to keep her there with him forever, he knew it wasn't possible.

At least not yet.

He had to take things slow.

For now.

He arrived at the stable to find Cooper shoveling hay into one of the stalls.

"Mornin," Dalton greeted him as he placed his hands on the wood railing, peering through the slats at his friend.

"Mornin'," Cooper replied. "When'd you get back?"

"Last night," he answered.

Cooper propped the pitchfork against the stall wall and stepped out into the wide walkway. "Where'd you stay?"

"My place."

"It's ready?" Cooper asked curiously.

"Almost."

Cooper cocked an eyebrow at him, clearly wanting more details.

"Katie stayed with me last night."

Dalton waited, watching Coop, expecting him to say something, but he didn't, so he spoke. "Say it."

"Say what?" Cooper asked. "What do you want me to say, Dalton?"

"What's on your mind?"

"You sure you know what you're doin'?"

"Me?" Dalton asked, incredulous. "You're askin' me that?"

"Come on, man," Cooper snapped. "Katie's not one of those groupies you can just toss to the side when you get done with her."

"Who said I was gonna be done with her?" Dalton countered heatedly.

Cooper studied him for a moment and then his eyes widened. "Oh, shit."

Dalton grinned, unable to help himself.

"You went and fell in love with her?"

"Don't sound so shocked, bro. It was bound to happen sooner or later."

"Yeah? I figured that, but I was bettin' on later. Much, much later."

"Well, stranger things have happened."

"I'm not sure they have," Cooper retorted.

"Sure they have. Look at you," Dalton said, nodding his head toward Cooper's house. "You're shackin' up with a woman you're gonna marry in just a few months. Can't say I saw that one comin'."

Cooper grinned, clearly proud. "Okay, you're right. Stranger things have happened."

Neither of them said anything for a moment, but then Cooper's expression turned serious. "Man, just be careful with Katie."

Dalton cocked an eyebrow, waiting for Cooper to elaborate. He couldn't understand why his friend was giving him the talk about women, but he damn sure intended to find out.

"She's quiet, that one. Don't you find it strange that no one knows anything about her?"

"I know plenty," Dalton stated firmly, his anger pulsing just beneath the surface.

"Do you?"

"Yeah, I do," he snapped.

"Where does she live, Dalt?"

Okay, fine. He didn't know as much as he wanted to know, but they were moving in that direction. "It hasn't come up yet," he told his buddy.

"No? Then why'd you ask Tessa?"

"Because I wanted to know."

"But you couldn't ask Katie directly?" Cooper asked.

"Man, I don't know where you're goin' with this, but I suggest you get there fast." Dalton was quickly losing his patience. As good of a friend as he considered Cooper, he never expected the man to look down his nose at him when he just wanted the guy to be happy for him.

Sure, Katie had some secrets. She didn't open up as easily as he would want her to, but that was part of her appeal. Eventually, she would tell him everything. And in the meantime, they'd take things slow.

He thought about waking up with her in his bed, the way she'd felt when he slipped inside her first thing, the tight grip her pussy had on his cock. No protection.

Okay, so slow wasn't exactly working out that well for them. But she hadn't said anything when he mentioned that they hadn't used a condom. In fact, her expression hadn't changed, which he took to mean she had already known.

"Well, I was hopin' you'd be happy for me, man," Dalton said, pushing away from the railing. "Sorry to rain on your fucking parade. I didn't realize you were the only one allowed to be happy."

"Damn it, Dalton," Cooper yelled. "That's not what I'm sayin'. I just don't wanna see either of you get hurt. That's all."

"Good. Then we're on the same page." Dalton turned and walked away. Cooper had said his peace, and Dalton made a mental note to avoid any personal conversation where Katie was concerned because clearly the guy wasn't ready to be happy for anyone but himself.

Goddammit.

Somehow, Dalton managed to shake off the conversation he'd had with Cooper earlier that morning. At least long enough to get some things done around the ranch. Since he wasn't yet on the payroll, he was limiting what he did, especially since they'd taken on a few additional volunteers to get through the colder months. He spent a little time with the horses, checked on the few animals they'd recently acquired for a small petting zoo for the children who visited, and then he took one of the four-wheelers out to check on a new section of fence that was being put up.

With nothing else left to do, he made his way back to his house, showered and then decided to head down to The Rusty Nail for a beer. The place was deserted, but it was early afternoon on a Sunday, and even though the big television on the wall was playing whatever football game the few people wanted to watch, the rest of the town was probably spending time with their families.

"What's up, man," Jack greeted him when he marched up to the bar, sliding onto one of the empty stools. "Didn't know you were back in town."

"Got back last night," Dalton told Jack, who was obviously managing the bar solo that afternoon. "How're things goin' round here?"

"Slow and steady," Jack offered with a smile.

Jack Rollins was Tessa's little brother, although "younger" was probably the more apt description because the guy was in no way little. He was a behemoth, in all honesty. Six foot six inches, probably right at two hundred fifty pounds of solid muscle, the guy made Dalton look like a fucking infant. And that was saying something because Dalton wasn't a small guy either.

"Tessa off tonight?" Dalton asked when Jack leaned his elbows on the bar, his eyes slowly scanning the room.

"Yep. Told her I'd fill in."

"What about Eric?"

"The four of them were goin' on a double date," Jack offered.

Dalton could only assume Jack was referring to Cooper, Tessa, Izzy and Eric. He knew Izzy and Tessa were close, and by default that meant Eric was probably around a lot. Not that Dalton gave a shit. Really.

"On a Sunday?" Dalton inquired.

"Some movie came out last week. They were headin' down to Austin to check it out."

Dalton sipped his beer, watching Jack as he scoped out the room. The guy was a contradiction. Funny one second, intensely serious the next. He was seriously protective of his sister, which wasn't necessarily a bad thing when Tessa ran a bar that had been known to have its fair share of fights break out. Sometimes on a nightly basis.

Jack seemed intently focused on someone in the bar and Dalton glanced over his shoulder to see what the younger man was looking at. He noticed a handful of guys sitting at a table near the wall. They were getting a little rowdy, but not more than usual. Then again, it was still early and if they kept at it, they'd probably be unruly before the night was out.

"Have you heard from Adam?" Dalton asked, referring to Jack and Tessa's oldest brother.

"He's doin' good. On the force now. Loves that shit." Jack turned his full attention back to Dalton for a moment.

"Dallas PD, right?"

"Yup. He's talkin' about moving back here in a couple of years, transferrin' to one of the local PDs."

"That'll be good," Dalton said, lifting his beer to his mouth again. Jack's attention was back on the group of guys and Dalton tried to tune everything out to see what they were talking about. Another quick glance over his shoulder and it was then that he realized just what had Jack on edge.

"Little cock sucking bastard," the guy sitting closest to the wall said to the other. "Oughta string his ass up by the ankles and take a bull whip after him. Gotta beat the faggot out of 'em. Only way to take care of the problem."

Yeah, well, Dalton would disagree.

Suddenly, his irritation from the conversation he'd shared with Cooper that morning lit a fire in his gut and the next thing he knew he was on his feet. Slamming his beer on the bar, he turned and headed toward the four guys.

"Did I just hear you correctly?" Dalton asked, none too kindly.

"What's that, Dalt?" the guy asked, sounding as though he considered them to be friends. He got that a lot, especially around Devil's Bend. Because they hung out at the same bar he frequented, they assumed he should be added to their list of friends.

Not the case here. No fucking way.

Without preamble, Dalton leaned down to the guy and gripped him by the front of his shirt, yanking him hard enough that he came up out of his seat.

"What the fuck?" one of the others shouted as she jumped to his feet.

"If I ever hear you say anything even remotely close to what just spewed out of your nasty fucking mouth, I will beat you so bad, your own momma won't recognize you. Are we clear?"

The guy glared back at him and Dalton returned the sneer, daring the bastard to say something else. He was hanging by a thread and he just needed a little tug before he went over the edge.

"Are we clear?" he repeated.

"Yeah," the guy said, none too kindly.

Dalton released him with a shove, sending him back to his seat. He made eye contact with each man at that table, memorizing their faces. This wasn't over, he knew that much. Small town cowboys were filled with testosterone and when they got their asses handed to them in front of anyone, chances were they were going to retaliate.

Not wanting to spend another second in their company, Dalton headed back to the bar. That was when he noticed Jack staring at him. *Yeah, buddy, I got your back,* Dalton thought to himself.

Jack might think he was safely secluded in that little closet he'd kept himself holed up in all his life, but Dalton knew better. From the first time they'd been introduced, Dalton got the impression Jack was hiding something. It hadn't taken him long to pick up on it either. With the sheer number of women who hit on Jack night after night, Jack never taking a single one of them home, Dalton had figured either he was planning to become a monk or he was gay. And when he'd seen Jack eyeing a few of the cowboys who'd come into the bar, Dalton figured it was safe to assume the latter.

The guy was clearly in some serious emotional pain, keeping his secret for so long. And now Dalton understood why. Living in a small town meant dealing with bigots on an entirely different level. Due to the population being so small, those assholes often filled the majority and rather than stand up for what people believed in, they gave in, whether they actually had an opinion or not.

Well, Dalton had never been part of the in crowd, he'd never given in to peer pressure and he damn sure wasn't going to start now.

"Can I get another beer?" Dalton asked Jack, taking his seat at the bar once more.

If he had to guess, the night was going to get really interesting.

Good thing he didn't have anything better to do.

CHAPTER NINE

Katie fell into bed later that night too exhausted to think. For having woken up to such an incredible morning, the rest of the day had gone to shit, which was why she found herself crawling into bed at ten, rather than staying up late to do her homework. For the first time in a long time, she just didn't give a shit.

She was tired.

And she wanted to spend a little time reliving the most wonderful night of her entire life. The night she'd spent in Dalton's arms.

Part of her wished she could just throw on some clothes and show back up at his place, surprising him. But she knew she couldn't. If she had any chance of putting distance between them, she needed to start now. With Christmas rolling up on them sooner than she expected, she had her chance to put some time and space between them. He was going to his parents' house in Georgia, and she had her own things to deal with. Maybe she could get some extra hours in at work. Heaven knew she needed it.

Just when she was drifting off, forcing her thoughts back to Dalton and not on the endless responsibilities that she had, her cell phone chirped.

A smile curled the corners of her mouth before she even looked at the screen. There was only one person it could be.

What she saw next had her sitting up in bed abruptly.

Get down to the bar. Urgent.

The text wasn't from Dalton, but rather from Tessa. Jumping out of bed, she quickly got dressed, pulling on the clothes she'd discarded after taking a shower earlier in the day. She pulled a hoodie over her head and stopped at Sarah's door on her way out. Knocking softly, she waited for Sarah to answer. When she did, she pushed open the door. "I gotta run down to the bar. Something's wrong."

Sarah's eyes widened, but she didn't ask for any details. "Okay. I'll be here."

Katie nodded and then grabbed her purse and her keys before running out the door, barely taking the time to lock it behind her.

Fifteen minutes later, Katie was pulling up to the bar, noticing the parking lot was empty. It wasn't unusual for The Rusty Nail to have fewer people on a Sunday, but this was a little ridiculous.

She heard the sound of the music blaring before she opened the front door, and when she stepped inside, she realized just why no one was there.

The place was in shambles, tables turned over, chairs askew, glass broken all over the floor and beer spilled everywhere.

"What happened?" she asked when she saw Tessa using a broom and a dustpan to clean up some of the broken bottles near the bar.

"Some assholes attacked Jack and Dalton."

"Oh my God. Are they okay?"

Tessa nodded her head toward the stairs that led to the office on the second floor.

Not knowing just what she was supposed to do, Katie made her way around the bar, placing her purse on the shelf and grabbing a rag. She continued to glance over at the stairs, but she managed to keep herself from running over there.

"Go check on him," Tessa insisted. "I didn't call you down here to help clean up. He was asking for you."

Katie's heart leapt into her throat and she tried to swallow around it.

"Jack's out back with Cooper. Dalton's alone."

Katie nodded in understanding and then tossed the rag on the bar before heading to the back. They'd had plenty of fights break out at the bar, but she'd never seen this much damage done. She had no idea what prompted this, but from the looks of the place, she had no idea what to expect from Dalton.

Rather than walking in, Katie rapped her knuckles on the door, waiting for Dalton to invite her in. A second later, his gruff voice instructed her to come in so she did.

"Oh crap," she said on an exhale when she saw Dalton sitting on the couch, holding an ice pack to his eye.

"You should see the other guys," Dalton said with a smirk. His lip was split, his eye swollen and there was blood on his shirt.

"What happened?" she asked, walking in and closing the door behind her.

"Some fucking bigot was talkin' shit. Apparently, he didn't like me reprimanding him. Rather than take me on like a man, him and one of his friends jumped me from behind. The other two took on Jack. They'll probably need to go to the hospital."

Holy crap. Katie tried to imagine what the other guys looked like as she lowered herself to the couch beside Dalton, studying every mark on his too handsome face. Funny how he could still be so beautiful even when he was all dinged up.

"I'm gonna be fine, darlin'," Dalton told her, reaching out and taking her hand.

"Then why did you need me down here?"

Dalton's eyebrows scrunched down as though he was trying to translate her statement into English. When it was obvious he didn't know what she was talking about, she clarified. "Tessa texted me. Told me to come down here. Just a minute ago, she told me you were asking for me."

"I think that was just Tessa interferin'," he told her with a tilt of his lips. "But I'm glad you're here."

Katie nodded, not sure what to think. Why would Tessa do that? Why would Tessa call her in like that? Granted, she was glad she had because seeing Dalton, Katie wasn't sure he needed to be left alone.

"What prompted the argument?" Katie asked, squeezing Dalton's hand when he tightened his grip on hers.

He leaned his head back against the cushions and closed his eyes before he spoke. "They were talkin' shit."

"About you?"

"Nope," he said simply.

"I'm not sure I understand what's goin' on here, Dalton."

He peered at her through one eye, smiling. "You don't need to get in the middle of this."

Clearly, she wasn't going to get any details from him, which meant she would have to talk to Jack. "Stay here," she told Dalton. "I'm gonna get you more ice."

Dalton nodded, his eyes closing once again.

Shutting the door softly behind her, Katie went back downstairs and down the narrow hallway that led to the back exit. She stepped outside to find Cooper talking to a furious looking Jack. She'd seen Tessa's brother pissed before, but she wasn't sure she'd ever seen him like this. Whatever happened, it was clear that Jack was taking it personally.

"You okay?" Katie asked Jack as she approached him slowly.

"Never better," he grumbled.

"Hey," Cooper greeted, rolling his eyes at Jack. "Tessa call you?"

"Yeah," Katie replied. "Texted me. Told me to come down."

Cooper nodded, glancing back at Jack briefly. "He's gonna be fine. Once he calms down. You check on Dalton?"

"Yeah. I need to get him more ice for his face."

"He okay?" Jack asked, looking at her for the first time.

"Seems to be," she told him honestly. His *never better* statement from earlier didn't qualify as a legitimate answer as far as she was concerned, so she repeated her question. "How 'bout you?"

"Fine," Jack retorted. "Thanks for comin' down."

Katie nodded, watching both men closely. They'd obviously been talking about something when she interrupted and neither of them were going to tell her what was really going on so she decided to leave them be. "I'll be inside helping Tessa if you need anything."

"Thanks," Cooper said as she was opening the door and stepping back into the bar.

She found Tessa continuing to sweep things up, putting chairs back on all four legs. Katie figured Dalton could wait a few minutes, so she helped her boss, grabbing a mop and a bucket. For the next hour, Katie followed Tessa around, mopping where Tessa had just swept, until finally the place looked relatively in order.

"What's goin' on, Tessa?" Katie asked as she was putting the mop back in its proper place, following Tessa into the storeroom.

"Dumbass people," she mumbled.

Just when Tessa would've passed her to go back into the other room, Katie stopped her with a hand on her arm. "Why won't anyone tell me what happened?"

Tessa stopped, looking Katie directly in the eye for a brief moment before she finally answered. "Some assholes were talkin' shit. Threatenin' to beat some guy for being gay."

Katie's mouth opened and her hand came up to cover it. "Oh, my God. That's awful."

"Yeah, well…" Tessa began, letting the sentence drift off.

"What?" Katie asked, knowing there was more to the story.

"Dalton threatened the guy and they retaliated."

That made sense. That was usually how fights broke out around there. But she knew there was something that Tessa *wasn't* telling her, so she waited for her to continue.

Tessa sighed heavily and looked up at the ceiling. "They were talkin' about Jack."

"What?" Katie exclaimed, surprised by her own response.

"Yeah. I don't think they knew what they were intentionally targeting him, but turns out they hit a sore spot."

"Is Jack…?" Katie kept her voice low.

"I've suspected it for a while, but he's never openly admitted it, Katie. Please don't say anything."

"I wouldn't. Oh my God. Why would someone do that?"

"No idea. Stupid people, I guess."

"Is he gonna be okay?" Katie asked.

"I'm sure he will," Tessa told her. "My baby brother doesn't let much get him down."

No, he didn't. Katie knew him well enough to know that Jack was resilient. Considering all the shit he'd gone through in his life, he would easily bounce back from this. But she had to wonder whether his secret would now be out. And worse, would those guys that targeted them tonight return?

"Thanks for helpin' me clean up," Tessa said, touching Katie's hand briefly.

"Sure. Anytime. I'm gonna check on Dalton."

Tessa nodded and left the room, while Katie followed her to the bar, remembering the ice she'd promised him earlier. After scooping some into a plastic bag, she returned to the office where Dalton was resting. She didn't bother to knock on the door, instead opening it to find Dalton staring up at the ceiling.

"How're you doin'?" she asked, once again closing the door behind her.

"Better. Thanks for comin' down here."

Katie held out the ice bag for Dalton to take. He took it from her hand and set it on the arm of the couch before holding up his hand to her. When she reached for him, he pulled her down beside him, wrapping his arm around her.

"This doesn't usually happen," he explained.

Katie smiled. "If you think I'm upset that you beat up some asshole, you're wrong."

"Then what are you upset about?" he asked.

"It just freaks me out to see you like this," she told him truthfully.

Katie looked up at him and he turned his head so their eyes met. He leaned forward and pressed his lips to her forehead briefly. "I'm sorry."

She had no idea what he was apologizing for, but Katie didn't respond. She couldn't. Because if she did, she would probably blurt out that she loved him and that was the last thing she needed to tell him. She was supposed to be putting space between them, not getting closer.

Seemed the universe wasn't onboard with her plan just yet.

She hoped like hell that it would get there soon because Katie wasn't sure how long she'd be able to convince herself that walking away from him was the right thing to do.

CHAPTER TEN

Wednesday night

As he geared up to head back to Georgia, Dalton decided to spend his last night in town at The Rusty Nail, wanting to see Katie before he left town. He hadn't seen her much since Sunday, just for a few hours when she worked at the bar last night. He had tried to see her on Monday, but she informed him she had to get her homework finished or she risked failing one of her classes. Who was he to argue with that? She had responsibilities and he definitely didn't want to get in the way of them.

But tonight, he hoped to talk to her a little, maybe convince her to dance with him once or twice. He had resigned himself to stay off the stage. Not because he didn't want to get up there and entertain the crowd, but he just wasn't sure he'd be able to give the crowd his full attention and he wasn't going to half-ass it.

Walking into the crowded bar, he noticed there was a guy up on stage, singing to the crowd. He stopped for a minute, trying to see if he recognized the man. His voice sounded familiar, but his face was cast in the shadow of his hat. Noticing Jack and Eric working the bar, he managed to squeeze through the hordes of people and found an empty spot near the wall.

"What's up, man?" Eric greeted. "Beer?"

Dalton nodded, turning his attention to Jack who was attempting to fill orders; however, his gaze continued to slip up to the big guy on the stage. He gave Jack a run for the money on height, Dalton could tell that from where he was sitting. Wide shoulders, thick arms, the guy looked like he worked out a lot. Or maybe he had some sort of manual labor job that got him looking like that. Dalton didn't know. He could see blond hair peeking out from beneath his black Stetson, but because of the distance, he couldn't make out his features enough to recognize him.

When Eric brought back the cold bottle and set it in front of him, Dalton stopped him before he wandered off again. "Who's the guy up on stage?"

"Brett Basson," Eric informed him simply.

"Why do I recognize the voice?" Dalton asked.

"He's been in here a coupla times."

"Has Coop heard him?"

Eric nodded as he wiped down the bar.

"I think we need to get David in here to listen to him," Dalton told Eric, referring to Cooper's father, the man who recently took on the position of Cooper's manager.

"Well, the big man's supposed to be here next week," Eric told him.

Dalton nodded, tilting his beer bottle to his lips and studying the guy up on the stage. He had great presence, and the crowd seemed really into him. Someone else seemed to be really into him, too, Dalton noticed. Jack was stealing frequent glances while continuing to serve customers who came up to the bar.

"Hey."

Dalton turned at the sound of the female voice from behind him. His lips had already curved up into a smile before he even turned around. "Hey, darlin'," he greeted Katie.

"Didn't know you were comin' by tonight."

"Wanted to get one last night in before I head out."

"You going to your parents?" she asked before rattling off a list of drinks to Eric. Once she'd given the order, she turned back to face him.

"Gonna be gone for a few weeks. Staying at my mom and dad's for a couple of weeks, then headin' back to Nashville to work on the album before the tour starts up again."

"Well, you be careful," she said, her tone much too friendly for his piece of mind.

Dalton reached for her, pulling her over to him and pressing his lips to her ear. "Stay with me tonight."

Katie pulled back, her eyes raking over his face. She didn't look enthusiastic about his offer and her words backed it up. "I'm not sure that's a good idea."

Dalton cupped her face, swiping his thumb over her smooth cheek. "Please."

He saw her swallow hard, her gaze dropping down briefly. "I don't know, Dalton."

He wasn't above begging, but he wasn't sure that was going to benefit his cause at the moment, so he decided to play it cool for a little while. "Think about it. I'll ask you again before the night is over."

She managed a small smile, but then they were interrupted when Eric placed her drinks onto the waiting tray.

Dalton followed her with his eyes as she made her way through the crowd, delivering drinks and chatting with the customers. He finished off his beer, not looking away from Katie until she was swallowed up by the people surrounding her. That was when he noticed the cowboy on the stage was putting his guitar down, clearly taking a break.

When Brett approached the bar a minute later, Dalton raised his hand to get his attention. The guy nodded as he squeezed through the people surrounding the bar and then joined.

"Hey, Dalton," Brett greeted, reaching out his hand.

Dalton returned the gesture, and then got to his feet, slapping the bar. "Got a minute?"

"Sure."

Jack came over, looking at Dalton. "Can we get two beers?"

He noticed the way Brett and Jack glanced at one another briefly, looking away just as quickly. Well, hell. Looked like these two had something in common. Dalton smiled to himself as Jack disappeared to get the beers, returning a moment later, his eyes still spending time raking over Brett's face.

"If you see Coop, will you send him upstairs?" Dalton asked Jack before urging Brett toward the stairs. He didn't bother waiting for an answer; he just hoped Jack had paid attention to him in the first place. The guy seemed just a little preoccupied with the singer.

Once they were upstairs, Dalton opened the cheap plastic blinds that covered the window overlooking the bar.

"How long you been singin' in bars?" Dalton asked, breaking the ice.

"A few years now," Brett answered, tipping his beer bottle to his lip as he stared down at the crowd below.

"You lookin' for a manager?" Dalton spared him a glance.

"You offerin'?" Brett countered.

"I might just know someone who's lookin' for talent."

"And you think I'm that talent?"

Dalton liked the guy already. His straightforward responses were a nice change of pace. He hadn't had many conversations with up and coming artists, but the few he had encountered were usually either hotheaded, thinking they deserved to be in the spotlight, or they were too star struck to have a legitimate conversation. Brett was neither.

"It's possible," Dalton answered. "I've got someone I'd like you to meet."

Brett didn't answer, just tipped his beer back again and kept his eyes trained on the bar below.

"Do you live here?" Dalton inquired when it was obvious Brett wasn't going to say anything.

"Austin," Brett answered simply. "Spend a lot of time checking out the bars in surrounding areas."

"You've been here before," Dalton said.

"A couple of times. One of the better places to hang out."

Dalton agreed with Brett on that count. He'd actually been impressed with the place from the moment he stepped foot in the door. Since his career took off, he didn't get to spend much time in the small town bars, but he tried to get back to them any chance he had.

Then again, The Rusty Nail had become one of his preferred hangouts for more than just the stage. Katie was more of a lure than the chance to get up on stage these days.

Dalton continued to watch out the window when he noticed Jack heading toward the back. He figured the guy was sneaking outside for some air. He spared a look at Brett, noticing the man was following Jack with his eyes as well.

Part of him wanted to say something to Brett, to encourage the guy to go talk to Jack. The other part knew he had to keep his mouth shut. Despite his realization after the altercation on Sunday, Jack Rollins hadn't come out of the closet. Nor did he know whether the tall, blond cowboy standing beside him was actually gay. Most importantly, none of that shit was his business and he'd do them all a favor if he just kept his opinions to himself.

"If Coop shows up, I want you to talk to him. He recently changed managers."

"His father, right? David Krenshaw?"

So the kid kept up with the local news. That was good. "Yep. His ol' man will be in town for the holidays. Be a good idea for you to meet with him."

"Why're you doin' this, Dalton?" Brett asked, turning his dark blue eyes on him.

"David's lookin' for some talent. If you ain't interested, just say the word. I'll drop it. Ain't no skin off my nose."

"I'm interested," Brett said firmly.

Dalton slapped the guy on the back before turning back to the door. "Good."

He didn't wait for Brett to follow, but he knew the guy was close behind him. When he reached the main floor of the bar, he peered over his shoulder to see Brett going out the back exit.

Dalton smiled again. Looked like Brett needed some air, too.

Another thing those two had in common.

Now it was time to mind his own business. And his business was the black-haired, gray-eyed waitress who was casting him a look that spoke of some serious promises for later tonight.

Katie wasn't surprised to see that Dalton had hung around after closing time. He had spent most of the night sitting at the bar, chatting with Eric and Jack, and then Cooper when he arrived a couple of hours ago. She noticed when he slipped off to the office with the cowboy who'd been center stage most of the night twice, once alone and then again with Cooper.

Not that she was keeping tabs on him or anything.

The thought made her smile. Yes, she was tracking his every move, memorizing every smirk, every look he sent her way. All because she knew their time together was coming to an end. He was going home for the holidays and she had made up her mind. She was going to insist that he move on when he came back.

Her secrets were weighing heavily on her heart and the last person she wanted to hurt was Dalton. She loved him. There was no doubt about that. He was the only man she'd ever loved. Possibly the only man she would ever love. But he deserved better. He didn't need the baggage she carried with her and she wasn't going to be his burden.

So, when he had asked her if she'd stay the night with him tonight, she had given it serious consideration and decided she would. But this really had to be the last night she spent with him.

Sure, she was probably inviting more heartache, but she just couldn't say no to him. Not when he was the one person plaguing her every thought from the moment her eyes opened in the morning, to the instant they closed at night.

Well, maybe not the only person, but he was certainly taking up a lot of the real estate in her mind at the moment.

"Did you decide?"

Katie turned around to see Dalton standing behind her. She had just tossed the dishrag into the bucket beneath the bar.

"Yeah," she told him. "I'll stay."

The smile he gifted her with had her heart ripping in two.

"Wanna follow me back to my place? Or I'll take you and bring you to pick up your car in the morning."

"I'll follow you." She wasn't sure when she would leave, but she needed her car or she would have to depend on him. Since she was contemplating sneaking out, she had to think about the easiest way to do that.

"Good night, kids," Eric called out as he emerged from the back room.

"Night," Katie replied. "I'll see you on Friday night."

Eric nodded as he moved toward them. "I'll be here."

After Dalton said his good-byes to Eric, he took her hand and led her out through the back doors. She had parked in the back lot, knowing that the place would be full. It always was on a Friday, and especially when they had live music.

Dalton helped her into her car and she waited to pull out of the parking space until he was in his truck, his headlights shining through the darkness.

The bar wasn't far, and at three o'clock in the morning, there wasn't anyone else on the road, so it took all of ten minutes to get to Dalton's house, including the slow drive down the narrow dirt road that led to his house at the back of Cooper's ranch.

Dalton was faster than she was and opened her door for her, helping her out and then holding her hand as they made their way into the house.

"You hungry?" he asked, locking the front door behind them.

Katie took stock of her surroundings, noticing there was more furniture in the house. It wasn't filled to capacity, but there were a couple of additional pieces. She followed him into the kitchen, noticing there were small appliances – a toaster oven, can opener, and a coffee pot – set out on the black granite countertops.

"I could eat," she told him, setting her purse on the breakfast bar.

"Scrambled eggs and bacon?" he asked, opening the refrigerator and peering at her around the door.

"Sounds perfect."

Dalton nodded his head toward the room behind her and Katie turned. "The television is set up. We can eat in there."

"Okay."

While he worked in the kitchen, Katie kicked off her shoes as she fumbled with the remote. While she hit button after button, she slid into the brown leather recliner, noticing that it was big enough for two people to sit comfortably. It took her about ten minutes to figure out the system, but she managed. She was pretty sure she had heard Dalton chuckle at her as he cooked, but she pretended not to notice, keeping her smile to herself.

After finding a movie channel, she placed the remote on the small table beside the chair. A few minutes later, Dalton joined her with two plates overflowing with food. He handed them over and then retreated to the kitchen once more, returning with two glasses of orange juice.

They discussed his less-than-adventurous trip to the grocery store while they ate and when they were finished, Dalton took the dishes to the kitchen, but he wasn't gone long before he plopped down beside her once again. She curled up against him, completely aware of his body beside her, the scent of his cologne, mixed with beer and cigarette smoke from the bar wafted in her direction, sparking her awareness even more.

Turning her head, she noticed he was watching her, not the movie. There was an intensity in his gaze, one she hadn't seen before. Not like this.

"Come here," he murmured, readjusting his position so that she was straddling his lap, staring down at him while he looked up at her. "I'm gonna miss you."

"And I'll miss you," Katie replied honestly. Although she saw the end of their relationship in sight, there was no need to deny the truth. She would miss him. Terribly.

But they still had tonight.

And Katie wanted to take advantage of every second.

She reached down, unhooking his belt buckle, and then releasing the button and zipper while she kept her eyes locked with his. When she had his jeans released, she eased her hand inside, stroking him slowly. Velvet covered steel slid against the palm of her hand. Dalton's eyes closed briefly, but then opened, gazing up at her as though she controlled his destiny.

And maybe for tonight she did.

They could be Katie and Dalton, two people who were attracted to one another. They could leave the rest of the world outside of Dalton's front door for just a little while. And tomorrow…

Tomorrow, they would both move on, and have the memory of tonight to hang on to.

CHAPTER ELEVEN

Dalton wasn't familiar with the emotion that was consuming him. He'd never felt anything like this, and he wasn't referring to the physical reaction his body was having to Katie stroking his dick in her soft, smooth hands either.

Although that was incredible.

But the way she was looking at him, as though she could read his thoughts or see into his soul... That was what was threatening to choke him up.

He was tempted to tell her that he loved her, but he bit his tongue, holding the words in. He didn't want to spook her, didn't want to send her running. He wanted to make her feel the same way he did, make her want him until there was nothing more important in the world than what they meant to one another.

She wasn't there yet. He could see it in her stormy gray eyes. She was holding back for whatever reason. And he was okay with that. For now.

"Oh, damn, baby," he said through a sharp exhale.

Katie was sliding off his lap and onto the floor, his dick still in her hands. She was blinding him with a need so fierce, he wasn't sure he was going to survive it.

Assisting her, Dalton lifted his hips and pushed his jeans and boxers down his thighs. Katie pulled them the rest of the way off while he tugged his shirt over his head and tossed it onto the floor with the rest of his clothes.

And then he watched her.

With one hand, she was stroking his cock slowly, gently, the other cupping his balls. He spread his legs farther apart, giving her better access, keeping his eyes on her as she leaned forward and wrapped her lips around the engorged head of his cock. The only thing sexier than her mouth wrapped around his dick that he'd ever seen was when she came. Which she would do very, very soon.

In the meantime, Dalton sucked in a breath, enjoying the raspy sensation of her tongue against the sensitive underside of his shaft, the way she sucked on the swollen head every so often.

Dalton reached for the ponytail holder at the back of Katie's head, sliding it off so he could slip his fingers into the silky strands, holding her head gently while she took him into her mouth, deeper with every downstroke.

His cock was pulsing, his balls drawing up against his body, but he wasn't ready to come. Not yet. He wanted to be inside her when he did. And the only thing stopping him from doing that was the panties she had on beneath that skirt.

Gripping her hair more firmly, he halted her motions, her eyes widening as they met his. "As sweet as your mouth is, and as much as I'd like to watch myself come in your mouth, that's not in the cards tonight. Come here."

Katie got to her feet, but she didn't join in him the chair immediately. She stood in front of him and slowly stripped off every stitch of clothing she had. First the sweater and skirt, then her bra and panties.

He observed every move she made, grazing every smooth inch of her skin with his eyes as she bared herself to him. And when she was as naked as he was, he reached for her hand, pulling her back onto his lap. She straddled him, her eyes meeting with his once again.

For the first time since she walked in his house, she kissed him, the thrust of her tongue into his mouth obliterating his senses. She tasted so damn sweet. And when she lowered herself onto his cock, taking him in hand and guiding him into her scalding hot depths, he feared he was going to come far too soon.

Gripping her hips to keep her from moving, he plundered her mouth with his tongue. He wondered whether she realized they weren't using a condom again. He knew he should've mentioned it, should've taken the precaution, but he was immobilized from the overwhelming pleasure, his brain cells scattering.

When she cupped his face in her small hands, pulling back and staring down at him, he knew he was a goner. And then she smiled, her eyes lighting up as she said, "Make love to me."

He damn sure wasn't about to tell her no.

Releasing the grip he had on her hips, he returned her smile. "Ride me, Katie."

Her smile turned a tad wicked, but her hips moved and his breath caught in his throat. She started off slow, her pussy gripping him as she took him as deep as she could.

"Oh, fuck," he growled. "That's it, darlin'. Ride my cock."

Her movements quickened, the way she rocked her hips back and forth, taking him in and slowly releasing him. And Dalton did his best to withstand the sensual torture for as long as he could, but he knew he was about to be at the point of no return. She felt too damn good.

He assisted her by guiding her hips, pulling her down onto his cock as he thrust up into her, fucking her harder and harder.

"Dalton," she moaned. "Oh, God."

Her fingers slid behind his head, her nails digging into his skull as she tipped her head back, her breasts jutting out toward his waiting lips. He sucked one beaded nipple between his lips, gently nipping her with his teeth. She cried out, her grip on his head tightening as her pussy clamped down on him.

"Rub your clit, Katie. Make yourself come on my dick."

Katie released one hand from behind his head, reaching down between them. Dalton followed the movement, watching as she used her middle finger to seek the hardened nub hidden between her swollen folds. He lifted her hips slightly, his feet planted firmly on the floor, his body sliding down into the chair as he used all the traction he could find to fuck her, watching his cock tunneling in and out of her while she teased her clit.

"Oh, damn, baby." Yeah, he wasn't going to last long. It was too much.

"Dalton," she cried out, her internal muscles clamping down on him almost painfully.

He didn't slow his thrusts, pulling her toward him as he pushed deep inside. "Fuck, Katie. Come for me, baby."

He was tempted to close his eyes, but then he didn't need to because Katie's entire body went rigid in his arms, her fingers pulling his hair, her nails digging into his scalp as she shattered right there in his arms. Unable to hold back any longer, he let go, his cock pulsing deep inside her as he pulled her down onto him one last time. He held her there, his hips flexing as he buried himself as deep as he could.

Cupping the back of her head, he held her against him, listening to her breathe as he tried to sort out the emotions that were boiling inside him. Now, more than ever he wanted to tell her that he loved her. But he knew now certainly wasn't the time. Never in the heat of the moment.

He would tell her.

Eventually.

Katie spent the night wrapped in Dalton's arms once again. However, she didn't sleep. Not a wink.

No, she lay awake and thought about everything that had happened between them over the last few months. She thought about all the good times they'd had and her reasons for why it all had to come to an end.

As much as she wanted to pretend to be someone else, she knew she couldn't. Her secrets would catch up to her. There was no doubt about that.

She'd spent too much time shucking her responsibilities as it was and she had more important things to worry about than Dalton or the love she'd developed for him. In another life, maybe they could've had something, possibly something that defied any love ever established.

But not this life.

Her cards had been dealt and she couldn't change her hand at this point.

It was time to move on, time to end this before he learned the truth.

She glanced at the clock on the nightstand. It was already after six and the sun would be coming up soon. She couldn't be there when Dalton woke up. He was leaving today and she didn't think she was capable of saying goodbye to his face. Not without revealing how she truly felt about him.

Easing out from beneath his arm, she took her time, not wanting to wake him. And when she was free, she dropped her feet to the floor and stood. Glancing back at him one last time, she admired him. He was truly the most beautiful man she'd ever met. Inside and out. And her love for him would never die, but he deserved so much more than what she had to offer.

Katie tiptoed out of his bedroom, not bothering to close the door behind her. She didn't want to risk any unnecessary noise. As it was, everything she did seemed to be amplified, at least to her own ears. Instead, she hurried to the living room, pulling on her clothes as quickly as she could, grabbing her purse and walking out the front door. As she sat in her car, she stared back at the house for a moment.

And when the single tear slid down her cheek, she knew it was time to go. She'd already gotten in over her head and she wasn't strong enough to resist this man so she had to do things her way.

By the time she reached the main road that would lead her back to her apartment, the tears were steadily streaming down her face. She didn't try to stop them. It was her way of letting him go.

She wasn't who he thought she was. She would never be that girl. The innocence, it was a front. A cloak that securely hid the life she'd been living for far too long. The life she couldn't turn her back on. Sometimes there were circumstances that were out of your control and no matter how much you wished things could be different, you knew deep down that it wasn't possible. And Katie knew.

She'd known since the day she turned eighteen.

CHAPTER TWELVE

Five weeks later

End of January

Dalton knew he had no choice but to go back to Devil's Bend. At least for a little while. He'd spent the last month with his parents, overstaying his welcome he was sure. Although they never questioned why he was still there, he knew they worried.

But he hadn't been able to talk to them. Not about this.

He was acting like a fucking pussy over a girl and it was even beginning to get on his own fucking nerves.

Which was why he was going back to Devil's Bend to get his house in order. Right before Christmas, he had received an offer on his house in Nashville, one that he hadn't been able to refuse. So he'd managed to have his things packed up and sent to his new place, with Cooper overlooking the delivery. He should've been there, but it had been around that time that his world came crashing down around him.

At Christmas. What a fantastic present that had been.

Katie, the woman he'd fallen in love with, had entertained thoughts of spending the rest of his life with had told him that she didn't want to see him anymore. She didn't even give him a chance to talk to her, to find out just what her reasons were.

When he tried to call her cell phone, she didn't answer. When he tried to reach her at The Rusty Nail, she refused to take the call.

Sure, he could've hightailed it back before now, but he'd been too confused to go after her. He still had no idea what the hell had happened. Aside from the fact that he'd woken up alone the last night he'd been in Devil's Bend, he'd had no notice that things were going to go south. Not like this.

Tessa had reached out to him once or twice, but he had tried to avoid the conversation. Katie was Tessa's friend and her employee, and the last thing Dalton wanted was to stir up shit for Katie. He might not know exactly what was going on with her, but whatever it was, she'd decided to put up a wall between them. And despite Tessa's good intentions, Dalton wasn't interested in bringing others into the mix.

He fully intended to find out what was wrong, but unfortunately, the timing wasn't right. He figured Katie knew that when she'd called it quits.

He was currently in the middle of his next album and he had a tour date rapidly approaching.

As much as he wanted to drop everything and go find her, to insist that she tell him what the issue was, he had too much on his plate.

But now he had the chance. He just had to get through the next couple of hours and he'd be back on the road, back in Devil's Bend for a few days before the tour kicked off. Oddly, for the first time since his career got off the ground, he wasn't looking forward to hitting the road. But he knew he had to. He couldn't let his fans down. Not the people who supported him. They deserved one hundred percent from him and he fully intended to give them that.

For the last couple of weeks, he hadn't been sure just how he was going to make that happen though. His thoughts constantly drifted back to Katie and what they'd had, what they'd shared. No matter what her reasons were, he knew she felt it too. They hadn't just had a brief affair. What transpired between them was more than that.

But that was exactly what she told him it was in one of the few texts she'd sent back to him.

Didn't mean he believed a single word.

Fucking hell. Dalton just wanted to get out of Nashville. And after that session, he knew it was time. He couldn't stay focused. He'd finally hit a wall.

Devil's Bend was calling his name and he was ready to hit the open road. Hours from now, he'd be back in the one place he'd been thinking about for the last month. Back where his life hadn't been a shitty number of endless days and nights spent thinking about what could've possibly gone wrong.

Now he had the chance to find out.

Maybe it would bring a little closure, if nothing else. After all, every time he closed his eyes, he saw images of Katie, could hear her seductive voice in his head, the sexy things she had said to him in the middle of the night back when he spent his evenings or early mornings talking to her on the phone.

When he remembered those instances, he found himself trying to recall any sign of what was to come. The one thing he always seemed to fall back on was her insistence that she was always busy. The more he thought about it, the more he didn't understand. She worked at The Rusty Nail three nights a week, and she took online classes which left her with an endless supply of homework, or so she said.

But he just couldn't seem to make it all add up.

Something else was going on. He could feel it.

Dalton wanted to assume that school was keeping her burning both ends of the candle, but he just couldn't imagine her taking so many classes that she spent every waking hour doing homework. She had admitted that she was working on her degree in accounting. So, sure, he figured a lot of studying was necessary for that sort of work, but seriously. How many hours could one person spend in a week on homework? And how was she able to spend time with him when she had if that was the case?

Dalton pushed open the doors of the office building where the recording studio resided, the brisk January air slapping him in the face. Shoving his hands in the pockets of his jacket, he felt around for his keys as he continued toward the parking lot.

"Mr. Calhoun!"

The sound of his name being screamed by one reporter after another was grating on Dalton's nerves. Up to this point, he'd done his best to ignore them, but they didn't seem to be taking a hint.

"Is it true that you're dating a stripper?"

Dalton came up short.

Turning to locate the face that owned that voice, he waited to see if they'd continue. A smarmy grin told him exactly who the culprit was.

"What did you say?"

"Rumor has it that you're dating a stripper. Care to comment?"

Where the fuck did these people come up with this shit?

Then again...

There was a warning bell chiming in Dalton's head. The damn thing was loud enough that he couldn't completely ignore it.

But he tried.

"No comment," he mumbled and turned back the way he had been heading. It would do no good for him to stop and listen to the bullshit. He'd heard it all.

Four fucking hours. That's the amount of time he'd just wasted in the studio, unable to get his focus where it needed to be. At this point, his throat hurt and he wanted to spend the next few hours without having to say a word, maybe by the time he was back in Texas he'd feel at least sub-par.

"No comment? We have it on good authority that you've been seeing Katie Renee Clarren, stripper extraordinaire. Stage name Sunshine."

Dalton saw red and his flash-temper got the best of him. It wasn't that he was prone to violence, but the one thing he detested was when someone went and talked shit about someone he cared for. Unfortunately, being in the limelight, Dalton saw it more often than not. But this time, the smarmy bastard grinning like an idiot had gone too far.

Stomping back to stand nose to nose with the asshole who was spreading vicious lies, Dalton growled. "Don't let me hear you say her name, understand me?"

"So it's true?" the asshole asked, clearly pushing his luck while glancing around as though someone else actually might care what he had to say. "You're seeing Katie? Is it serious? Do you care that she takes her clothes off for other men?"

Dalton was tempted to punch the dickhead in the face, but that would only add fuel to an unnecessary fire at this point.

Ignore his shit. Move on.

The voices in his head were doing their best to sway him in the opposite direction, but something kept his feet rooted in place.

"What the fuck are you talkin' about?" Dalton growled, keeping his voice low.

"Katie Renee Clarren, twenty-three years of age, five-feet-two-inches, black hair, gray eyes—"

Dalton couldn't help himself, he gripped the front of the reporter's shirt and pulled him even closer.

"Lay off, man," the reporter spat. "I'm just relaying the facts and based on your reaction, I assume it's true. Wait a minute…" the guy paused, looking seriously confused. "You didn't know, did you?"

Dalton shoved him, not hard enough to knock him to the ground but just enough to make him stumble backward.

"Look, Dalton, I'm sorry, man. I didn't mean to break the bad news to you. Look at it like this, at least she's not a hooker," the bastard said, laughing. "At least not that we know of."

The red haze was consuming Dalton by now, but he managed, by the grace of the Lord Almighty, to turn and walk away. This asshole had no idea what he was talking about.

Katie. A stripper?

No fucking way.

Don't believe everything you hear, he reminded himself.

How many times had someone made up some bullshit rumor about him? And even half the time, when they did get part of the story right, they butchered the rest, probably on purpose.

This was no different. Katie was a waitress, not a fucking stripper.

She would've told him, right?

Pinching the bridge of his nose, Dalton opened his truck door and climbed inside, slamming the damn thing a little too hard. He shoved the key in the ignition and twisted, the big, powerful engine roaring to life with a ball-rattling rumble.

He darted a look in the backseat, checking that his bag was back there. It was. And now he was on his way to Texas.

As he pulled out of the parking lot, his stomach roiled and his head was screaming.

And that was when he took a left, laying on the gas and leaving a trail of rubber in his wake.

Too bad, he should've taken a right if he had intended to go to Texas.

Katie couldn't curb her edginess. She attributed that to the amount of time she'd spent in the bathroom these last few days, hovered over the toilet, puking her guts up. And it had only gotten worse from the moment she opened her eyes that morning. She was sick to her stomach and nearly jumping out of her skin on top of that.

Dalton was on his way back.

Or at least he was supposed to be according to what she'd overheard last night. She had been innocently waiting at the bar for Eric to fill her drinks when Cooper had mentioned the news to Tessa. So she hadn't purposely been eavesdropping, but she knew. And it didn't make her feel any better.

She hadn't talked to him for a month, and even before then, she'd only communicated by text, answering as little as she could without completely blowing him off. It was the least she could do.

Not that she deserved any praise whatsoever. What she had done to him was appalling, even to her. She'd shunned him completely, after all they'd been through together. She loved him; there was no doubt about it. She was trying to protect him.

She continued to remind herself of that. She wasn't a bad person, didn't get off on hurting people and this… what had happened had damn near destroyed her, but it had to be done.

Katie could only imagine all of the questions going through Dalton's head. All of the answers she never gave him. He'd stayed away longer than he originally said he would, and she didn't very well blame him. In the middle of the night, when she crawled in from work, she fought the urge to call him. She just wanted to hear his voice.

But as much as she wished she could tell him the truth and life would continue to go on the way it had been, she knew better. Men didn't understand the sort of secrets she held. Especially not men as untainted as Dalton. He would never be able to deal with the truth.

She'd just clocked in at The Rusty Nail and was wrapping her apron around her waist as she made her way out to the bar when Cooper approached.

"Did you hear?"

A sudden odd ringing sounded in Katie's head, along with a strange heart stutter, all triggered by the sound of Cooper's voice. She had no idea what he was about to tell her, but she got the feeling it wasn't good.

"Hear w-what?" she stammered.

"Dalton's not comin' back right now."

"He's not?" A sense of foreboding washed over her, making it hard to breathe. "Did he say why?" she managed to ask.

"No, he didn't go into detail. Said somethin' 'bout needin' to take care of a coupla' things. I figured he'd call you."

Katie shook her head, answering the silent question. No, Dalton hadn't called her, not in weeks. But Katie hadn't told anyone that she'd broken things off with Dalton. There would be too many questions, ones she couldn't answer. But the fact that he wasn't coming back now… that in itself told her more than she wanted to know. Something had happened. And she had a feeling it had something to do with her.

She had a feeling that life, as she knew it, had just crumbled around her. Because, if Dalton had found out about her other life, then there was a good chance Cooper and Tessa were going to find out soon enough.

It's your fault for keeping all those damn secrets, she told herself.

And it was true, but Katie had her reasons.

Or at least she thought she did.

Katie's shift seemed to crawl by. At one point, she had found herself watching the clock, something she rarely had the opportunity to do. She blamed it on whatever was making her sick. Maybe she had the flu.

Right.

The flu.

When closing time came, she was anxious to get out of the bar. As soon as her cleanup was finished, she made a beeline for the door, not bothering to tell anyone she was leaving.

It wasn't until she was walking into her apartment that she actually took a deep breath.

Not that it helped.

"Wow, you're home early," Sarah, her roommate, greeted. "I figured you'd be out with Dalton. What happened?"

"He didn't come back," Katie whispered, still feeling a little stunned. "Do you think he knows?"

"Oh, crap," Sarah mumbled, pushing to her feet.

"Where's…?" Katie asked before her friend could wrap her in a stranglehold and attempt to put Katie's world back together the way she had so many other times.

"Sleepin'. It was a good night."

Sarah was Katie's roommate, but she was also so much more than that. She was her best friend, her confidante, and the only person who'd stood by Katie for the last five years.

"Come on, sit down," Sarah encouraged, taking Katie's hand in hers. "Have you talked to him?"

"Who?"

"Dalton. Good grief, woman. Snap out of it."

Katie shook her head as though trying to do just that. It wasn't easy because for the better part of the last few hours, she'd been wandering around in a fog, fearing the worst.

"No," Katie admitted. For the last month, Katie had been pretending that she was still communicating with Dalton, more for Sarah's benefit than anything. She didn't want her best friend to worry about her. Granted, she was pretty sure Sarah knew better. She was tired of pretending. "Not since before Christmas. He doesn't try to contact me anymore."

It was what she wanted, she reminded herself. In fact, that was something she had reminded herself of every day since she'd last seen him. She was the one who set this in motion. Rather than be truthful and tell him who she really was, Katie had kept it all to herself, hoping to spare him the heartache.

"Is that what all this has been about?" Sarah asked, her disappointment etched on her pretty face.

Katie nodded. She was tired of lying, tired of acting as though everything was perfect in her already fucked up world.

"Why didn't you tell me, Katie?" Sarah asked incredulously. "Why would you keep that to yourself?"

"I… I just didn't want you to worry."

"Right. Like I haven't been worried that you've spent the last few weeks walking around like a zombie, making yourself sick… Oh. My. God."

Katie met Sarah's piercing blue gaze, waiting to see what she would say.

"Are you…?" Sarah moved closer, taking Katie's hand in hers. "Honey, are you pregnant?"

God, she hoped not, but she could no longer pretend that wasn't an option. Not that she'd ever been pregnant before, but she'd done enough reading up in the last few days to believe it was a real possibility. "I haven't taken a pregnancy test," Katie told Sarah, glancing down at her lap.

"But it's a possibility?"

"Yeah." Admitting that aloud actually felt surprisingly good. It took some of the weight off her shoulders. Not that it made anything better, but it helped.

"We need to take a test," Sarah stated firmly.

Katie lifted her eyes until their gazes met. "We?" she asked with a small smile.

"I'm here for you, Katie. You know that. You're my best friend in the entire world. I'd do anything for you. You know that."

Katie did know that. But during all of this, she had shut out the one person she knew she could depend on.

"Do you want me to run out and get one now? There's a twenty-four hour pharmacy not far from here."

"No," Katie said adamantly. "Not now. Today though. I promise." It was after three in the morning; Katie did not want Sarah to go anywhere, especially not on an errand for her.

"Okay. After my shift this morning, I'll stop and pick one up."

Katie nodded. She didn't move, trying to put together the next words; tried to formulate the questions that had been plaguing her. She swallowed hard and met Sarah's eyes once more. "Do you think I should? You know, reach out to him?" Katie asked Sarah, dropping to the couch when the cushion hit the back of her knees.

"Are you ready to tell him the truth? Because if you're not, what good is it going to do?" Sarah questioned.

Sarah had a point. Katie wasn't looking to tell him everything that was going on. It would defeat the purpose of all her suffering for the last month. And it wasn't as if he was going to look at her and say all was forgiven. She'd lied to him. She'd omitted the truth for weeks on end and there was no way he could forgive her.

After all, she was a stripper. A woman who took her clothes off for cash.

Didn't matter that she hated it; despised going to work at the club. But it was a necessary evil, one that paid the bills and kept her little world spinning.

"He knows," Katie whispered, fighting the tears that were clogging her throat.

"You don't know that."

Katie shook her head. "He knows and now he knows I lied to him."

"How could he know?"

Katie shrugged while she said, "He's a celebrity. People dig up dirt on him all the time. Maybe someone figured it out."

"But y'all have been broken up for weeks. Why would anyone care?"

Katie processed her friend's questions, but the words weren't what bothered her. Sarah's expression said it all, confirming Katie's worst fears.

"I should've told him."

"I won't argue with you there," Sarah stated, not helping at all.

Katie stared at the wall, wishing like hell that life had been easy, that she'd been given the opportunity so many other people had. Instead, she'd had to make difficult – no, make that impossible – decisions that were now going to come back and bite her in the ass.

Knowing that sitting around wasn't going to help the situation any, Katie pushed to her feet and headed for her bedroom. She snagged her purse and her cell phone on the way.

Maybe Dalton didn't want to hear what she had to say, but now that the truth was out, she needed to explain. It wasn't going to fix anything, but maybe if he heard it from her… maybe then he'd be able to forgive her one day.

CHAPTER THIRTEEN

"Sonuvabitch," Dalton groaned as he tossed and turned, grabbing the cheap-ass motel room pillow and yanking it over his head.

He should've turned his damn cell phone off.

But he hadn't and there'd been a reason for that.

Honestly, he'd been hoping that Katie would call. Every fucking night for the last month, he'd been hoping she would call to tell him that something had happened. That she would never purposely turn her back on him. That she wanted to be with him.

That call had never come.

But she did call last night. More than once. Only he hadn't answered any of her calls, not wanting to hear the disgusting truth.

Disgusting? A little judgmental, huh?

Dalton squeezed his eyes shut, trying to force that damn voice out of his head. He had every right to be pissed. Katie had lied to him.

And she was a fucking stripper, for chrissakes.

That doesn't make her a bad person.

"Shut. The. Fuck. Up," he told that damned voice in his head. There was no way in hell that Dalton was going to rationalize what Katie did. At least he had that closure he'd been searching for. The truth was brutal, but he was no longer left wondering just what he'd done to fuck things up.

She was a fucking stripper.

But it didn't matter anymore. What she did in her spare time wasn't his business and by God, he didn't want to have anything to do with her.

Then again, it wasn't as if it was his choice. Katie's voicemail had pretty much told him everything he'd been wanting to hear, but nothing that made anything better.

"As much as I had hoped Cooper was wrong, that you weren't staying away because of me, I guess the truth lies in me talking to your voicemail for the tenth time. I don't know exactly what's going on, Dalton, but I've got a pretty damn good idea. I'd say that I was sorry, but you know what? I'm not sorry. This was the very reason I did what I did. If you heard the truth, then you've already pre-judged me. I knew it would come to that sooner or later. I thought you were one of the good guys and I was trying to spare you the pain."

One of the good guys, huh? Was that why she hadn't bothered to tell him she was a fucking stripper in the first place?

"Anyway, I'm sorry things came to this. Walking away from you was the hardest thing I've ever done. I… Well, let's just say I haven't felt this way about anyone before. I… God, I can't even say it. I really am sorry, Dalton. I was trying to spare you. But don't worry, you're not the only person I've ever let down. And I doubt you'll be the last. Believe it or not, I was trying to protect you. I didn't want you to get hurt. I love you."

Those last three words nearly knocked him sideways.

Goddamn it!

What could he have possibly done to make her think he would turn his back on her?

Then again, he'd been lying on that hard ass mattress for the last few hours, trying to force his eyes to close all while picturing her taking off her fucking clothes for a bunch of assholes. For the life of him, he couldn't seem to wrap his mind around the fact that the girl he found himself falling in love with was a fucking stripper. And a liar.

"Fuck!" Dalton roared, throwing his pillow across the room and knocking something off the dresser in the process.

Why the fuck did this happen to him? What the hell did he do to deserve all this shit?

And when did he become such a fucking whiner?

Since the day he turned eighteen and realized his entire path in life had been knocked off course thanks to a stupid ass decision and some shitty friends, Dalton hadn't felt sorry for himself. No, he'd vowed not to.

Yet here he was, thinking about all of the ways people had done him wrong, starting with his so-called friends when he was a senior in high school, months away from graduating.

Drug charges. That had been the beginning of the end for him, the start of the disappearance of all his hopes and dreams. Thanks to the people he'd trusted, those who'd said they were his friends, everything he'd wanted had crashed and burned at his feet.

Dalton had never blamed anyone but himself, although the drugs that had been found in his car that night weren't his. In fact, he'd never done a single drug in his life. Not one single fucking time. Not even so much as smoked a cigarette.

Well, except for liquor.

But that hadn't mattered at the time. It was his car, he was driving, and all the kids he'd considered friends had pointed their fingers at him.

"Dude, chill the fuck out," Dalton yelled at Jeremy, his buddy riding shotgun. "Worst case, I'm gonna get a speeding ticket."

"Right. Speeding ticket," Jeremy retorted.

Dalton pulled his Mustang over onto the shoulder, glancing in his rear view mirror to see the cop pulling up behind him. Dave and Alan were turned in their seats, watching out the back window.

"Fuck," Dave muttered.

Dalton continued to watch, noticing how Dave and Alan were getting antsy.

"Seriously?" Dalton laughed. "What the fuck are you so freaked out about? I was the one speeding."

"Just shut the fuck up," Jeremy snapped at the two guys in the back.

The next thing Dalton knew, there was a tap on his window and he turned, plastered on a smile and rolled down the window. "Officer?"

"Do you know how fast you were going?" the officer asked without any pleasantries.

"Probably close to eighty," Dalton said truthfully, figuring it would be better not to lie.

"Try eighty-five in a sixty. License and insurance," the cop requested.

Dalton handed over both, keeping his eyes trained on the cop. The guy was shining his flashlight into the car, first over at Jeremy and then to the backseat where Dave and Alan were sitting.

"Don't move," the cop instructed before heading back to his car.

"Fuck," Dave exclaimed again.

"Dude, what the fuck is your deal?" Dalton asked, twisting in his seat to face his friends.

"Nothin', man," Alan snapped, punching Dave in the arm.

The hair on the back of Dalton's neck stood on end. He knew something was up, he just didn't know what. Did one of them have a warrant or something? They were both a couple of years older than Dalton. They'd known each other for a while, but they hadn't hung out all that much.

The cop returned a few minutes later and shined his flashlight in the car once again. "You don't have any guns, knives, or other illegal weapons in the car do ya?"

Dalton noticed the cops tone had turned friendly and that didn't help his bullshit meter. It'd already redlined thanks to the freak out that Dave was having in the back seat. He shook his head and added, "No, sir."

"Would you mind if I checked?"

"Nope. Do your worst," Dalton said confidently, smiling at the cop before opening the door slowly. The cop took a step back and allowed him to exit the vehicle.

"You boys go ahead and get out, too," the cop ordered the others. "This'll just take a couple of minutes."

When Dave exited the car, Dalton realized he was sweating profusely and it was then that he knew something bad was about to happen. He just didn't know how bad it was going to be.

His dreams of joining the FBI had died right along with the felony charges that had been brought up against him. As it turned out, a certain amount of marijuana could get you in some deep, deep shit.

That was where Dalton had found himself.

But he'd been given a second chance with his music career, although for whatever reason, he'd just stumbled upon that one thanks to some wild nights in a karaoke bar. Right place, right time.

Sure as shit beat the wrong place, wrong time, Dalton thought to himself as he remembered that night when the red and blue lights had flashed in his rear view mirror. He'd tried to reassure his friends that it would be cool. A speeding ticket was nothing to freak out about.

Yeah, well, as it turned out, they hadn't been worried about speeding. And neither was Dalton when he'd been cuffed and charged with drug possession.

Marijuana for fuck's sake.

Forcing himself out of bed, Dalton headed for the bathroom. Why the hell did he do this to himself? That part of his life was over. He'd done his time, paid the price and here he was.

For the first few years after he'd started his music career, the drug charges had loomed over him, every reporter in the country had jumped all over that shit. But Dalton had persevered, moving past it and forcing the public to as well.

He'd been wrongly accused.

Sort of like Katie?

"Fucking shit," Dalton grumbled, turning the plastic knob on the shower.

He did not want to think about her. He did not want to think about the fact that men saw her naked nightly.

Not that she didn't deserve an explanation.

She'd get one. As soon as Dalton could get over the rage that burned like diesel fuel in his blood stream. Until then, he'd just return the favor. He would ignore her the same way she had him.

And with any luck, he'd be able to forget about her.

Right. Because that's what you want, you stupid shit.

Yeah, shut up, subconscious.

CHAPTER FOURTEEN

Katie stared in disbelief at the little white stick sitting on the bathroom counter, tears forming in her eyes as she tried to hold back the sobs that threatened to rip from her chest.

A soft knock sounded on the door, followed by Sarah's concerned voice. "Katie? Let me in, okay?"

Without feeling herself move, Katie reached for the knob, flipped the lock and then stepped back to where she was. Sarah came in, leaving the door open. In the reflection of the mirror, Katie watched as Sarah leaned down and looked at the little screen on the white stick.

"You're pregnant, Katie."

Katie nodded. She couldn't do anything else.

"Oh, honey," Sarah said soothingly, wrapping her arms around Katie and pulling her close.

Katie rested her chin on Sarah's shoulder and stared at the reflection of herself in the mirror. She didn't even recognize that woman anymore. Thankfully, she didn't have to look at herself for long because the tears broke free, clouding her vision and she sobbed uncontrollably right there in her best friend's arms.

She had no idea how long they stood there like that, but the next thing she knew, Sarah was helping her to sit on her bed.

"I want you to rest for a little while," Sarah told her. "I'll take care of everything here."

Katie nodded. She didn't have the energy to argue.

When Sarah left the room, Katie crawled up into her bed, pulling the covers over her and resting her palms on her stomach.

A baby.

Dalton's baby.

What had she done?

Oh, God, what had she done?

The tears came again, and this time she didn't try to stop them. She cried for herself, for Dalton, and for their unborn child.

Just when she thought life couldn't be any crueler than it already had…

CHAPTER FIFTEEN

Three months later – April

"Thank y'all!" Dalton screamed into the microphone that was attached to the earpiece in his left ear, his guitar now hanging in front of him, his head soaked in sweat and his heart pounding double time. It'd been one hell of a night and honestly, Dalton wasn't quite ready for it to be over. "We love you, Austin! Good night!"

Taking his hat off, he tossed it into the crowd, not able to see it once it fell past the bright stage lights, but the noise that erupted from the VIP section told him someone was delighted to have received it.

There was a chorus of "One more! One more! One more!" that resounded throughout the enormous amphitheater where they were performing the last stop of a hellacious thirty-concert tour.

God he loved this shit!

With a smirk to the crowd being broadcast via several big screens behind him, Dalton tilted his head as though considering their request. He wasn't actually thinking about it because what the fans wanted, the fans got. This had been one of the best tours he'd done in his career and he fully intended to go out with a bang.

He was pretty sure they were on goal, too. After all, he'd set it up so that Brett Basson opened for him, and just as he had suspected, the crowd loved him.

But that wasn't all that he'd had in store for the Austin crowd. Working with Cooper's father, David, Dalton had managed to get Cooper to join him up on stage. But the kicker was when he managed to secure Cheyenne Montgomery as a guest appearance. Dalton didn't know Cheyenne all that well, but Cooper and Tessa had pulled a few strings, working with Tessa's cousins to have her call him. The rest was mere details. Cheyenne had agreed to join them up on the Austin stage and they'd blown the roof off the place in the first few minutes.

And now they were gearing down, getting ready for the lights to go out.

But he had one more thing up his sleeve before that happened.

Pretending to come up with an idea, along with a strategic head nod in agreement got the crowd going wild. Dalton then turned toward the left side of the stage, locating his partners in crime before crooking his finger to signal them back out. When Cooper Krenshaw and Cheyenne Montgomery made their way back in view of the audience, the sound level went to astronomical levels.

"What do ya'll think?" Dalton asked Coop and Cheyenne, speaking right into the microphone. The noise dropped significantly, although his ears were still ringing. "Think we should give 'em one more?"

Coop looked out at the crowd then glanced over at Cheyenne. Another round of that dramatic feigned consideration and then Coop was nodding and grinning, getting the crowd riled up even more. "Why the hell not?"

"I don't know," Cheyenne said sweetly, causing hundreds of people to start laughing and cheering. "What'll they want us to sing?" she asked, pretending to be worried.

"Good question," Dalton replied, turning back to the crowd who was gearing up, chanting again.

Cooper moved over to Cheyenne and whispered into her ear, making the crowd go wild. Cheyenne played along, her eyes opening wide as she looked back at Cooper and then over to Dalton. "Is he serious?" she asked, her own microphone amplifying her raspy voice through the overhead speakers, garnering her a loud "I love you, Cheyenne! Marry me!" from one of the cowboys on the floor.

"Of course, I'm serious," Cooper answered for Dalton before walking over to stand beside him, leaning in close to his ear. Cooper whispered his suggestion, making Dalton laugh.

"Bro, they ain't gonna go for that," Dalton said smiling. The truth of it was, Cooper hadn't mentioned a song at all. He hadn't mentioned anything because even a whisper would've been picked up by the microphones. They already had a song in mind. That was all part of the plan.

"Sure they will. Ask 'em," Cooper replied, nodding his head toward the crowd.

Dalton glanced at Cheyenne, then to Cooper before giving a brief side nod and a shrug that said what the hell.

"All right, y'all," Dalton addressed the crowd. "Coop seems to think y'all might not wanna hear 'Angel in Blue Jeans'."

Before the words were completely out of his mouth, the crowd was screaming once again.

"I think that's a yes," Cheyenne stated, grinning.

"See, bro, I told you they'd wanna hear it," Dalton added.

"I dunno," Cooper pretended to be concerned. "They haven't heard this version yet." That earned them some high-pitched screams, a few piercing whistles and a huge round of applause. "All right, fine. We'll do it. But I'm warnin' y'all, this is a little different."

Dalton shot a look over to Cooper along with an award-winning grin before the three of them lined up to face the crowd. As planned, three stagehands ran out bringing stools for them to sit on, another hauling Cooper's guitar to him. The three of them got comfortable, taking a little longer than necessary while the band got ready behind them.

As usual, Cooper started out his hit song in that low crooning voice that drove the women crazy. The song he'd written for his soon-to-be wife, Tessa, had topped the charts for months, and Dalton even received requests to play it from time to time. With Coop's permission, he'd given it some attention a time or two. But it had been one night several weeks ago when Dalton had stopped in Devil's Bend for a three day break, meeting up with Cheyenne and Cooper that they'd messed around with it a little at The Rusty Nail.

From the first time I saw her
Her smile spoke to my soul
My heart found a home
Right there in the arms of my angel in blue jeans

Dalton eyed the crowd as Cheyenne came in, her voice soft and sweet. The crowd hadn't expected it. She sang her portion, which was a modification of the original song, turning it into a duet. They'd perfected the lyrics after that one night at the bar and had a good time messing around for their hometown folks. This was the first time they'd actually performed it for an audience of this size.

Cooper and Cheyenne continued, belting out the song, alternating as planned. Then the music changed and Dalton smiled. With his voice lowered, he kicked in his part, which was a modified country version of a rap, made popular in recent country hits by others. The crowd exploded in screams, making it difficult for anyone to hear. They got the gist of it though so with a grin, Dalton continued his verse.

On and on they went until the song was complete and the crowd was on their feet, cheering and clapping.

And as was generally the case, Dalton added another tick mark to his list of best nights ever.

♥ ♥ ♥ ♥ ♥

Katie elbowed her way through the crowd on her way to the bar, setting her tray down on the scarred wood top as she smiled up at Eric.

"How's it goin'?" he asked as he pulled the spigot, filling a mug of beer.

"It's nuts. I'm surprised we're this busy for a Wednesday night," she admitted, adjusting her ponytail at the back of her head.

"Blame Tessa. She announced a celebration for the final concert of the tour. Of course, she's backstage at said concert enjoying it while we're here covering her ass." Eric's huge grin belied his bellyaching about Tessa not being there.

"Tonight's the last concert? Really?" she asked, her stomach taking a tumble from her nerves, or maybe that was the tiny flutter she'd felt in the last couple of days. Either way, her sudden distress had nothing to do with Tessa or Cooper, or the fact that she was now four months pregnant and no one other than her best friend knew.

Granted, if it wasn't for the oversized sweaters she'd been wearing, more than just Sarah might've figured it out. She was beginning to show quite a bit. For the last month, she'd noticed her once flat belly had begun to round out. How they hadn't noticed at Diamonds and Lace, she didn't know, but regardless, she was giving her notice this week, unable to keep up the charade any longer.

But tonight, she wasn't worried about the fact her cash flow was about to come to a disturbing halt. No, her bout of anxiety came from hearing that he'd be back home – *he* being Dalton. Katie wasn't the least bit worried about Cooper. She was worried about coming face to face with Dalton when he did finally make it back for good.

For good.

Damn. Why didn't that sit well with her? It'd been three months since she had had any communication with Dalton and even then, she'd only been allowed to talk to his voice mail.

In recent months, she'd gotten an earful about the tour. Cooper had agreed to join up with Dalton at a few stops, but for the most part, he'd spent the last few months right there at home, keeping the equestrian center running. Turned out, one of the Walkers had come down to help out during Dalton's lengthy absence. From what she heard, Cooper had asked for some help from Tessa's cousins and one of them had taken him up on the offer. Braydon Walker had been a brief resident of Devil's Bend, thus a regular at The Rusty Nail until just recently when he headed back home to Coyote Ridge.

Through the grapevine, Katie had recently learned that after this tour Dalton was going to come back to Devil's Bend. There'd been some discussion about him staying back in Nashville, but the final answer had confirmed her worst fear. He was coming home permanently, no more tours or extended trips scheduled for at least a year.

It had been after learning the last part that her stomach issues had begun.

She would have to see him again.

Of course, Katie wished them all well, but she wasn't particularly excited about having to face Dalton again. Not on a daily basis at least. Things were so weird between them, as had been noticed on the few visits he'd made back in the last three months. Although they rarely spoke, they were trying to be civil because of so many eyes on them. They might've broken up, but their friends didn't seem to be privy as to why. Hard to feign even being friends when Dalton hadn't so much as said two words to her, aside from the required pleasantries.

Along with not wanting half the town to know that she wasn't the sweet, innocent girl they thought her to be, Katie also didn't want her boss to find out that she moonlighted as a topless dancer at a strip club in order to make ends meet. Again, that wasn't going to be the case much longer, but still. She didn't want Tessa to find out. Knowing Tessa, she would insist on trying to help her, and Katie would have to refuse, leaving an awkwardness between them that would make Katie hesitant to keep working for Tessa. And Katie really wanted her job at The Rusty Nail. Being there, interacting with customers, talking to her friends… it really was the only time she felt normal.

But she hadn't had a chance to talk to Dalton. Not about that and not about the more important topic, the tiny life growing in her belly. She really didn't know how much Dalton might've told Cooper or Tessa about what he'd learned, although she was inclined to believe he hadn't said anything. As far as she could tell, Tessa was none the wiser. The woman would've questioned her, Katie was pretty sure of that.

"Here you go, kiddo," Eric said, interrupting her thoughts. He handed over two longnecks and the three shots she'd ordered before she had headed out the last time.

Arranging them onto the tray so that she wouldn't risk dropping them on the floor, Katie made her way back into the throng of people.

After delivering the drinks and collecting the money, including a few hefty tips, she worked her way through the room, tossing empty beer bottles and checking on the customers. Every table they had was full tonight and the dance floor was packed as well. There wasn't a live band on stage, but the music from the fancy sound system that had been installed gave them the atmosphere they were searching for.

When she worked her way back to the bar once again, Katie motioned for Jack, who was assisting another customer. She waited patiently for him to head her way and when he did, she smiled, still feeling incredibly guilty although she seriously didn't believe Tessa or her brothers were any wiser as to her side job. One of these days, Katie feared she was going to blurt it out just to get the twenty tons of guilt off her chest.

But not tonight.

"Mind if I take a break?"

"Go ahead. I think we're windin' down for a little while."

"Thanks, I'll be back in thirty if that's okay."

"Sure thing," Jack said with a smile before turning back around, laughing at something Eric was saying to one of the customers.

Katie headed upstairs to the office that rarely got any use. Tessa generally spent her time outside if she took a break at all, Eric never left the bar, and Jack, Tessa's younger brother, refused to go up there because he said he wasn't interested in being stuck with the paperwork. The only other person who'd ever used the office regularly was Adam, but he was up in Dallas these days.

Once she was inside the small room, Katie closed the door behind her, retrieved a bottle of water from the small, antiquated refrigerator that they kept stocked. She was pretty sure they did it for her since she really was the only one who used the pseudo office as a retreat when she took her breaks.

After a few sips of her water, she sat down at the desk and reached for the phone. Glancing at the clock on the wall, she knew she needed to wait three more minutes before she could place the call or she risked an unnecessary altercation. She tried to avoid those at all costs these days.

Not only did she not want any pointless incidents, Katie just wanted a little peace. She was tired, to be honest. It seemed like she was working herself into the ground these days, what with working at The Rusty Nail on Tuesdays, Wednesdays, and Saturdays and then over at Diamonds and Lace, the strip club she'd been employed at for the better part of the last four years, on Thursdays and Fridays. Her only days off were Sunday and Monday and even then she really didn't have any time for herself. There was too much going on.

Damn.

That reminded her that she had homework that was due tonight. There was no way she was going to hit the midnight deadline, but she'd still have to go right home and finish it. Her instructor might accept it being a couple hours late, but for sure, he wasn't going to give her a pass to hand it in too late. She'd already used up every extra pass she had.

Katie was taking online classes at a local university, working toward her degree in accounting. She was crazy; there was no doubt about that. Taking some of the classes online was a recipe for disaster, but she knew there was no way she could manage to take day classes with everything else that she had going on. So, she had to settle for the occasional B minus just to make things a little easier on herself.

Another look at the clock, Katie realized it was time.

Grabbing the receiver, she quickly dialed the number and she listened as the ringing began.

One ring.

Two rings.

Three...

"Hey, baby, it's me," she said softly into the phone. She forced a smile, sending up a silent prayer that this conversation was going to go well.

If not, she wasn't sure what she was going to do.

CHAPTER SIXTEEN

Friday morning

"Damn it's good to be home," Dalton drawled when he stepped into the barn early Friday morning. After their final concert on Wednesday night, he had foregone a hotel room in lieu of coming back to Devil's Bend. It would've been a waste to stay so close although he'd been ready to crash in the closest bed as soon as he walked off the stage. But he had been looking forward to being in his own bed again. He wasn't disappointed that he'd done it either.

Thursday had been about relaxing, hanging out at the house and trying to get a few things unpacked. Although his house was complete, located at the far end of the Dream Chasers ranch, he hadn't had much of a chance to move in. Since he'd opted to make his Texas home permanent, he'd sold his Nashville one and stayed with his parents or on the road for the better part of the last four months, which meant the movers had relocated all of his belongings with the help of Cooper's manager – *slash* – father while Dalton had been on tour.

Needless to say, he still had a lot of work to do in order to feel like he wasn't living out of a box. Since, technically, he really was living out of boxes, it was quite literal and very much a pain in the ass.

"Glad to have you back," Cooper replied, his voice muffled as he stepped around Sacred Spirit, the most recent gelding to have been acquired by the center.

"How's she doin'?" Dalton asked, referring to the horse Cooper was brushing.

"Better. She's calmed down some. Braydon's been working with her quite a bit. She's not quite ready to go out with the kids, but maybe a few more months. She'll get there though. I have faith," he answered, crooning to the horse as much as answering Dalton.

"How's Braydon doin'?" Dalton asked, referring to Tessa's cousin who had come to stay at the ranch while Dalton was away. He was living on the premises and handling some of the chores, as well as giving direction to the volunteers as needed. Dalton hadn't realized Braydon had taken to the horses, but he couldn't say he was surprised. The few times Dalton had seen the man, he'd looked like he was deep in thought, and doing everything he could to stay busy.

Dalton knew what he was going through. He'd been plagued with the same need to fill every spare minute with something to do, no matter how trivial.

"Doin' good. Doesn't seem to be goin' anywhere anytime soon. Tryin' to keep him busy."

"I see you've got a group coming out today," Dalton said, glancing over at the giant board on the wall that listed upcoming events.

"Yep. Day care center. About ten kids."

"Mind if I take that one?" Dalton asked, sliding his fingers over the wood bar on the outside of the stall, gripping the board and resting his boot on the bottom rung.

"You sure? I've got another group coming in tomorrow mornin', and I'm meetin' with my dad then so I won't be able to get that one."

"You gonna be able to get up that early?" Dalton joked. "What with the bachelor party tonight and all."

"I'm sure I'll be fine," Cooper said, frowning.

The guy had made it known that he didn't really care for a bachelor party, but Tessa had overruled his arguments.

"All right. Well, I can take that one too," Dalton told him. Anything to keep himself occupied. Since it seemed that his personal life had fallen right off the edge of a cliff thanks to the shit storm that had become his life, better known as the overwhelming thoughts of Katie, Dalton wasn't interested in any downtime. Keeping busy was the only way to keep his mind off her.

As if that was working.

"Have at it then," Cooper acknowledged. "If you need help, just let me know. I'm gonna run Harmony and Havoc into town tomorrow. Time for their shots."

Speaking of…

As though the two giant huskies had been waiting for Cooper to call their names, they frolicked into the barn, nudging one another as they vied for first place.

Dalton knelt alongside them when they approached, receiving his customary greeting from Harmony and a sniff or two from Havoc. Glancing over his head, he noticed that Sacred Spirit was getting a little antsy. Probably thanks to the dogs.

Yeah, she'd get used to them. Everyone else did.

"Talk to you later then," Dalton told Cooper as he pushed back to his feet, and then turned on his heel to head the opposite direction, the dogs falling into step with him.

He needed to go check on the horses, noticing that several of the stalls were empty. One of their volunteers must have already taken the other geldings out for their morning walk around the giant covered arena, which meant it was time for Dalton to get to work.

"Hey, Dalt!" Cooper called.

Dalton turned and continued walking backward toward the exit. "Yeah?"

"Tessa wants you over for dinner on Sunday."

"Tell her I wouldn't miss it," he hollered before turning around once more.

Dinner with Cooper and Tessa had become somewhat routine for him when he was in town. Now that he was going to be there more often, he really needed to let Tessa know that the gesture wasn't necessary. He was quite capable of cooking for himself, and if that failed, he could always grab a bite in town. Not that he minded at all because hanging out with Cooper and Tessa was about the only way he could keep his mind off things he shouldn't be thinking about in the first place.

Like Katie.

And the fact that she lied to him.

Damn it. He did not want to think about her now.

His attempt at keeping his mind off Katie wasn't working nearly as well as it had been when he was on tour. Being back in Devil's Bend was a constant reminder of the woman. He had yet to talk to her, aside from a polite hello a time or two, and he didn't have any intention of saying much more to her, but clearly, his brain thought that having a running commentary of *what ifs* flowing through his head was productive. He had news for his brain… It wasn't.

In fact, the more Dalton thought about her and the way she'd looked the last time she'd been at his house … naked and riding his cock for all she was worth … It made his head hurt just to remember.

His first instinct after she did her little disappearing act had been to confront her. Now that he knew the truth about who she was, he wasn't sure he even wanted to see her again. The second had been to confront Cooper about it, but he had the distinct feeling that no one in Devil's Bend knew that their beloved waitress was a fucking stripper.

It wasn't his place to fill them in on it either. And he wasn't really made that way. Creating gossip just for the hell of it was not on his list of things to do. He spent his days fending off asshole reporters who liked to speculate on his life as it was. He wasn't about to do that to someone else.

"Hey, Dalt!" Austin Paxton called when Dalton approached. "How's it goin'?"

Dalton offered the young man a forced grin and followed with a lie. "Never better. How 'bout you?"

Dalton could tell Austin was excited when he was around. The kid wasn't even out of high school and it was obvious he harbored a little hero worship where Dalton was concerned. Since Austin was usually tongue-tied, he considered this a step in the right direction, especially since they hadn't run into one another for at least three months.

"Good. Just gettin' the horses ready."

"You wanna help me with this group when they get here?" Dalton offered, remembering he was actually supposed to be working.

"Me? Really?"

Dalton laughed. "Yeah, you. No one else out here to volunteer. So what d'ya think? You wanna give it a go?"

"Yes, sir."

"Awesome." Nodding toward the barn, Dalton told the kid they would need to get the horses saddled, at least a few of them. Then they could wrangle one more volunteer to help out.

And by that point, maybe, Dalton would've forgotten all about Katie. At least for a few hours anyway.

♥ ♥ ♥ ♥ ♥

"Sissy! I need your help!"

Katie brushed her hair out of her face, blowing a couple of strands with a huff, a hint of frustration escaping with the exhale. She knew she shouldn't be irritated. It wasn't Lexi's fault, but Katie was exhausted and she had no one to blame but herself. Last night had been an incredibly long night, so the early morning wasn't helping.

"I'm comin'," Katie hollered, keeping her voice as steady as she could. It was incredible how Lexi picked up on the slightest nuance in Katie's tone, easily detecting her moods.

"Now!" Lexi screamed.

Katie ran through the small apartment, frustration replaced by a sliver of panic as she made her way to her little sister's bedroom as fast as she could.

Before she got there, Sarah peeked out of her bedroom, looking as tired as Katie felt. "She okay?"

"Probably," Katie answered. "Sorry we woke you. Go back to sleep. I'll try to keep her quiet."

Sarah nodded and then closed the door softly.

Katie made it to the end of the hall, calling out to Lexi as she did. "What's wrong?"

"I can't find my pink shoes!" Lexi exclaimed.

Crap.

At least it wasn't something that required medical attention, but in all fairness, when it came to Lexi, this was a critical matter.

Katie took a deep breath and stood stone still in the bedroom door. There was her little sister, sitting cross-legged in the middle of her floor, her stringy dark hair falling down over her shoulders, her little hands in her lap, fingers white as she rocked back and forth.

"We'll find them, Lex," Katie assured her. This was not what she needed today, but she couldn't very well blame Lexi. "May I come in?"

Lexi looked up at her, eye contact minimal as she nodded her head and looked away. Only after she had been approved to do so did Katie step into her little sister's room. One of the fastest ways to set Lexi off was to approach her without warning.

"Do you know where you last saw them?" Katie asked.

That earned her a glare, followed by, "In my closet where they belong."

Right. Closet.

Katie made her way over to Lexi's closet. Not surprisingly, the room was clean. Spotless, in fact. Everything was properly in its place, to Lexi's exact obsessive-compulsive standards.

Katie's heart ached when she thought about the hell her little sister went through on a daily basis. According to the doctors, there wasn't anything Katie could do to fix Lexi's obsessive-compulsive disorder, but she could help her to adapt. On top of that, they had to deal with her attention deficit hyperactivity disorder. Which was exactly what Katie had been doing ever since their mother hauled ass back when Katie turned eighteen. That had been a truly suck ass day that Katie was sure she would never forget.

Opening the closet, Katie glanced down at the row of shoes on the floor, all in perfect order by color: Black to red to dark blue to lighter blue to yellow to… Nope, no pink shoes.

Crap.

Just for grins, Katie peered up at the top of the closet. Nope. No shoes there either. Not that she had really expected them to be there because the top shelf was reserved for Lexi's dolls. The ones she didn't allow to be on her bed. All in perfect order from biggest to smallest.

"There's one more place I need to check," Katie assured Lexi. "You stay right there. I'll be right back."

Lexi nodded as she continued to rock back and forth, wringing her little hands together in her lap.

Running to the only bathroom in their tiny apartment, which didn't take much effort since it was directly across from Lexi's room and right next to her own, Katie threw open the hamper and rummaged through the dirty clothes.

Just as she suspected, Lexi's pink shoes were in the hamper, but finding them wasn't the hard part. Now she had to try to explain to her sister why they were there in the first place. And to make sure that Lexi didn't have a panic attack because they were buried with the dirty clothes. Lexi had an incredible distaste for dirt.

A quick glance in the mirror above the sink was just what Katie didn't need. She looked like hell and the dark circles beneath her eyes certainly weren't helping matters.

It'd been a really rough morning. Lexi had woken up early, forcing Katie out of bed at five o'clock when she shouldn't have had to get out of bed until at least seven. But that wasn't unusual in her little three-person household. Especially not when Sarah had to go to work early, and definitely not these days when Lexi seemed to be getting more and more antsy.

"Found them," Katie called from the bathroom, more of a warning to Lexi that she was coming back.

"Where were they?" Lexi yelled, staring up at her as Katie stepped through the door of her room. She quickly took a step back when Lexi began that humming sound that she had been doing for the last few years whenever Katie would invade her personal space. Or rather, the space she deemed personal, which was her entire bedroom.

"May I come in?" Katie asked, trying to rein in her patience.

"Where did you find them?" Lexi asked again, nodding her head.

Katie took a step inside and placed the shoes beside her sister.

"I remembered putting them under the counter in the bathroom," Katie lied. Telling her eight year old sister that her beloved shoes had been mixed in with the dirty clothes because Katie had been too tired when she'd come home at three o'clock in the morning to pick them out of the pile on the bathroom floor wouldn't have gone over well.

As she expected, Lexi studied the shoes, not responding.

"We need to go in a few minutes, Lex," Katie said softly. "You've got a field trip today and you don't wanna be late."

Katie couldn't remember where the child care center that she had Lexi registered at for three days a week had planned to take them, but she hoped wherever it was, Lexi would enjoy herself.

Thankfully, she'd managed to find reasonable childcare at a place in the neighboring town that actually seemed to enjoy Lexi's attendance there. They completely understood her diagnosis, and had even insisted that they would work with Lexi in order to help her acclimate to her surroundings, as well as the other children. For the most part, Lexi was actually doing well there.

That was three years ago. And to be honest, Katie wasn't sure what she'd do without them. Well, the center and her part-time nanny, better known as her best friend Sarah, who watched Lexi at night when Katie worked. They were her lifeline most of the time and she doubted they even realized it.

After gathering her purse and her cell phone, Katie went back to get Lexi, finding her sister standing just inside her bedroom door, her pink shoes on her feet. She was waiting patiently to leave, studying the doorframe of her bedroom, and as was her routine, she didn't leave her room until it was time to go.

Just another oddity that Katie had gotten used to over the years.

One of many.

CHAPTER SEVENTEEN

"Did y'all have fun today?" Dalton asked, making sure he kept his tone upbeat as he addressed the fifteen eight year olds forming a line behind him. The kids must've heard him because they cheered, and a chorus of "yes" and "we don't wanna go" could probably be heard for miles.

"Thank you so much, Mr. Calhoun," Bethany, the center's director, said for the umpteenth time, her gaze a little too intimate for Dalton's peace of mind.

"You're very welcome," he answered, making sure not to hold her gaze for too long. "And please, call me Dalton." Mr. Calhoun was his father, but he wasn't going to tell her that. As it was, he was a little worried there were a few too many stars in her eyes when she looked his way.

Dalton continued to walk through the barn, holding hands with one little girl who'd insisted on sticking close to him throughout the day. According to Bethany, it was just short of a miracle because little Lexi wasn't very fond of most people.

Not that he minded one bit. Lexi was quite cute and very polite, almost freakishly so at times. She didn't speak unless spoken to and even then, she sounded like she was light-years older than eight.

"How about one more treat before y'all head out?" Dalton asked, glancing over his shoulder at the long line of kids making their way behind them in an orderly manner as instructed.

He received an overwhelming agreement so he continued on his way toward the small area that Tessa had cordoned off for the petting zoo. At the moment, they didn't have but a handful of animals populating the various pens, but Dalton knew it would be enough to satisfy this bunch.

As they approached, Austin made his way to the front of the group and offered a quick overview of the animals they had, and what they were going to be able to do. They would only be taking two kids at a time into each pen which meant their little detour was going to take a little longer than expected, but Dalton wasn't in a big hurry. It didn't seem that Bethany was either.

Taking a seat on one of the benches just outside the pen, Dalton was surprised when Lexi sat down beside him rather than joining the rest of the kids gearing up to visit the animals.

"Do you wanna go see the rabbits?" he asked softly, glancing down at the little girl who was still holding his hand like the world might swallow her up if she let go.

"No, that's okay," she said quietly.

Dalton shot a look over at Bethany to find the young teacher staring back at him as if he'd hung the moon.

Shit.

He knew that look, and he knew that he was going to have to do some serious damage control if he was going to get out of this one without hurting her feelings.

"Come on, Lexi," Austin called to the little girl. "I've got a friend I think you'll wanna meet."

Dalton watched the young man as Austin approached the little girl slowly. It hadn't been hard to detect how skittish Lexi was from the moment she stepped foot into the barn just two short hours ago. She'd come in latched onto Bethany's hand and hadn't joined in when they began giving them the kid-friendly version of the equestrian center. The version that was catered solely for these visits with day care centers, church groups, and a handful of organizations that worked with at risk youth.

"What is it?" Lexi asked, seemingly interested, yet still reluctant.

Austin squatted down in front of her, keeping a good two feet between them. Dalton had to hand it to the young man, Austin had a way with kids. The boy couldn't have been more than sixteen, maybe seventeen, yet he handled the group of eight year olds as though he did that every single day.

Dalton watched as Austin glanced to his left, then to his right and then leaned forward just a little bit. "Can you keep a secret?"

Turning his focus on the little girl still gripping his hand tightly, Dalton noticed the way Lexi's eyes widened and her cheeks puffed slightly from her small smile.

When she nodded, Austin continued, "We've got puppies."

Lexi's eyes lit up like saucers and her hand slipped from Dalton's as she leaned toward Austin. "Really? Can I see them?"

"Of course you can. Why don't we bring Ms. Bethany along with us, too?"

Dalton nearly laughed aloud when the boy shot Dalton a glance that said, "You're quite welcome and you owe me one."

When Lexi took hold of Bethany's hand and pushed off the bench, ready to follow Austin to the puppies, Dalton took the opportunity to make his way over to the goats to watch as a couple of kids fed them from their small hands. He didn't make eye contact with the teacher because he already got the feeling this wasn't going to end well. No matter how he handled it.

A solid half hour later, Dalton was waving good-bye to the kids in the day care van while Austin stood beside him. Once the van was out of sight, Dalton turned to head back to the barn. They needed to get the animals settled and then the afternoon volunteers would come in to ensure the various chores were taken care of.

"She gave you her number," Austin said chuckling.

"Shut it," Dalton offered with a laugh of his own.

"Oh, Dalton, you're so handsome. Oh, Dalton, I think I love you. Oh, Dalton…" Austin said in a high pitched, singsong voice.

Dalton knocked Austin's hat wonky before taking off to the barn, ignoring the continued mocking from Austin. Bethany hadn't been quite that bad, but Dalton had also managed to use a small group of eight year olds as his battle shield for most of the day, giving her little opportunity to get a word in edgewise.

"Mind if I head out early?" Austin asked a little while later when they'd double-checked all of the latches and locks on the small pens that housed the animals used for the petting zoo.

"Nope, I don't mind. I'm thinkin' about headin' home for a bite. I'll be back in a bit to check on the afternoon help. Anything I need to finish up for you?"

"No, sir. I got it all taken care of. I'll be back bright and early tomorrow."

"Good deal. See you then," Dalton answered as he started toward his truck.

"Hey, Dalton," Austin called back.

"'Sup?"

"Would you mind if I start helpin' with the groups more?"

Dalton stopped walking and turned back to the younger man. "Is that what you want?"

They had a handful of helpers that volunteered from the high school and a few through a program with the local church, and although they didn't have a set job description, Dalton was all for letting the kids do what they felt they were most suited for.

"I'd like to give it a try," Austin replied.

"You have brothers or sisters?" Dalton asked curiously.

"Yeah," Austin grinned. "Two. My brother's five and my sister's seven. I keep promisin' them I'll bring them by one of these days."

Dalton considered that for a minute. "How 'bout this? You bring your brother and sister up here next Sunday and give them the tour. Just like you would the daycare kids. If I like what I see, I'll let you lead a couple of the tours durin' the week. How's that?"

Austin's face lit up and he nodded. "That's great. Thanks."

Dalton watched as Austin rushed off toward his truck, nearly running the entire way.

He couldn't help but remember a time when he got that excited about something. Long before music took his life in a direction that he hadn't really anticipated.

And just as quickly, he shoved those memories away because they had no place here. As far as he was concerned, those dreams had vanished.

Katie couldn't remember a single Friday night in the history of Friday nights that she actually wanted to go to work. It didn't have anything to do with not being able to go out with her friends and it wasn't that she had anything against the people she worked with at Diamonds and Lace. They were fine. It was the actual *work* that bothered her.

But it was really hard to say no to the kind of money she received for stripping.

Granted, if there was any other way for her to make that kind of money she'd do it in a second. With childcare, school, a nanny, and Lexi's therapy sessions, it wasn't that she had much of a choice. As much as she enjoyed working at The Rusty Nail, it just didn't pay the bills and anything else was off the table because of the amount of hours she'd have to put in just to make even a fraction of what she made in two nights at the club.

Not that she could explain that to anyone and have them look at her like she was anything but trash. It was the consensus amongst most people which was why Katie made a point to keep her side job as far from her personal life as possible.

At least that had been the plan, only Dalton now knew her secret. And now she feared that at any given moment, everyone she cared about was going to find out that she was a fraud.

Katie knew what people said about her, knew that they all considered her the sweet, innocent little waitress who was putting herself through school, avoiding dating because her focus was on her education. That's what they thought because that was the exact persona she had developed for herself, feeding into it whenever possible.

If they only knew.

Not many people even knew about Lexi or the fact that Katie had been pulling mother duty to her little sister since she was eighteen years old. Lexi had been three when their loser of a mother disappeared and Katie certainly hadn't been equipped to handle a mentally challenged three year old at the time. No more than she was equipped now that Lexi was eight.

But somehow they'd made it and a lot of it had to do with this stupid job.

Walking in through the back doors of Diamonds and Lace, Katie greeted Terrence, the burly, black bouncer that worked the door. "How's Mona?"

"Fantastic," Terrence answered with a quick smile. "She's about ready to pop, but she's hangin' in there."

"Tell her I said hello," Katie offered quickly, hurrying toward her dressing room. It wasn't that she didn't want to stop and chat with Terrence about his pregnant wife and their unborn child, but tonight she was running late and the last thing she needed was for Dwayne to come charging through there to ride her ass about it.

Her boss wasn't much of a people person, but even considering that, Katie knew he'd been lenient toward her. He knew about Lexi, knew that Katie was practically a single mom, although she wasn't really a mom at all. She and Dwayne had one of those tolerable relationships. He gave her a couple of free passes as long as she came in, kept her mouth shut and got her job done.

Katie had agreed, but only because Dwayne didn't push her to interact with the customers. She danced on stage and did the occasional lap dance, although she steered clear of those whenever possible. Considering the other girls were more than willing to rake in the money that Katie was willing to pass up, it all seemed to work out.

But that meant that Katie spent more time on stage. Which, if anything could be considered a blessing, that was it. Only because when she was up there, she could get lost in her own head while forgetting about her problems all at the same time. Not an easy feat, mind you.

That and she didn't have to deal with all of those wandering hands.

But tonight, more than ever, she just wasn't feeling it. Not that she hadn't been on a downhill slide for the last few months, ever since she'd put distance between herself and the only happiness she'd ever known.

But Dalton didn't want to have anything to do with her and she had predicted it in the beginning. Sure, part of her had hoped that he would fight for what they'd had, but just like everyone else in her life, he turned and walked away without looking back.

It was your own fault.

Katie ignored the voice, not wanting to deal with the guilt. It was her fault. No need to rub it in.

And Dalton had plenty of other reasons to not want to talk to her anymore. After all, Katie had lied to his face. That she could definitely understand because it was something she beat herself up over and over again.

With hurried movements, Katie pulled off her leggings and her T-shirt after kicking off her sandals. She flipped through the clothes hanging on the metal rack in her personal dressing room – another perk of this particular establishment – before yanking one of the outfits off its hanger. Picking out the limited amount of clothing that she was going to wear tonight seemed somewhat redundant to her, but it was a task she endured on the nights she came to work.

Once she pulled on the sequined turquoise bra and matching thong, Katie slipped into an oversized man's white dress shirt that she kept on before she went up on stage. She would've worn it all the time, but Dwayne would have her hide and avoiding an argument with him was always high on her priority list. The shirt wasn't much, but as far as she was concerned, it offered a plentiful view of her body, which Dwayne repeatedly informed her was the whole objective when she was in the main part of the club.

Even with the shirt on, she still felt naked.

Sliding onto the stool at the small makeup table, Katie did what she did best. She plastered her face with goop in order to make her look older. Dwayne had wanted to exploit the fact that she looked so young, but even after three years working at Diamonds and Lace, Katie had never given in to him. It was bad enough flaunting her naked body to men she would never even talk to, but she damn sure had no intention of supporting some sort of taboo teenage fetish that they harbored.

A sharp knock sounded on her door, followed by, "You're on in five."

"Thanks," Katie called out to whoever was kind enough to remind her that her doomsday clock was still counting down.

As she stared back at the woman she no longer recognized, Katie sent up a silent prayer, just like she did every single night.

Lord, please let me get through this night. Please forgive me for my sin. And, just because, please know that I'm only doing this for Lexi. Everything I do is for Lexi.

CHAPTER EIGHTEEN

Dalton never would've pegged Cooper for the type of guy to go to a strip club as a way to celebrate his last hoorah to bachelorhood. Yet here they were, sitting at a table, beers in hand with naked women flaunting themselves back and forth in front of them, hoping for one of them to request their services.

The hypocrisy wasn't lost on him.

Dalton was well aware of the fact that he'd condemned Katie for working in a place like this, yet he had no qualms about coming in and enjoying all the place had to offer.

It didn't matter that the strip club that they were at … er, hold up. Amend that. This was a *gentleman's club* as the sign out front boasted – as if it really made a damn bit of difference what they called it, it was still full of nearly naked women.

Regardless of the fancy ass words in the name, Dalton had to give the place a little credit. Diamonds & Lace *Gentleman's* Club was somewhat classy, if one could actually use class as an accurate adjective when describing a strip club. Truth was, he had definitely been in seedier joints than this one back in his younger days. He just wasn't one to frequent these sorts of establishments anymore and it had nothing to do with the fact that he was past that stage of his life.

He still had a healthy appreciation for naked women, beer, and hanging with the boys. But when it came to his women these days, he just preferred them to be in his bed, not flaunting their assets for a bunch of horny cowboys drinking cheap beer while losing the last of their common sense.

That and there just wasn't enough time in the day, to be honest.

Then again, for the last few months, the women he'd busied himself with were one-nighters at best. And even that had been infrequent. It was hard to be with a woman when he closed his eyes and the only person that he saw was the one woman he couldn't have.

But Dalton had vowed not to think about Katie tonight.

Despite his rule to focus on his surroundings, it still didn't make their outing any easier to wrap his mind around. A strip club? Cooper?

Nope. If he weren't seeing it with his own two eyes, he never would've believed it.

Even though Diamonds and Lace served up a damn good steak, Dalton still didn't understand how they'd ended up there in the first place. Since he wasn't much for questioning his friend's motives, Dalton had just gone with the flow.

Granted, he'd gone a round or two in his head on whether this was actually a good idea or not. After all, he had no idea where Katie worked, or whether she was still stripping. And truth be told, he really didn't want to find out.

But nevertheless, here they were and it was true, the venue Coop had chosen to spend the last few hours of his wild and wicked single days did have some kick ass cuisine which made up for everything else. Dalton would admit that he was quite fond of a good steak, and to his surprise, he'd just finished one off that had left him wanting more. Rather than look like a backwoods redneck, he had opted not to rake the leftovers from Coop's plate although he'd been damn tempted.

Truthfully, Dalton would've preferred to be hanging out at The Rusty Nail, gnawing on some chicken wings, downing some shots, singing a little, chatting it up with the locals… the same shit they did most nights when he was in town.

Although, he had been avoiding that place for quite some time. When Coop or Tessa questioned him, he gave them the answer he'd rehearsed over and over again. He had too many other things to focus on. Like work.

Tipping his chair back on two legs, Dalton used the same motion to sip his beer as he leisurely surveyed the room. The place was nice; he'd give it that. He wasn't much into the whole strip club scene, but he wouldn't deny an appreciation for this one with its friendly girls, fantastic food, and elegant décor.

Then again, elegant might've been taking things a little too far. It wasn't like it was a palace. The walls were dark, the floor was dark, but the lighting didn't blast him in the face the way he was used to when he was on stage, and the girls working the room were pretty. Since that was the gist of the décor, yeah, maybe elegant was going a little overboard.

Dalton would blame it on the beer.

Not that he was paying much attention to the women. That wasn't why he was there tonight and Coop knew that. He'd come along to help his buddy bid farewell to singlehood, but only because he hadn't wanted to throw Cooper to the wolves without backup.

Right, keep telling yourself that.

Dalton downed half his beer in one gulp, purposely ignoring that damn voice in his head that had been prominent over the last three or so months.

Tonight was about enjoying himself, not thinking about anything – or anyone – else.

And he was enjoying himself.

At least that's what he was forcing himself to believe.

He was actually a little (translated to a helluvalot) surprised that Tessa had allowed Cooper out of the house in the first place. He'd damn near fallen over when he found out this had been her idea and when she'd practically shoved Coop into Dalton's truck a short while ago, his jaw had been scraping the floor.

Honestly, Dalton had been expecting bingo for Coop's bachelor party.

However, Tessa never ceased to amaze him. Dalton didn't have any question as to what his friend saw in her. She was smart, funny, pretty, maybe a bit on the neurotic side at times. And on top of that, she was a little tame for his taste, but to each his own and all that shit. Or at least he'd thought she was, then she went and informed them that she'd booked a night at the club for them.

Who were they to argue with a pretty woman?

Dinner, drinks, and a couple of lap dances later – no, she did *not* approve of that last part – and they were enjoying the hell out of themselves.

Granted, neither he nor Cooper had been on the receiving end of one of those lap dances. He knew when to keep his shit in his pants and with his name and his face plastered all over God's creation anytime he so much as fucking sneezed without warning, Dalton knew better than to attract any unnecessary attention.

He'd been in the paper more than he cared to be in the last few months. Going headstrong into his music and gearing up for some of the farm concerts they'd been focused on had sent quite a bit of attention his way.

It beat having his name in the paper for dating a fucking stripper. Thank God, that shit had died down. He'd had to stop showing his face in Devil's Bend for a short time, but his disappearing act had worked like a charm.

Didn't mean he'd managed to get his mind off the only woman who had managed to spark anything in him and the only one capable of holding his attention for longer than five minutes.

Katie Clarren.

The sweet little waitress at Tessa's bar had captured his eye the moment he stepped foot into The Rusty Nail back when Coop had summoned him to the little backwoods town he'd landed in. The same place Cooper now called home.

Not that he was thinking about her anymore.

Right.

It still pained him that he'd lost her long before he ever even had her. But he wasn't about to take the blame for that little fuck up. He hadn't been the one who had lied.

The moment his eyes had met Katie's across that crowded bar, Dalton had realized there was something incredibly hot about the petite dark-haired beauty and her sexy little girl-next-door good looks. One of the best things he had liked about Katie… She didn't give a shit who he was, although he had recognized a little giddy excitement in her pretty gray eyes which he had to admit was a boost to his ego.

Too bad she used that sweet innocence to take money from naïve cowboys who thought they might just have a chance with her.

It wasn't easy, but Dalton had managed to stop thinking about her for at least a few hours every day. Mostly when he was asleep. But even then, she'd occupy his dreams. When he was awake, she was frequently invading his thoughts.

Like now.

Fuck.

There was no doubt about it, Dalton still had a hard on for the pretty little waitress. So much so, he found his wandering eye had ceased to wander too much in recent months even when he'd tried his damnedest to fill his waking hours and sate the lust she'd inspired in him all those months ago. As it turned out, other women just didn't do it for him, but he'd had to learn that the hard way, too.

Getting over her seemed to be an ever-increasing problem for him, one he wasn't sure how he was going to handle, but he was up for the challenge.

"How long do we have to stay here?" Coop leaned over as close as he dared and grumbled near Dalton's ear.

"Your ol' lady will think you're the world's biggest pussy if you come home before nine o'clock," Dalton answered with a laugh, his chair landing back on all four legs.

"Nine o'clock! Are you fucking serious? What time *is* it?"

"Seven thirty, bro."

"Fuck."

"Exactly," Dalton chimed in as he watched as a new girl took center stage, the previous one rotating to the secondary stage to the right.

Oh, fucking hell.

He would know that walk anywhere.

His eyes didn't stray beyond the short little number with the long, silky hair. He couldn't see her face, but he didn't need to. His vision wasn't obscured because he was sitting near the back either. She had some sort of fancy mask over her face, apparently part of her costume. Damn. Despite the fact that he could only see her from the neck down, that woman captured his attention like no one else. Even knowing what she was up there doing, Dalton had to admit that she was kind of hot. Okay, no. *Kind of* wasn't the right word. She was fucking hot. How was that?

Goddammit, this was not supposed to be happening tonight. What were the fucking odds that they would stumble into the same fucking strip club where Katie worked? Even without seeing her face, he knew it was her. He fucking knew it, and he wanted nothing more than to charge up on that stage and whisk her away from all of this.

Dalton glanced down at his beer, realizing it was empty. Third one and he was ready for another, especially if he was expected to sit there and act like a monk while Cooper passed the minutes before he could get home and engage in some pre-marital sex while Dalton had a date with his fucking hand. The only thing he was grateful for was that he didn't have to sleep in Cooper's guest room any more. Those two damn sure didn't have a lot of consideration for their houseguest; at least not once they were in their bedroom. Even the night Dalton had pounded on the wall, answering the call of what he assumed was their headboard, he was met with a growling Cooper who told him he was more than welcome to go sleep in the barn.

Yeah, no thanks, buddy.

At the time, the new stable and the new barn hadn't been built yet, and his house had just been a bunch of lines on a sheet of paper. These days, having a bed to sleep in while he was slipping through town whenever possible was the only thing he cared about, which was why he hadn't given his house much attention.

When he wasn't in Devil's Bend, which had been quite a bit these last few months, he was burning a hot trail from state to state focusing on his tour. That had been the only way he could keep his mind off things he knew were better left alone.

Although Cooper pretended not to notice all the flesh shimmying and shaking around him, there was no doubt the guy was going to need to burn off a little steam when he got home.

Too bad Dalton wasn't going to have that option.

Nodding at the waitress when she asked if he wanted another beer, Dalton gave the room another once over. The girl on center stage, the one he was pretty damned sure was Katie, caught his eye again as she slowly unhooked that teeny tiny thing she called a bra and allowed it to slide seductively down her arms until it fell to the floor. He gripped the empty beer bottle so hard, he was surprised the damn thing didn't shatter. Even from where he sat, he could see there wasn't any silicone injected there. Nope, her pert, yet plump breasts were au natural, and he recalled every single fucking time he'd held them in his hands.

Not only did she have an incredible body, all trim and curvy, there was something about the way she moved. Almost as though she was making love to herself as she swayed to the music, using that pole every now and again for effect. The cowboys in the front row were definitely enjoying themselves. Too bad that damned mask obstructed his view because he was actually quite interested in seeing all of her.

Glutton for punishment; that's what he was.

He was mesmerized by her long, dark shiny hair as it caressed the gentle curves of her ass when she dipped down, glided seamlessly over her gleaming tan skin as she slowly stood back up, offering the cowboys in the front row a perfect view of her bare ass. If it hadn't been for the barely there turquoise thong separating her ass cheeks, they would've gotten a lot more than just that. Her skin was coated with what looked like some sort of body glitter and the lights did crazy things as she spun around that pole like a woman who'd been trained in the fine art of seduction. He could almost imagine wrapping his fist in all that hair again, holding her head back as he thrust his tongue deep into her mouth.

That's Katie, you dumbass and you're done with her, remember?

Thank you, subconscious… For the not so subtle reminder that he was acting like an idiot.

The last thing he wanted was for them to realize that was Katie. That wouldn't go over well at all, so Dalton turned his attention to the others at the table, trying to listen in on the conversation. Eric was telling a story about something that'd happened at the bar the other night while Tessa's brothers, Jack and Adam, chimed in from time to time. Eric seemed about as interested in being in the club as he probably was about going to the opera, and the way he kept his eyes from wandering past the edge of the table was pretty damned amusing.

Of all five of them, Tessa's older brother, Adam, who was down here for only two days, seemed the most comfortable. He'd already paid for a couple of lap dances, bought some chick several drinks, but didn't seem to be working too hard to take her home. Every time a naked ass sashayed past, he'd take a hearty swallow of his beer and allow his gaze to linger for a little while.

At least one of them was having some fun.

Jack, on the other hand, looked like he was ready to bolt at a moment's notice. If Dalton wasn't mistaken, Jack hadn't glanced once at any one of the nearly nude women flaunting their God given – albeit surgically enhanced – gifts all around him. Not that Dalton was surprised. Had this been a Chippendale's, Jack might've been a little more interested. Not that Jack would've admitted to that, but Dalton knew. He might be the only other one at the table privy to that information, but he knew Jack was firmly rooted in the closet and it was only a matter of time before he came barreling through that door. The guy was holding on to a secret that would eventually tear him apart, but it wasn't Dalton's place to say anything.

"I'll be back," Dalton interrupted, talking to the guys at the table as he pushed his chair back. He was ready for that next beer, but nature was calling his name and she was getting louder by the second.

Keeping his hat tipped low, hoping no one would recognize him, Dalton wound his way through the scattered tables on his way to the restroom at the back of the place. It seemed to take a decade just to get there. Diamonds and Lace was probably the biggest strip club he'd ever been in. Hell, it was bigger than most of the bars he had played in when his career had just been getting started.

Everything was bigger in Texas, wasn't that how the saying went?

He smiled at the thought, heading down the dimly lit hall that ended with a door labeled "Men."

Dalton did his business, washed his hands and then headed back out, not wanting to hang out any longer than necessary. There were a couple of drunk cowboys chatting it up just outside the door as he slipped by, once again keeping his head tipped down, the rim of his Stetson shielding his face.

Had he been looking where he was going, he might've been able to stop the collision course that he was unknowingly on. But since that wasn't the case, Dalton didn't notice the petite, dark haired woman coming right for him until it was too late.

Their bodies collided, his hands immediately coming up to grab her arms, trying to keep her from falling over from the impact. He managed to catch her, but not before she stumbled, her arms flying, a wad of cash fluttering to the floor as her arms went askew, knocking her mask clean off her head.

That wasn't the only thing that went askew.

As Dalton looked into that face, his breath slammed to a halt while his brain scrambled. Thinking it might help, he shook his head, wondering if maybe he'd been knocked out cold and he was now seeing things. It was one thing for people to tell him that she was a stripper, or for him to suspect that had been her up on that stage. But it was something else entirely to see for himself.

"Dalton," Katie whispered, surprise etched across her face.

Sonuvabitch.

Nope, he didn't have a concussion and he wasn't seeing things. Although, for the first time in his life, he wished he was.

There standing before him, naked except for the tiny black G-string covering not nearly enough of her was that sweet, innocent little angel who'd fogged his brain so many months ago. The one he dreamed about. The one he'd actually had stupid thoughts about for months on end.

"Katie."

Dalton realized he was still holding her arms, his fingers gently surrounding her slender biceps. He released her and took a step back, then another until there he was a safe distance away.

As he stared down into the prettiest gray eyes he'd ever seen, Dalton saw the last few months before him. All of the nights he'd fought to not think about her, all of the times he'd remembered holding her in his arms, fucking her senseless, all of the days he had hated himself for not confronting her… And as his startling realization turned into anger, then morphed into rage, he glared at Katie.

"I can explain," she said quickly.

Not wanting her to give him any of the gory details as to why she was sexing it up in a strip club while her alternate persona catered to cowboys with the help of her sweet smile at The Rusty Nail, he stopped her before she could continue.

"Yeah. Don't bother."

And with that, Dalton pushed past her, ignoring her when she called his name.

CHAPTER NINETEEN

Sunday night

"How're things goin' with you?" Dalton asked Braydon Walker who was sitting at Tessa and Cooper's kitchen table, snatching a foil wrapped potato and dropping it onto his plate.

"It's goin'," Braydon replied in his usual standoffish way.

The guy had come to stay with Tessa and Cooper to help out with the equestrian center while Dalton was on tour. Even though Dalton was now back for good, it didn't look like the guy was going anywhere anytime soon. Not that Dalton minded. He happened to like the Walker brothers. They were a bunch of good ol' boys that he'd had the pleasure of hanging around with a time or two.

"How's the family?" Dalton asked, taking the plate of potatoes when Braydon handed them over.

"Good. Talked to my ol' man this mornin'," Braydon offered, glancing over at Dalton. "Sounds like they've got it all runnin' smooth in my absence."

Dalton could tell that Braydon wanted to talk about himself about as much as Dalton did. Although he'd tried to keep the questions impersonal, he still felt as though he'd hit a nerve. Rather than make Tessa's cousin uncomfortable, Dalton opted to change the subject.

"What about you?" Dalton asked Tessa, who was doctoring her own potato with butter and sour cream. "Everything in place for the weddin'?"

Tessa smiled, her face lighting up as her eyes slipped over to Cooper. "We're getting' there. Only a few more weeks to go."

Cooper grinned just as big as his fiancée, holding his knife and fork above his steak. "Countin' down the days, darlin'."

"You glad to be back?" Braydon asked, his question directed at Dalton.

"Damn straight. Life on the road ain't all it's cracked up to be."

"I couldn't imagine it is. But the tour went well?"

"Better than well," Dalton answered Braydon's question. "Wish you could've made it to the last show. Probably the best one yet."

Braydon nodded, shoveling steak into his mouth while he spared Dalton a look every now and then. When he finished chewing, he shot off another question. "I heard Cheyenne Montgomery was there. How'd that work out?"

"The woman can fucking entertain a crowd," Dalton stated. "They loved her."

"We're lookin' at puttin' together an official tour," Cooper chimed in. "The three of us."

"Is that right?" Braydon asked, glancing back and forth between Dalton and Cooper.

"That's the plan. She seemed to be on board with the idea," Dalton confirmed.

Braydon's cell phone rang as they sat there eating and Dalton watched as the guy peered down at the screen before hitting a button to silence it. Dalton quirked an eyebrow at Braydon. "Everything okay?"

"Yep," Braydon answered gruffly. "My twin. I'm sure he's just checking up on me."

"You talk to him lately?" Cooper asked.

Dalton looked up from his food to see Tessa and Cooper watching Braydon intently. Looked like the guy was about ready to bolt from the table from the scrutiny in their gazes.

"Nope. Don't need to."

Cooper made eye contact with Dalton briefly, a signal that meant there was a story there. A story Dalton probably didn't want to know. Whatever demons Braydon was running from, Dalton felt his pain. But he damn sure didn't want to add to the guy's stress, so he turned his attention on his food, hoping for his sake the topic would die.

"Where's Katie these days?" Tessa asked when the silence had hovered over the table for longer than a minute. The woman never did let dinner conversation dwindle.

"No idea," Dalton answered quickly, focusing his attention on prepping his baked potato and avoiding as much eye contact with Cooper and Tessa as possible. When it came to the subject of Katie, he had absolutely no intention of discussing her with anyone, including his closest friends.

"I thought the two of you were datin'," Cooper added, his hands stilling as he held his knife and fork over his steak.

From the corner of his eye, he realized Cooper and Braydon had both turned their full attention on him, which was both unsettling and disturbing. This was supposed to be dinner, not an interrogation, yet he felt oddly as though he were under the spotlight.

Dalton knew he couldn't get out of this quite as easily as he wanted to, so he shrugged. "Nothin' serious. We just went out a coupla times."

"Sure looked like more than 'nothin' serious'," Tessa offered, stressing the last two words.

Dalton dared to look up, meeting her concerned gaze. "Really, we're cool. We just decided to back off a little. What with the tour and all."

"Now I know you're lyin'," Cooper added, his fork and knife hitting the glass plate.

Dalton closed his eyes briefly before sitting up straight and looking directly into the eyes of his closest friend. He opted not to go on the defensive, waiting for Coop to follow up on his accusation. Dalton had learned a long time ago that jumping to conclusions only got him in a world of unnecessary hurt.

"The two of you backed off long before the tour," Cooper stated, reaching for his beer. "In fact, I'm pretty sure it was about the time you went to your folks' place for Christmas."

"Not true," Dalton lied. He had managed to be civil to Katie the few times he'd seen her at The Rusty Nail over the last few months. Granted, he had tried to avoid going there on the nights she worked, but there had been a handful of times he hadn't been able to get out of it. He didn't want to make anyone suspicious, although he had no real reason to keep her fucking secret for her in the first place.

Anger surged through his insides, obliterating his appetite. He tried to hide it, not wanting to upset the meal, especially with Braydon sitting there, watching on quietly.

"What's really going on?" Tessa questioned, returning her focus to her food as though she was just making casual conversation. "Did the two of you break up?"

"We weren't *together*," Dalton barked, squeezing the neck of his beer bottle as he took a deep breath to calm himself. "Sorry. No, we didn't break up. We weren't together in the first place." Not that he hadn't wanted to be, but Katie… well, Katie clearly had other ways of spending her time. Time she insisted she didn't have. The woman had claimed that her schoolwork was getting in the way, but from what he saw last night, it damn sure wasn't homework that was keeping her up late at night.

A bold-faced lie.

But he couldn't very well tell Tessa that. From what he knew, Tessa and Katie were close, which surprised the shit out of him considering the double life that Katie was living. Whatever her reasons, the woman had done a fantastic job of snowing everyone, including her close friends.

Sure, it would've been easy to blurt out that she was a stripper and that he couldn't stand the sight of her because she had lied to him, but that wouldn't solve anything. And it wasn't exactly true. The bigger problem was that Dalton did want to see Katie. He wanted to figure out why she felt it was necessary to lie to him in the first place.

The urge to do exactly that grew stronger and stronger every day and now that he was back in Devil's Bend for the foreseeable future, he had the feeling he was going to confront her. He just hoped he could do it without losing his shit. Why it bothered him so damned much in the first place confused the hell out of him, and Dalton was tired of the mixed feelings as much as he was tired of thinking about her all the fucking time.

"I was thinkin' about invitin' her to dinner," Tessa admitted, drawing Dalton's attention.

"Don't," he growled. "Damn it. Ignore me." He was going to have to ignore himself. This anger wasn't who he was, and he was getting overwhelmed by the emotion, so much so that he was barking at his friends. He was supposed to be having a good time, living the high life, enjoying his new outlook on life.

Instead, he was being a dickhead.

"Sorry. Again," he mumbled. "Invite whoever you want." *Just tell me when so I can make other plans*, he thought to himself. "Can we talk about somethin' else?" he asked, desperately needing to change the subject. As it was, he knew Tessa and Cooper were on to him and the last thing he wanted was for them to get in the middle of something they knew nothing about.

Forcing himself to eat, Dalton shrugged them off when they asked a few more questions, grateful when they started talking about the bar and about what Braydon would be doing for the next week. While they went back and forth regarding an upcoming act on Saturday night, and taking care of horses, Dalton's thoughts drifted to that first date with Katie.

"Tell me about you," he encouraged as they sat across from one another at the small booth.

When Dalton had asked Katie out, he truly hadn't expected her to say yes, so when she did, he'd made the suggestion that they get breakfast after her shift ended. Another agreement from her and Dalton had been walking on a cloud ever since.

And here they were, sharing a meal.

Katie was surprisingly easy to talk to, and Dalton assumed that was because she didn't look at him as though he might break out in song and serenade her. Not that he hadn't thought about it.

The idea made him smile.

"What are you grinnin' about?" Katie asked, taking a sip of her orange juice.

"Nothin'," he said with a smirk. "So, I hear you're in school."

"Yeah. I'm workin' on my bachelor's degree. In accounting."

"Accounting?" Dalton laughed. "Sorry. I'm sure that's a very noble profession, but it doesn't sound all that much fun."

"I like numbers," she said with a grin. "Although, I'm questioning my sanity these days. I'm takin' online courses and they're kickin' my butt."

"So you're working at The Rusty Nail in the evenings and taking online courses during the day?"

"Something like that," Katie answered, her smile faltering just slightly.

Dalton studied her, curious as to what she wasn't telling him.

"How long have you worked at The Rusty Nail?"

"Two years. Since I was twenty-one."

"Where'd you work before that?"

Another fading smile and Katie was studying her plate. "I… Uh… I worked at a grocery store once."

"Didn't work out, huh?" he laughed, hoping to get her to smile again. He hadn't meant to bring her down.

"Nope, it didn't." This time Katie looked up at him, pasting a smile on her face. It looked incredibly forced, but Dalton didn't call her on it.

"Do you live at home with your parents?" he asked.

"No."

Dalton had expected her to elaborate, but when she didn't, he searched his brain for another question. Before he could ask, she popped off one of her own.

"Tell me about you. I know you're a singer, and I love your music, by the way. Did you always want to be a singer?"

"Not so much, no," he said truthfully. "I had other big dreams when I was younger but some things got in the way. So here I am."

Thinking back on that first night they'd spent talking, he could clearly see where things had started going wrong. Katie had been elusive, not wanting to talk much about herself. And then when she'd turned the questions on him, he'd answered with as little detail as possible.

What a couple they were. Now that he thought about it, he doubted they ever stood a chance in the first place. That didn't stop him from thinking about what might've been.

Because when it came down to it, Dalton knew that he still loved her. And no amount of anger was helping him get past that either.

♥ ♥ ♥ ♥ ♥

Her day off couldn't have come at a better time. Not because she had anything planned though. No, Katie had absolutely nothing to do on a Sunday night except spend a few quality hours with her sister and her best friend Sarah, both of whom Katie felt like she didn't get to spend nearly enough time with these days.

It'd been a while since they'd done anything more than their usual routine, but that was Katie's fault. Shaking up Lexi's life, even with the smallest change in schedule was a gamble. Tonight she was up for the challenge because she wanted to take the two most important people in her life out to dinner.

She had spent the better part of the day dropping hints to Lexi, letting her know that they were going to have dinner at Charlie's, one of Lexi's favorite places to go when she was actually in the mood to leave the house.

The moment had arrived for them to go and Katie was rushing around, trying to make sure that she had everything in order. Lexi would expect the house to be a certain way before they left and when they returned. What had brought about that compulsion, Katie wasn't exactly sure, but she didn't try to rationalize Lexi's behavior anymore.

"Sarah? You ready?"

"Yes, ma'am," Sarah replied with a huge smile as she stopped just outside of Lexi's bedroom. "How 'bout you, kiddo? Can we have a girl's night?"

Lexi nodded, her smile tipping her little lips.

"Awesome! Let's go," Sarah said with way too much enthusiasm.

There was a reason Sarah had opted to get her degree in psychology and her interaction with Lexi was probably the biggest reason. Every time Katie watched the two of them together, she knew her best friend was destined for incredible things. She admired Sarah's patience, and everything else about her.

The trip into town didn't take long, Sarah offering to drive. The woman might've had the patience of a saint when it came to Lexi and her frequently changing moods, but she had absolutely zilch when it came to driving. Considering the small population of Devil's Bend and the way Sarah reacted to the minimal amount of traffic she encountered, Katie tried not to think about the way the woman drove in the neighboring cities.

"What're you gonna have for dinner, Lex?" Sarah asked as she helped the little girl from the back seat, Katie standing on the opposite side of the car, waiting for the pair to join her.

"Can I have a milk shake?"

"Of course you can," Katie told her sister as Lexi reached for her hand, gripping her fingers tightly.

"Can I have chicken strips?"

"Definitely," Katie replied.

"What about mashed taters?"

"If that's what you want."

"Okay. Then that's what I want."

Katie grinned as they stepped into the restaurant. As usual, the place was bustling, most of the booths filled and the tables, too. There was one empty spot in the back and Sarah led them directly to it. Although they were packed, the service was always prompt and tonight was no exception. They were able to order their drinks and their food within minutes of their arrival.

Lexi was surprisingly quiet, so Katie opted to talk to Sarah, wondering what was on her little sister's mind, but not wanting to dig too deep. The night was going too well.

"He's back," Katie told Sarah, realizing she'd opted to pick the most serious topic she could have for their one night out that week.

"Have you talked to him?"

"Nope. But I saw him on Friday night."

Sarah's eyes widened and Katie was grateful she didn't have explain all of the details. "He was at Cooper's bachelor party."

"At D and L?" Sarah questioned, leaning forward, her curiosity obviously piqued.

"Yep."

"Did he see you?"

"Unfortunately."

"And?" Sarah inquired.

"And he ran out. I wanted to explain, but he told me not to bother."

Sarah's eyes darted down toward Katie's belly. "Do you think he knows?"

"I doubt it. But I've got to tell him. He deserves to know."

"Yeah, he does," Sarah agreed.

They'd both been on the same page as far as that was concerned from the beginning. There was no doubt in Katie's mind that Dalton would be an incredible father and she had to tell him. Until now, she hadn't had the opportunity because it wasn't like he'd tried to reach out to her. And she wasn't interested in leaving that sort of information on his voice mail either. "He'll have to talk to me sooner or later."

"You need to tell him now, Katie. You're not gonna be able to go much longer without people finding out."

No, she wasn't. As it was, last night when she told Dwayne that she wasn't going to be able to work there for a while, he had called her on it. Obviously, if you were paying attention, her growing belly was pretty unmistakable. Especially when she was practically naked like she was up on that stage. Curious, Katie had asked him why he hadn't said anything. Dwayne, being Dwayne had shown his true colors. He was a greedy bastard and he informed her that she was one of his most popular requests.

Not that she'd been happy to hear that. Had that been a lifestyle she wanted to be in, it might've stroked her ego just a bit. Instead, it actually creeped her out a little.

"I told Dwayne that Thursday's my last night there."

"Good. I'm not sure how you can keep doing it without people realizing."

"It's all about what you want to see," Katie told her friend.

"Maybe. But pretty soon, that," Sarah said with a widening grin as she glanced down at Katie's belly, "is gonna be all anyone can see."

Katie laughed. True.

Her hand went to her belly, a gesture that had become so natural lately, she didn't even know when she was doing it half the time. When she was at The Rusty Nail, she made a point to avoid touching her stomach, although it took a lot of effort.

At first, the idea of having a baby had been terrifying. She had cried for several days after taking the pregnancy test. But then she'd sucked it up and went to the doctor, receiving confirmation that yes, she was pregnant. From that moment on, Katie had felt a little lighter.

Taking care of Lexi hadn't always been easy, and Katie knew she wouldn't have been able to manage without Sarah, but it had been something that gave her purpose. She hated their circumstances, hated her mother for abandoning them, but she knew this was what she had to do. Despite her challenges, Lexi was a sweet, beautiful, smart girl and Katie loved her more than she loved anyone.

The thought of being a mother no longer freaked her out, it actually gave her something to look forward to. But she knew, without a doubt, she had to tell Dalton. And she had to tell him soon.

Because keeping in him in the dark about this was not something she was okay with.

CHAPTER TWENTY

Thursday night

Dalton had absolutely no idea why he was there or what he thought he might prove by going down to Diamonds and Lace in the first place. After nuking a TV dinner in the microwave and scarfing it down, he had needed something to do. Being back in Devil's Bend was a lot harder than he thought it would be. Knowing where Katie was and what she was doing wasn't helping matters either.

Cooper had called, asked if he wanted to stop by the bar, but Dalton had declined. He'd made an excuse that he had an errand to run and high-tailed it out of his house as fast as he could. He damn sure didn't want Cooper to stop by and see his truck. That would be the first clue that he was lying about the errand.

So here he was, sitting at one of the tables at Diamonds and Lace, waiting for the night's main act to come on stage. He already knew it was Katie, thanks to the chatty waitress who'd brought him his first beer. He was pretty sure the blond with the big tits had made him from the moment he walked in the door, but so far, she hadn't gone all fan girl on him. Yet.

The night was still young though, just a little later than the last time he'd found Katie shaking her ass on stage for all of the horny cowboys vying to get close enough to see all her goods.

God, the thought of those bastards ogling her just made him want to punch them in the face.

And yes, he was a damned hypocrite because his ass was sitting right there, at a table along the wall, waiting for her to come out.

What he was trying to prove, he had no fucking clue but for some reason, Dalton still wanted to see her. No matter how hard he tried, he couldn't get her out of his head and the wide-eyed surprised look on her face when he'd run into her in that hallway just a few days ago was still engrained in his brain.

"Hey, honey, can I getcha anything?"

Dalton raised his beer toward her, signaling to let her know he was good, or maybe he was asking for another. He didn't know. Shit faced drunk sounded like a damn good mood to be in right about now.

As he watched the waitress strut away, his ears were assaulted by a low, throbbing base line that rumbled through the building. The lights on the stage began to flicker, the strobe lights dancing across the black curtain that hung along the back wall.

A rowdy group of guys up near the front began to whistle and cheer, building the hype and the excitement throughout the place.

Next thing Dalton knew, there she was.

Aww, damn.

As much as he wanted to hate what she was doing, he still had a vast appreciation for Katie's incredible body. He much preferred her to be flaunting all of those delicious curves just for him though. Maybe in his bedroom, sprawled out on his bed…

Not helping, cowboy.

Dalton didn't figure she could see much past the lights, but he tilted his hat a little lower, hoping to conceal himself from her view in the event she glanced out at the crowd. He found himself mesmerized by every move of her body, from the sensual sway of her hips, to the way her hair caressed her skin. Damn it.

Dalton's body hardened, but it wasn't completely from desire. One of the cowboys in the front started yelling out, telling her how much he loved her, and how he wanted to marry her.

That shit pissed him off.

"How 'bout a dance just for you," one of the wandering girls said as she passed by, her long, blood red fingernail making a line across his chest.

"No, thanks," he grumbled, his eyes glued to the only woman in the room he had any interest in.

"Are you sure, honey?" she asked sweetly as she moved even closer, the sharp smell of her cheap perfume stinging his nostrils.

"Positive," he growled, not bothering to look up at her.

He knew he should've been polite, offered her a "thanks, but no thanks" smile but he couldn't bring himself to do it. Hell, at this rate, Dalton was going to wind up in the parking lot on his ass when one of those bouncers decided he was more than they cared to deal with tonight.

His anger was ratcheting up. The last few months had helped to ease it some, but sitting here, while Katie flashed her ass for every Tom, Dick and Asshole waving money at her only set him back again.

"If you're interested in a dance, that one won't help you out," the other girl offered as she lingered beside him.

That bit of news grabbed Dalton's attention and he tilted his head toward her, not quite making eye contact, but lifting his head enough that he could see her face. Pretty blonde hair, bright blue eyes, a body to die for... Yep, she looked like half of the other girls in there.

But she still didn't hold a candle to Katie.

"She avoids the crowd if at all possible," the girl continued, her white silk robe falling open to reveal a barely there matching G-string and nothing else. Her breasts were firm, a little too much for his taste, her nipples a tantalizing shade of brown. Overall, she was incredibly attractive. Didn't explain at all why his body didn't give a damn that she was standing there half-naked.

She didn't do a damn thing for him.

Now Katie on the other hand... Lord, have mercy.

"So no lap dances for her?" he asked curiously.

"Not if she can help it. Not to mention, tonight's her last night here."

Dalton lifted an eyebrow, trying to hide his surprise. "She's leavin'?"

"That's the rumor," the woman replied.

Interesting. Not that it changed the fact that Katie was currently peeling off her bra slowly, with a wicked gleam in her eyes. He still preferred that sweet look she had offered him a time or two to that vixen routine she had going on. And when in the hell did she start wearing that much makeup?

"I'll check on you in a bit, honey," the blonde said, smiling down at him as she ran her hand across her flat stomach.

"I'll be here," he offered, turning his attention back to Katie as he tipped his beer back.

When the music changed to an even more seductive tune, Dalton knew he was in for it. His current case of blue balls was threatening to turn into a fierce shade of electric blue before the night was over.

And he didn't know what the fuck he was going to do about that now that he was here.

♥ ♥ ♥ ♥ ♥

God Katie was tired. And sore.

Too much dancing in those freakish heels that Dwayne insisted she wear and now her feet were killing her. Another reason she was grateful that tonight was her last night to dance up on that stage. Even if she could've hidden her protruding belly, there was no way she would've been able to wear those heels for much longer. Her ankles had already started to swell.

It was nearly three o'clock in the morning and Katie was more than ready to sneak out to her car and head home so she could fall into her bed. At this point, she didn't even care if she changed into pajamas; she just had an overwhelming desire to schedule an appointment with her pillow. An eight-hour session would be fantastic.

"Saying goodbye forever, huh?" Terrence asked when Katie approached the back door where he was stationed.

"God, I hope so," Katie admitted honestly, earning a brilliant white smile from the big man.

"Give me a hug, kid." Terrence pulled her into his big, burly arms and Katie went easily. There were few people she would miss in that place, but Terrence was one of them.

"Take care of yourself," Katie told him. "Tell Mona I said goodbye and when that baby's born, give her a kiss for me."

"Will do."

Katie took a step back when Terrence released her, trying to hold her emotions back. That seemed to be an overwhelming problem these days, what with the pregnancy and all.

"Need me to walk you to your car?" Terrence offered as he held the door open for her.

"I'm good. Thanks though." It wasn't as if she had far to walk. For their safety, the girls were given the parking spots closest to the back door and to ensure no one was lurking around who shouldn't be, the parking lot was lit up like the surface of the sun.

Even with that small measure of security, Katie double-timed it to her car because despite all of the lighting and the big man standing guard by the back door, she had always hated this part of the night. More than once, she'd been confronted by a drunk guy who was hoping to get a little more than just a dance. And more than once, she'd kindly had to refuse. Only one of those times had the guy gotten physical, but that had been enough to scare Katie senseless.

So much so that she'd relied on Terrence's kind offer of an escort for months after that. Only recently had she begun to feel a little safer, at least enough to walk the thirty or so feet to her car on her own.

Once she was in her car, she locked the doors and started the engine, not wanting to hang around to invite trouble. A minute later, she was pulling out onto the street, heading toward Devil's Bend. The drive took roughly thirty minutes at this time of the morning with little traffic to fight through and on days like this one, she was grateful for that. She was too damned tired; keeping her eyes open was a bigger chore than even driving.

It wasn't until she was pulling down the street that led to her apartment complex that she noticed there were headlights in her rear view mirror. A cold chill ran down her spine at the thought of some guy following her from the club. As it was, it was after three in the morning and the entire town of Devil's Bend was probably tucked into their nice warm beds.

Everyone except her.

Her attention swung back to the headlights shining into her rearview mirror. Had they been there the whole time? How had she missed that?

Was she supposed to go home? Or somewhere else? And if the latter, where?

Holy crap.

The never-ending questions weren't helping her at all.

Her skin began to tingle from the warning that her brain was sending, and her hands were now shaking as they white-knuckled the steering wheel. Katie glanced at her small apartment complex off on the right side of the road. The place was so small; she didn't stand a chance of losing her tail in the parking lot so she knew not to bother with that.

Maybe she could go into town.

No, that was stupid. The only place that might have people hanging out was The Rusty Nail and they would just be Eric or Tessa closing up.

Katie didn't want to bring them into this if she could help it.

When her cell phone rang, Katie nearly leapt out of the moving vehicle. Her heart raced like it was a contender in the Kentucky Derby. She glanced down at the screen, hoping it was someone who might be able to help her as she pulled into the small complex. It was that or she would end up on the wrong end of a dead end road.

She hit the talk button and waited, unable to get her voice to work enough to greet the caller.

"It's me, Katie," came the familiar voice on the other end of the line.

"Dalton?"

"Yeah. Pull into your apartment. I just want to talk."

The relief had her nearly dropping her phone. That was until her brain made the connection that Dalton was the one following her. As happy as she was that he wasn't some creeper stalking her, Katie still didn't want to face him.

Not like this.

Darting a look into the rearview mirror, Katie noticed the makeup that was still caking her face.

Shit.

"Come on, Katie. Just talk to me."

Katie couldn't even find the words to answer him, but she did find enough brainpower to direct her car into her parking spot. The one right next to her was empty, meaning that the young guy living in the apartment below hers was probably spending the night with his girlfriend, something he did quite frequently these days.

When she put the car in park, Katie pulled the phone from her ear and looked at it. She knew Dalton was still on the other end, but no matter how hard she tried, she couldn't utter a single word so she hung up.

And that's when she sent up another silent prayer. God should be used to it by now, she rationalized. It seemed she sought his help more and more these days.

Good thing too, because she saw what happened when she relied on her own instincts to do the right thing.

∞ ∞ ∞ ∞ ∞

Dalton knew it was risky following Katie home, but he couldn't help himself. Partly because he wanted to make sure that she got home safely, but more so because he wanted to talk to her.

All the questions he wanted to ask her seemed to be on constant repeat in his head and spending the last few hours watching her hadn't helped him one fucking bit. In fact, he wanted to fire them off one at a time and wait to see if she would lie to him again.

Since he hadn't come face to face with her tonight, he had opted to do a little investigative work on his own. It was funny how much a woman would talk when she thought she was going to earn a big tip. And that was exactly what Jessica, the blonde stripper with the big tits, did for most of the night. In his defense, he did leave her a big tip. Bigger than he had originally intended, but the information she had given him had cemented a few things for him.

One of them being that it was time to confront Katie and figure out just what the hell was going on.

Climbing out of his truck, Dalton took his time making his way behind the vehicles. Rather than invite himself in, which he was pretty sure would get him shot down in a heartbeat, he lowered the tailgate and took a seat while he waited for her to join him. He didn't care much that it was after three o'clock in the morning; he just had the driving urge to talk to Katie, to understand what was motivating her, to ask her why she felt she had to lie to him. The conversation with the stripper at the club told him so many things about this woman. But everything he had learned just didn't add up, which was why he still had a hard time believing half of it.

Katie didn't rush around to the back of the truck and, at one point, Dalton thought she might've disappeared on him. He didn't make a move to encourage her to get out of her car, but he did toss a glance over his shoulder to make sure she was still there.

She was.

Finally, after a good ten minutes, she exited the car and made her way around, her eyes not meeting his as she approached.

"Hey," he greeted, realizing she wasn't going to speak to him. She'd managed to avoid him completely on the phone as well, but he expected they would have to say something to one another being face to face.

Clearly, she didn't think so.

"Can we talk?" he asked when she didn't respond.

"It's a little late, don't you think?" she retorted with a snap.

"I would've tried earlier," he added snidely, "but you were working."

He noticed Katie's slight cringe at his statement and he felt like a world-class asshole.

"Fine," she muttered. "What do you want to talk about?" Her gaze slid up toward the second floor where he assumed her apartment was.

"Someone waiting for you?" he asked, not expecting the reaction that he received.

Katie's eyes widened and she wrung her hands together in front of her, but she didn't answer. The heat that scorched his insides was laced with fury. Did she have a guy up there? Was she seeing someone?

Surely, Tessa would've mentioned that she was. Or even Cooper. Based on their conversation the other night at dinner, he had to assume they would've said something. Then again, aside from trying to figure out why he wasn't seeing her anymore, they hadn't actually talked about her. He had assumed that was because *he* wasn't talking about her. Now he had to wonder.

"I'm really tired," Katie finally stated.

"I bet," he bit out.

Katie's eyes narrowed, but she didn't say anything. As he watched her face, he expected to see anger reflecting back at him. What he saw looked more like regret.

"Shit," he mouthed. "I'm sorry. I'm sure you're tired. It's been a long day," Dalton said, grabbing the back of his neck as he stared down at the ground. He was sure she really was tired. He got that. It didn't mean he wanted to leave or that he wanted to let her walk away from him. He wanted to talk, to find out what was going on with her because damn it all to hell, he just couldn't fucking stop thinking about her.

No matter how hard he tried.

When it was evident she didn't have anything to say to him, he dove right in, not holding anything back. "Why are you workin' there, Katie?"

The look he got would've singed the hairs on his head had he not had his hat on. He'd never seen Katie pissed off, not even when she had to deal with unruly cowboys at The Rusty Nail. No, this was an entirely different side of the sweet woman he'd found himself unable to stop thinking about.

"That's none of your business," she snapped, her eyes slamming into his.

"God, Katie, don't you get it?" he asked rhetorically. "I want it to be my business."

"Why?" she asked, her eyes raking over his face.

"Because I... Damn it. Because I do," he told her. Telling her that he loved her wasn't going to earn him any points, and he'd suffered enough at this point. Making that public knowledge would only add to his pain. "I thought you and I had something," he added, his own frustration getting away from him.

Katie's eyes darted down to the ground. "We did."

Hope sparked in his chest.

"But this," she said, motioning toward her face, "is why it can't work. You don't deserve this, Dalton."

"Don't deserve what?" he asked, thoroughly confused.

"I'm a stripper, Dalton. That's all I am."

"That isn't all you are," he retorted.

"Really?" she questioned, her gray eyes sparkling. "You've seen me workin', Dalton. I think it's safe to say that it's true."

"Fine, maybe you're a stripper. But you could've told me. Could've given me a chance to understand."

"Are you serious?" she snapped. "I tried to explain myself, Dalton. You ignored my phone calls, remember?"

"Hold up," he said, almost pointing his finger at her but pulling it back at the last minute. No, he couldn't allow her to put this all on him. "You're the one who told me it was over. You turned your back on me the minute I drove out of Devil's Bend."

"For your own good," she replied, her eyes softening.

"How was it for my own good? You'd been lying to me the whole time. I was the dumbass who thought we had something good going."

"I never lied to you," she bit out.

"No? You just conveniently forgot to mention that," Dalton lowered his voice slightly, "you were a fucking stripper?"

"You never asked," she answered angrily.

"Oh, sorry," he belted out. "I'll have to remember to add that to the list of first date questions for the future."

"You do that."

Okay, great. He'd succeeded in widening the gap between them. And to think it'd taken very little effort. Taking a deep breath, he tried to steer the conversation back to less hostile topics. "I thought we were dating, Katie."

"No, we weren't," she countered. "We went on a couple of dates, that does not constitute dating."

Okay, she had a point there.

"Maybe not, but I kinda figured the sex constituted a relationship."

"Well, you were wrong." Katie looked as though she was hoping the ground would open up and swallow her whole.

The sight made Dalton's chest hurt. He took a deep breath, let it out slowly. "Fine. We went on a couple of dates, had mind-blowing sex. And you know good and damn well that it was going somewhere."

"I didn't know that," she said harshly, and Dalton realized it for the lie that it was.

Damn the woman was hot. Especially when she was pissed. That was strange enough to think, so Dalton opted not to tell her as much.

"Why do you have to be like that?" he asked. "I thought we were friends."

"Holy shit, Dalton!" Katie exclaimed. "One minute we're dating, the next we're friends. Which is it? I'm getting whiplash trying to follow your questions. I'm sure you have a point. Could you possibly get to it?"

Dalton ground his back teeth together. So maybe he shouldn't have followed her home. Maybe he should've waited until they had an opportunity for a civil conversation at The Rusty Nail. Or even at a get together with Tessa and Cooper. It was obvious she didn't want to be alone with him, and Dalton still wondered whether it was because she was hiding something or someone. He wouldn't put it past her, she'd lied to him enough already.

When her gaze launched back toward the upstairs apartment, he realized she *was* hiding something. "Why should I be surprised?" he blurted, pushing himself to his feet before turning to close the tailgate. "You didn't bother to tell me you were a stripper, why would you bother telling me you had a boyfriend."

Katie's eyes widened, but she didn't tell him he was wrong. That hurt worse than when he'd run into her at the strip club, half-naked and counting her earnings for the night.

She took a step back when he came toward her. That made his stomach hurt. Although she seemed to be convinced that what they had wasn't the same as what he thought it was, Dalton really did think they'd made more progress than this.

This woman had caught his eye and held it from the moment he saw her. And the more he got to know her, the more he had liked her. And then he'd gone and fallen in love with her.

She isn't who you think she is. "Yeah, I get that," he grumbled beneath his breath, answering the voices in his head.

"What?"

"Nothing. You better go inside."

Katie turned toward the stairs, but stopped. She looked over her shoulder at him and for half a second, Dalton thought he saw tears shimmering in her eyes. But then they were gone.

Almost as fast as she was.

CHAPTER TWENTY-ONE

Katie slipped into her apartment trying to be as quiet as possible. She knew Sarah and Lexi would be asleep and she didn't want to wake them. Even though she wished she could talk to her best friend, she knew it wasn't fair to do it in the middle of the night.

On tiptoe, she bypassed the tiny apartment kitchen. She would have to forgo dinner, or rather breakfast. Or whatever a meal at this ungodly hour would be considered. She just needed to get some shuteye at this point, merely because she was ready to shut her brain down for the day.

By the time she got ready for bed, showering because she hated the way she felt after she came home from the club, Katie was wired. So much for the closed-eye conversation she was going to have with her pillow.

As was habit, Katie stopped at Lexi's doorway, leaning in to make sure her sister was asleep. When she confirmed that she was, she padded barefoot inside before making her way to Lexi's bed. As gently as possible, she pulled the soft, pink microfiber comforter up over her sister's little body and then slipped back out.

Sometimes, on nights like this, Katie just wanted to fall into bed and cry for the injustice of it all. She'd gone from young adult to full adult far too soon, having to become a mother figure at eighteen. And Lexi had lost so much by losing her real mother, having to deal with an inexperienced and not quite so patient Katie. They'd managed to make their own little family though, and at this point, Katie didn't know what she would do without her sister, but sometimes, she daydreamed about all the possibilities the future had once held.

All of those dreams she'd had: getting out of Devil's Bend, going to the big city, getting a place of her own, going to school, finding a job. Even at eighteen, her motivation had been getting away from her crazy mother, and how ironic was it that Katie had been planning to be the one to disappear and her mother had just beat her to it.

Katie crawled into bed, flipping off the bedside lamp before curling beneath the heavy blanket. As she stared across the room, the orange glow from the parking lot light filtering through the cheap plastic blinds, Katie fought the urge to cry.

Why? Why her?

Why had all her dreams come crashing around her? She'd been a good kid, made good grades, went to school every day. And then when she turned eighteen, she'd been planning to head off to college, get a degree and make something of herself.

Only that never happened and she'd resorted to stripping just to make ends meet. Four years as a fucking stripper and she had nothing to show but a steadily growing bank account, a baby on the way, and a broken heart that continued to weigh her down more and more each day.

Oh, and now she could add liar to her repertoire of skills.

In her defense, providing for Lexi was the only thing that mattered to her these days. Katie squandered every last penny, trying to make it by on the least she could so that Lexi would have what she needed. As far as Katie was concerned, as long as she had food and clothes, then she was fine. Lexi was who mattered. And now the baby.

Only on occasion, Katie did need something. She needed that human connection that she didn't seem to have. That she *never* had.

Sweet little innocent stripper.

God, she was pathetic.

She hated the pity parties she had, and she hated even more that they'd increased in number since the night Dalton had run into her at the club. Tonight's encounter wasn't going to help either. She still remembered the look in his eyes, then and now. He'd been hurt and angry. Which was the only reason she hadn't told him about the baby. She had wanted to, but she didn't want him to take pity on her. She was doing enough of that on her own.

Who the hell did he think he was just showing up at her apartment anyway? Following her home like that? He had to have been at the club. How else would he have known to follow her?

And now he knew where she lived, something she'd tried to hide from everyone she knew because she didn't want to disrupt Lexi's life by having friends. It was enough that she had Sarah, her best friend from high school. And she had Tessa, Cooper, Eric, and Izzy, although they were more acquaintances than anything else because even they didn't know about Lexi.

Nor did they know where she lived. And she didn't want them to either, which was why she used a post office box as her address, trying to keep herself off the radar.

Until now, until Dalton, it had worked.

As her eyelids drooped, Katie forced the thoughts away, choosing instead to focus on the good memories she had. The one she revisited most frequently these days was the first real date she'd had with Dalton.

"Let's get out of here," Dalton whispered.

Katie glanced over at the handsome cowboy with the sexy voice and smiled. It wasn't easy to do considering the situation, but just looking at this man made things seem that much better.

Maybe not for Tessa and Cooper, who were currently having a hush-hush conversation on the front porch. The night had gone terribly wrong, at least for Tessa, but Katie was glad to see that Cooper was there for her.

Allowing Dalton to link their fingers together, she walked alongside him toward his truck.

A few minutes later they were pulling down the driveway and out onto the main road.

"Where are we going?" she asked as she focused on the scenery outside of the truck.

"The lake," he informed her.

"The lake?" she asked, looking over at him.

His grin was enough to make her insides turn to mush.

"Yes, ma'am. I thought we'd go make out in the bed of my truck. That is, if you're game."

They'd done a little making out, if that's what some hot and heavy kisses were considered these days, but not much farther than that. Although she was a bit nervous, Katie was more than happy to spend some alone time with Dalton. For whatever reason, she enjoyed his company.

He made her feel safe. He made her feel important. And more importantly, he didn't treat her like she was just a sex object.

Then again, he had no reason to.

Katie tore her gaze off him and settled on watching the porch lights as they passed by in a blur. She wasn't going to think about the fact that she'd never told him much about herself. At least not the important details.

It wasn't the right time, she reminded herself.

Maybe one day. But not tonight.

Tonight she just wanted to enjoy their time together.

As Katie drifted off, she felt a single tear slide down her cheek. The first of many.

∞ ∞ ∞ ∞ ∞

By the time Dalton made it home, he was in a strange state of mind.

Not bad.

Not good.

After the argument he'd just had with Katie, he actually felt a little numb.

Strange, because that had never happened to him before. At least not that he could recall.

He was tempted to try to nail down the reason, but he couldn't come up with anything. Aside from the fact that his confrontation with Katie had actually hurt. Like a physical ache that he hadn't anticipated.

The only thing he knew for sure was that it all stemmed from what had started between him and Katie. No matter how much she wanted to deny it, there was no doubt in Dalton's mind that what they had started wasn't the usual brief relationship. It was more than that. So much more.

Fucking hell.

Marching into his house, he slammed the front door behind him. Damn good thing he lived in the country or he was sure someone would have questioned him, even at four o'clock in the fucking morning.

Unable to keep himself upright, Dalton made his way to his bedroom, still about the only room that was completely set up in his house. And the only reason that had happened was because of Katie. He fell facedown onto the mattress, fully clothed and closed his eyes.

Katie.

Son of a bitch.

Why did he care so fucking much? Why couldn't he just let it all go rather than try to stir it up and make it worse. It was clear she didn't want to have anything to do with him. And if he thought about it long enough, he should've been able to rationalize his reasons for not wanting her either.

But he couldn't get there.

Even knowing what he did, even after she pushed him away and put a ridiculous amount of distance between them, he still wanted her. And it wasn't all just sex.

At least he didn't think so.

As the memories of their time together swirled together, morphing into one giant commemoration, Dalton took a deep breath. He could clearly remember their first date, their second, and all of the other that followed. He remembered the first time he made love to her in his truck, and the nights she spent in his bed. He doubted he would ever forget any of it.

His mind drifted to that first night in his truck. What he had expected to be a simple hour or two between friends just talking and enjoying one another's company had turned into one of the most memorable nights of his entire life.

They'd had sex for the first time that night. And he knew... Damn it, he knew that she had been a virgin. But why wouldn't she have said something? How could she possibly just let that go?

Oh, hell, yes, he'd give his left arm for another few minutes with her in his arms, but at that point, he wasn't sure that was ever going to be an option. Not again anyway.

Yet he couldn't shoulder all of the blame.

It was obvious that Katie was hiding something else; he just didn't know exactly what. Another man, maybe? It was possible, but he wasn't so sure that was the case.

An easy assumption though, especially considering the way she'd reacted tonight at her apartment. She'd wanted him gone; there was no doubt about that.

But what about the look she gave him when she turned to go? He'd seen something there. Something that looked like remorse.

Or was that just wishful thinking on his part.

Flipping over to his back, Dalton toed off his boots and let them fall to the floor with a thud, first one, and then the other. As he stared at the ceiling, he found himself thinking back to that night when he'd taken her to the lake. The night he had taken her virginity.

Was that when things started going wrong?

That was the first night that things had heated up between them, turning into something so much more than just friendship. And it had been hotter than hell. So much so that he'd been concerned that a fire extinguisher might've been needed in order to keep them under control.

"Katie," Dalton pleaded, pulling back, trying to hold himself together. He didn't want to push her too far. Didn't want her to do something she might regret tomorrow.

"Please don't," she whispered. "Don't warn me that this isn't the right thing to do. That it isn't the right time. That it isn't the right place. You and I both know those are just social niceties and I'm so far passed that—"

"Are you sure?" he asked, cutting her off midsentence.

"More than," she answered, pulling him closer, pressing her breasts firmly against his rock hard chest while she nipped his lower lip.

"Oh, hell," Dalton mumbled, launching to his feet, his hands cupping her ass and holding her astride him.

Katie wrapped her legs around his waist and her arms around his neck, while he held her tightly.

"I've got you, Katie," he muttered, his lips pressed to hers. He'd always have her. He just didn't know how to tell her that.

Pulling himself back to the present, Dalton placed his hands beneath his head, sleep pulling him under. As much as he wanted to dig into the reasons for his feelings for Katie, or why he still wanted her after all this time, Dalton knew it was moot.

Katie didn't want him anymore.

And that's what bothered him the most.

So much so, that as he fell into a deep sleep, he acknowledged one final thing… He was in love with Katie Clarren.

What he was supposed to do with that knowledge, he really had no clue.

CHAPTER TWENTY-TWO

"You want to go *where?*" Katie asked, confused.

"To the horse place," Lexi said firmly. "Can you take me?"

"What horse place?" Katie had a pretty good idea of where Lexi was talking about, but she was clueless as to the reason.

"The one with the nice cowboy man," she told him. "He let me look at the puppies and the horses."

"What was this cowboy man's name?" she asked, scared of what Lexi's answer was going to be.

"Mr. Dalton."

Yep, her deepest fears were confirmed.

She recalled her conversation with Sarah just a few hours ago. Right before her best friend disappeared out the front door, off to handle her own personal life rather than take care of Katie and Lexi. She mentioned that as soon as she woke up, Lexi had started to go on and on about going to the horse place and meeting the nice man who talked to her.

Oh, crap. The field trip.

Katie recalled Bethany, the childcare center's director mentioning that Lexi had done incredibly well on the field trip. She'd even talked their ears off when they made it back to the center, telling everyone about the horses and everything she had learned.

Yes, Lexi was incredibly smart, but she had a central focus about things. When she found something she was interested in, she learned all that she could, to the point of being obsessed. Hence, the obsessive-compulsive disorder she'd been diagnosed with. And Katie had seen firsthand just what that would do to Lexi.

Which meant her only option was to give in to Lexi's request to take her back to the horse place.

"Was it called Dream Chasers?" Katie asked, hoping that maybe she was wrong.

Lexi's eyes lit up, her mouth curving into a brilliant smile. "Yes! That's it. Can we go? Can we?"

Crap.

"Can I take a shower first?" Katie asked, knowing that any other answer would've sent Lexi into a downward spiral, and as much as she didn't want to have to face *Mr. Dalton*, as Lexi had referred to him, she knew she wasn't going to get out of this one easily. Either face him or face Lexi's wrath.

Damn it.

So much for keeping her personal life secret.

"Yes. Go!" Lexi encouraged, pulling on Katie's arm. "Go shower so we can go see the horses."

Katie nodded, allowing Lexi to pull her to her feet. She was trying to come up with a plan, wishing like hell there was a way she could get out of this without having to face Dalton or answer any questions from Tessa or Cooper, but she knew Lexi. The kid was bullheaded at best and when she got her teeth into something, she didn't let go without a fight.

Katie didn't want to fight.

Not today.

As it was, she was drained. Emotionally at least.

Forcing her feet to move, she made her way down the hall to the small bathroom. It wasn't that she needed a shower because she'd taken one just that morning when she got home from the club, but at least this would give her a little time to possibly formulate another plan.

Not that she was likely going to come up with a way to distract Lexi. That never worked.

Then again, Katie had never been this motivated before.

An hour and a half later, Katie was pulling down the dirt drive that led to the Dream Chasers Equestrian Center.

Yeah, so much for a possible out. She'd come up with exactly zilch. And the few things she'd mentioned to Lexi had been shot down before they even came out of her mouth.

Her little sister was officially fixated on the horses.

At least she hoped it was the horses. Every conversation seemed to mention Mr. Dalton as well as the horses, but what did she know.

"Hey, lady!" Tessa greeted when Katie stepped out of her car. "This is a wonderful surprise. What brings you by?"

Katie glanced back at the car, seeing Lexi still buckled into the backseat. An assortment of lies formulated in her head, but nothing would come out of her mouth. What was she going to say? It wasn't as if she could pretend Lexi wasn't there. Or that the little girl wasn't with her. Seriously, they looked so much alike, it was scary. Even the girls at the daycare center had thought Lexi was Katie's daughter at first.

"I just thought I'd stop by to see how things are going," she lied.

"Hey, kiddo," Tessa greeted hesitantly, looking behind Katie. That's when she realized that Lexi had scrambled out of the car and was moving toward her with intent.

Once Lexi's small fingers slipped into hers, Katie looked back up at Tessa to see the other woman was studying them both.

"Is she… your daughter?"

"My little sister," Katie blurted. "Lexi, meet Tessa Donovan. Tessa, this is my sister, Lexi."

Tessa moved closer, but she did so slowly, almost as though she knew how to handle Lexi without being informed.

"It's very nice to meet you, Lexi."

Lexi didn't respond, but Tessa smiled down at her anyway.

"Did you know that I work with your sister?" Tessa asked, keeping a safe distance between them. "I also own this place." Tessa signaled her reference by raising her arm and motioning toward the huge buildings behind her.

"You own it?" Lexi asked excitedly. "Does that mean the horses are yours, too?"

"Yes, ma'am," Tessa agreed.

"What about Mr. Dalton. Is he yours, too?"

Tessa choked, her eyes bugging as she looked up at Katie and then back to Lexi. "No, Mr. Dalton does not belong to me, but I take it you've visited us recently, huh?"

Katie glanced down to see Lexi nodding in agreement.

"So what brings you out here today?" Tessa asked, this time turning her question to Katie.

"She wanted to come and see the horses."

"And Mr. Dalton," Lexi tacked on.

Tessa's smile widened and Katie was pretty sure she saw a mischievous gleam in her eyes.

"Well, good news," Tessa replied. "We've got plenty of horses in the arena right now, and Mr. Dalton is there, too."

Katie fought the urge to turn around and run back to her car. The thought of seeing Dalton wasn't terrible, but she wasn't sure how this was going to go. After all, bringing Lexi was just another way of exposing one more of her many secrets.

And she knew exactly what Dalton thought about the last secret he'd unearthed.

∞ ∞ ∞ ∞ ∞

Dalton had spent the morning in a fog. After three cups of coffee, his blurry brain hadn't cleared any, but he was wired for sound. That was one of the main reasons he was working with Sacred Spirit, the unruly gelding they'd brought to the center recently. He had to do something to stay busy, and the less he had to think, the better off he would be.

"Hey, Dalt! You've got visitors!"

Dalton turned at the sound of Tessa's voice.

What he saw, or rather who, had him stopping mid-step.

Katie? And Lexi?

What the hell was going on?

"Hey," he greeted as he approached the ladies.

"Hey," Katie replied, not meeting his gaze.

"Mr. Dalton! My sister said I could come see the horses today!" Lexi's enthusiasm had him smiling.

Sister? Holy shit. His gaze transferred back and forth between them, finally landing on Lexi when he realized Katie wasn't going to look at him. "Well, I'm so glad you're here, little lady." Dalton left Sacred Spirit alone in the arena while he joined Katie and Lexi on the other side of the fence.

"I'll get her put up," Tessa informed him, touching his arm gently as she passed him.

"Don't you go in there," Dalton warned her. "Sacred's in a mood this mornin'."

Tessa nodded. "Okay. Cooper's on his way down here. I'll let him get her then."

"Lexi, you wanna go see the puppies first?" Dalton asked the little girl as he made his way to her side.

"Yes, please," she confirmed, taking his hand when he held it out to her.

Glancing over at Katie, Dalton noticed she was watching the interaction between him and her sister, but she didn't say anything. She simply fell into step a few feet behind them.

Right then, Austin came waltzing up to them, his brother and sister charging along beside him. "Hey, Dalt."

"Mornin'." Nodding toward Katie, Dalton made the necessary introductions.

"Nice to meet you, ma'am," Austin replied.

"You, too," Katie answered softly, her gaze linked with Dalton's for the first time since she arrived.

Lexi gripped Dalton's hand a little tighter, but when Dalton looked down, he noticed she was watching Austin intently. "You wanna go see the puppies with Austin?"

"Hey, Lex," Austin greeted her. "This is my little brother, Matt. And my sister, Olivia."

"Hi," Austin's brother and sister said in unison. Lexi didn't respond, gripping Dalton's hand even tighter, but she was smiling.

"Come on, y'all," Austin said as he guided Matt and Olivia toward the pen where the petting zoo animals were kept, and the area where the puppies were being contained.

"You can go, Lex. I'll be right here with your sister. Okay?"

Lexi nodded, releasing Dalton's hand and glancing over her shoulder at Katie before smiling and hopping toward the others. When the four of them walked off together, Dalton pivoted to see Katie watching after Lexi.

"Didn't know you had a sister," he told her blandly.

Katie peered up at him, her pretty gray eyes widening. "You didn't ask."

That was the same thing she'd told him last night when he asked about her being a stripper. And just like then, her response felt like a slap in the face, but Dalton managed to hold his tongue.

Barely.

Only because he didn't want to argue with her. Last night had been hell. Significantly harder than he'd anticipated. Walking away from Katie, anytime, was damn near debilitating and last night hadn't proved to be any different.

"Look, I didn't come here to—"

Dalton took two steps and was standing directly in front of Katie. Before she could finish the sentence, he gripped her shoulders and leaned in until their mouths were less than an inch apart. "I don't want to fight with you, Katie," Dalton whispered harshly. "I've never wanted to fight with you."

Her eyes widened, but she didn't say anything.

And that's the moment Dalton snapped. He lost every ounce of his control.

Sliding his arms around her, he crushed her to him, pressing his lips to hers. At first, he didn't try to take things farther. But that lasted all of two seconds. Before he could question his own sanity, Dalton coaxed Katie's mouth open with his tongue, slipping inside. God, she tasted just like he remembered. Sweet. Like mint and coffee.

He groaned, unable to contain the pent up emotion that rumbled in his chest. And when Katie wrapped her arms around his neck, kissing him back just as desperately, he felt all of that anger that was encasing his heart crack. "Katie," he breathed her name against her lips, his hands sliding down her back. He kept them north of her ass, but just barely.

Guiding her backward, he stopped when her back was against the wall of the stable. They were just inside, hidden from any prying eyes and Dalton couldn't help himself.

Sliding one hand up, he cupped her face gently, not wanting to hurt her, but unable to contain the fiery need that ignited in his blood stream. He slipped his thigh between her legs, urging them open. Grinding his thigh against her pussy, he took the kiss to the next level. She was kissing him back, nipping at his lip, her nails digging into his back where she'd slid her hands beneath his T-shirt.

"Oh, God, Katie." He was losing his fucking mind. That was all there was to it. He had no idea how to stop the collision course they were on, but he didn't want to either. He wanted to devour her. He wanted to lift up her skirt, pull her panties to the side and drive himself into her, claiming her.

"Dalton!"

The sound of Austin's voice calling him was the only thing that stopped him. Pulling his mouth from hers, he didn't stop touching her, one hand at the small of her back, pulling her to him, the other cupping her face while he brushed his thumb over her soft cheek.

"What the hell is going on, Katie?" he asked, his voice low and gruff.

"Dalton. Hey, man. Where are you?"

"You better see what he needs," she whispered, her eyes still linked with his.

Dalton nodded, releasing her from his grip. "Don't go anywhere."

"My sister's here, remember?" she retorted, her eyes sliding away from his.

"Right."

Dalton took a step back, his eyes still trained on her for another second. Then he turned and rounded the wall that was separating him from Austin. "What's up, man?"

"I'm gonna take 'em to see the horses in the arena. That cool? Coop's over there."

Nodding his head, Dalton felt Katie come up behind him. To his surprise, she didn't try to go with Austin, and for whatever reason, that simple gesture had hope once again swelling in his chest.

Hope.

Damn it.

"If you need us," Dalton told Austin, "we'll be in the barn."

Austin nodded his head in understanding and then ventured into the stable, all three kids following behind him.

Taking a deep breath, Dalton considered just what this opportunity meant for him. What it meant for the things he wanted from this woman. He realized he was standing there, praying that Katie wouldn't walk away from him again. That whatever was happening here might be the second chance they needed.

That morning, when he had woken up, Dalton had lay in his bed, remembering his life from so long ago. The lies, the secrets. He'd been burned by people he thought were his friends. Maybe that was what had hurt him the most about her secrets. But as the sun's rays began to slip into his bedroom, he remembered his own secrets. Everything he'd kept from Katie.

And it pissed him off. He was a fucking hypocrite.

He wanted another chance with her. He wanted to make it up to her. Only he didn't know how that worked. He'd never tried to reconcile with anyone, choosing to walk away rather than stick around and fight for what he wanted.

After Austin walked away with the three kids in tow, Dalton turned to face Katie.

That was the moment he knew he was ready to make a change. If it meant groveling at her feet, begging for her forgiveness, he was ready.

His dreams of being in the FBI had died a long time ago because of circumstances beyond his control. But Katie... The woman standing in front of him was what he longed for. What he wanted more than his next breath.

And it was time to stop watching his dreams vanish.

It was time to go after what he wanted.

Starting with her.

CHAPTER TWENTY-THREE

Katie was pretty sure she was going to have whiplash due to Dalton's frequent mood swings.

Last night – or rather early that morning – he had seemed angry with her when he had followed her back to her apartment. But now… Now he was acting as though nothing had transpired between them over the course of the last few months.

What was wrong with this man? What made him think he could just take what he wanted, or forget the fact that he had crushed her all those months ago?

Then again, what the hell was she thinking? She'd been a willing participant a few minutes ago when she had practically tried to climb his body, wanting nothing more than to get close to him. When he had touched her, all her walls had come crumbling down.

Watching Lexi walk away with Austin, she steeled herself for what was to come.

Being alone with Dalton Calhoun was not good for her piece of mind.

Dalton took her hand and Katie allowed him to lead her out into the field that separated the barn from the stable. She hadn't been back to the center since they finished all of the buildings, but she got the impression that Dalton was choosing to go to the barn because it offered them a small amount of privacy.

Katie wasn't so sure that was a good idea, but she didn't argue.

A minute later, when they stepped into the shadows of the barn, Katie's nerves decided to disrupt her thoughts. She was alone with Dalton.

Alone and intently aware of him.

"Come on," he encouraged, gently tugging her arm.

"Where are we going?" she asked, glancing around and noticing all of the equipment they stored there. Surprisingly, there weren't any animals as she'd suspected there would be.

"Hay loft," he answered roughly.

Katie glanced up, noticing another level. It, in fact, did have hay up there, but she got the feeling they didn't actually store the hay there.

Dalton took a step back when they reached the wooden ladder that went straight up. He wanted her to go first, she realized.

After taking a deep breath and resigning herself to having this conversation with him, Katie grabbed the wooden rungs and began climbing. When she reached the top, she crawled onto the plywood floor, putting several feet between herself and the edge. Now probably wasn't a good time to tell Dalton that she was scared of heights.

Dalton propelled himself around the ladder like a man who'd done it a million times. He had to duck to avoid a few wooden beams that were attached to the ceiling, but he made his way around and then dropped onto a hay bale.

"Come here," he insisted. His tone left no room for argument, which put her on the defense instantly.

But rather than argue with him, she pushed to her feet and reached for his hand when he held it out to her. He pulled her toward him and then motioned for her to sit beside him.

"What's going on, Katie?" he asked bluntly, his elbows resting on his knees, hands hanging between his legs.

"You tell me," she replied, unsure where this was going. Seriously, the man had brought her here, what was she supposed to say to that?

"Did Tessa know you had a sister?" he asked directly, tilting his head enough to look over at her beneath the brim of his hat.

"No," Katie answered honestly. There were too many lies between them and now that Dalton had figured her out, she knew there was no reason to keep up the charade. And quite frankly, she felt a little better without the weight of all her secrets sitting on her shoulders.

"Do y'all live with your mom?"

"Nope," she told him. "She left when I was eighteen."

Dalton's head snapped toward her, his eyes studying her face. She didn't need to elaborate; he knew exactly what she was telling him.

"You've been raising that little girl since you were eighteen?"

Yep, he came to the correct conclusion all on his own.

Katie nodded.

Dalton pushed to his feet, pulling his hat off his head and shoving his hand through his hair. "Holy shit." He turned to face her, pressing his hat back on his head.

God, he really was the most attractive man she'd ever met. In his Wranglers and boots, Stetson on his head and a dark T-shirt plastered to the hard planes of his chest, the man made her mouth water.

"Is she…?"

He let the question hang, but Katie knew what he was asking. "Lexi has attention deficit hyperactivity disorder. She's predominantly inattentive, which you've probably noticed by how quiet she is. She has also been diagnosed with obsessive-compulsive disorder," she answered. "Some days are better than others."

"Holy shit, Katie. Why the hell would you have kept her a secret all this time? You've got friends who would help you."

Katie felt her ire rising. This man pretended to know her, but he seemed to forget that they hadn't shared their deepest, darkest secrets with one another during the brief time they were together. She didn't owe him any explanations. Pushing to her feet, Katie ran her hands over her skirt, sucked in a deep breath and let it out slowly.

Keeping her tone even and trying to pretend she didn't give a shit what he thought about her, she said, "I'm not sure why you're all of a sudden worried about me, Dalton. I've spent the last five years managing my sister on my own without needing help from anyone else. And just because you met her a few days ago, you don't have the right to question how I've managed my life or hers up to this point."

"Damn it, Katie. That's not what I'm sayin'," Dalton barked. "She's a great kid. You've done a fantastic job raisin' her. I just want to know why you thought you had to go this alone."

Katie's anger got the best of her. "Fuck you, Dalton. Alone is all I've ever been, don't you get it? No one sticks around. No one. And with my... choice of occupation, I don't gain a whole lot of respect. You think I would've wanted that for my sister? You honestly think I would've wanted to introduce you to her so that you could abandon her, too? You didn't know me. Not the real me. And then you find out that I'm a stripper and what did you do? You did exactly what I thought you would do. You looked down your nose at me. That's the reason I've done this alone. I don't want to depend on someone else who's gonna bail when things get tough. And trust me, every day is a coin toss with Lexi. Some good. Some bad. I'm in it for the long haul. I don't need any part-timers disrupting our lives, thank you very much."

Katie was fighting the angry tears that flooded her eyes. The last thing she wanted was for Dalton to see her cry. She was done.

Heading toward the ladder, Katie just wanted to get away from him. She didn't need his questions and accusations. She had enough guilt that she'd piled on herself, his wasn't welcome.

Before she could move passed him, Dalton put his arm out and stopped her, then easily pulled her into his arms. She tried to push him away, but his grip just tightened. And then the tears began to fall which only pissed her off more. She pounded on his chest, trying to get him to leave her alone, but the stubborn man didn't back down. He merely pulled her closer, crushing her to his chest, capturing her arms between them.

Right then and there, Katie broke down. She cried for the injustice of it all. For her baby sister being abandoned, for having to live her life with a debilitating disease that most people didn't understand, for the baby growing inside of her. And she cried for herself. For the fact that she had made decisions that she regretted, but couldn't take back. And she shed more tears for the man whose arms were wrapped tightly around her because, if ever there was someone she wanted in her life, Dalton was that person.

And the worst part of it all, Katie loved him. She had loved him for so long, but the hell she'd put them both through by walking away wasn't something she wanted to endure again. He had reacted exactly as she had expected him to, which was the only reason she'd broken things off with him. And leaving him was harder than anything she'd ever done before.

Katie wasn't sure that was something they could ever get past.

∞ ∞ ∞ ∞ ∞

Everything made perfect fucking sense.

Too much sense.

As he held Katie in his arms, her small body shuddering as she sobbed, Dalton hated himself for what they'd put each other through. They were both to blame. She had walked away from him without giving him an explanation and he had just let her go, not fighting for what they'd had. And she was right. When he had learned the truth, he had turned his back on her without giving her a chance to explain. He had jumped to conclusions, making her out to be something evil, something vindictive.

But she wasn't.

Katie wasn't manipulative. She wasn't out to hurt anyone.

She was trying to survive.

And now they'd come full circle.

"Katie," he whispered her name, pressing his lips to her forehead. "Baby, I'm so damn sorry."

Clearly that was the wrong thing to say because Katie pushed him, and this time he took a step back, giving her space.

"Fuck you," she snapped. "I don't want your pity, Dalton. I don't need it."

Sweet little Katie Clarren saying the "F" word… For some reason, that turned him on.

Dalton knew that everything he said was coming out wrong. But that was what Katie expected from him and he honestly couldn't blame her. He had turned his back on her the same way she had him.

That didn't mean he wasn't ready to repent. This woman did things to him that no other woman ever had and as much as he knew she deserved someone who would be there for her no matter what, someone who would fight to protect her, to take care of her, Dalton wasn't going to leave her alone. He wasn't turning his back on her again.

With an urgency that took him by surprise, Dalton closed the gap between them, cupping her face and tilting her chin so that she had to look at him and then melded his mouth to hers.

Her soft moan nearly ripped him apart, the way she gave in to him so easily, so thoroughly.

"Katie," he groaned, pulling his mouth from hers momentarily. "I can't do this anymore. I can't stay away."

To his surprise, she pulled him to her, their lips sealing together once more. The kiss erupted into a firestorm, a conflagration of sensual need. It overwhelmed him, stripped him bare.

"I've missed you," he whispered, sliding his hands down her hips and lifting her, forcing her to wrap her legs around his waist.

Dalton carried her to the hay bale. He lowered himself down, Katie straddling his lap, her skirt bunching around her thighs. He palmed the back of her head, his other arm banding around her waist, unable to let her go.

The kiss continued, Dalton thrusting his tongue into Katie's sweet, welcoming mouth. He'd missed this. Missed touching her, holding her. If she'd let him, he'd sit right there and kiss her all damn day.

"What are we doin', Dalton?" she asked, drawing back from him. Her arms wreathed his neck, and she didn't pull away, which he considered a good sign.

"I don't know," he told her honestly. "But I don't want it to end, Katie. I…" He couldn't complete the sentence, fearful that he was cutting himself open for her and she would just let him bleed out.

"I have to know," Katie said, her voice more insistent. "I have to know what you want from me. I'm still that same girl. I'm still a stripper, Dalton. Even if I'm not doing it for a while. I will have to eventually. As much as I hate it, that's the only way I can make a living, the only way I can make enough to take care of Lexi and put myself through school."

"What do you mean you'll have to do it again eventually?" he asked, trying to piece together everything she'd just told him.

When Katie tried to move out of his arms, he held her there, refusing to let her go.

"Talk to me, Katie. This is how we got here in the first place. You need to talk to me."

Katie's eyes met his and another tear leaked down her cheek. She kept her eyes on his as she reached for his hand, taking it in hers and then pressing it to her belly.

Dalton's heart stopped beating. He was pretty damn sure he was going to pass out as he glanced down at their joined hands, then back up to meet her eyes.

"You're…?"

"I'm pregnant. I've been wanting to tell you," she said quickly, obviously feeling the need to explain. "I didn't want to tell your voice mail, so I was waiting for a time we could talk. Last night just didn't seem like the right moment."

"Oh, fuck." He exhaled heavily, watching her closely.

The fact that he wasn't angry that she hadn't told him wasn't lost on him. Her explanation actually did make sense. She had tried to call him before but he hadn't answered and he had never returned her calls. The few times he'd come back during his tour, he had tried to stay as far away from her as possible. And he completely agreed, last night, that kind of news wouldn't have gone over well.

Dalton swallowed around the lump in his throat and pressed his hand more firmly to her belly. "Oh, God, Katie."

For the first time in as long as he could remember, Dalton actually cried.

He broke down right there and when Katie wrapped her arms around him, holding him tight, he let it all out.

Dalton had no idea how long they sat like that, but the next thing he knew, he was lowering Katie to the hay at their feet, his mouth pressed to hers. She tasted so familiar, so sweet.

Without thinking, his emotions guiding his every movement, Dalton slid his hand beneath Katie's skirt, then slipped his finger beneath her panties, finding her warm and wet. He continued to kiss her while Katie worked the button and zipper of his jeans, releasing him from the denim confines before wrapping her arms around his neck once again.

He tugged at her panties until they ripped, unable to take the time to remove them properly before he was guiding himself into her.

"Oh, fuck, Katie. Oh, God, baby." It was too good.

"I love you, Dalton," Katie whispered against his mouth.

He pulled his head back slightly so he could look into her eyes. Holding himself up with one forearm, Dalton lifted her leg, pulling it up against his hip as he ground his hips against hers, driving deeper into her welcoming body.

"I love you, darlin'. I've loved you this whole time."

More tears fell from Katie's eyes and Dalton couldn't contain his own emotions. While he continued to slide deep into her, he pressed his face into the crook of her neck. This was the only place in the world that he wanted to be. Right here, with Katie, wrapped in her arms, buried in her body. He could spend eternity right there and he'd never have one single complaint.

"Dalton. Oh, God, it's… it's been too long. I'm gonna…"

Katie's body tensed as her sentenced trailed off and Dalton let go, following her lead, coming deep inside of her.

Dalton didn't pull out of her right away, didn't want to move from where he was, so he hovered over her, careful not to put his weight on her as he did. He lifted his head and smiled down at her. "Have dinner with me tonight," he finally said, his thumb grazing her soft, smooth cheek. "You and Lexi. Let me cook you dinner."

"I don't know…" Katie's gaze slid away from his, but Dalton wasn't finished.

"Look at me, Katie." He waited until she did before he continued. "What we started all those months ago… we're right back there. I'm not letting you walk away again. I know you thought you were doing what was best for me, but you were wrong. What's best for me is you. Wherever you are, that's where I want to be."

Katie's eyes narrowed on his face but she didn't respond.

"I love you, Katie. I've never said those three words to another woman before. I've never felt anything for anyone like what I feel for you. I've beaten myself up for letting you walk away. I should've come after you, should've begged you to stay. Give me a chance to show you what you mean to me."

"I hurt you, Dalton."

Dalton hadn't expected that, but he nodded his head, unable to deny the truth. "You did. More than you know. But that was the past. This is now. The only thing we have is that. There's no time for regrets."

"I don't want Lexi to get hurt," she said softly. "She likes you, Dalton. That might mean a lot to you, but for her, it's a really big deal. She doesn't get close to many people. I don't want her to get close to you, just so you can turn and walk away."

"I'm not going anywhere, Katie."

Katie pulled her eyes away, looking behind him. He could tell she was considering his request.

Dalton tipped his head forward and pressed his forehead against hers. "Darlin', I'm a firm believer that things happen for a reason. You and me. Maybe then wasn't the right time. But now is. I know that and I hope you do too. As for Lexi, I'll love her with my whole heart."

Lifting his head, Dalton met her gaze once again.

He feared that he wasn't going to win this battle. No matter how hard he tried, they had too much history between them and she was too protective to let him back in. But he wanted in.

And he was tired of backing down. Tired of letting the universe dictate to him. He wanted to control his life; he wanted to choose what the outcome would be. And if he got hurt in the process, so be it. Otherwise, he was still hurt and he knew without a doubt that having to be around Katie all the time wasn't going to help. He was going to spiral out of control until he couldn't take it anymore. And then he'd be gone. Back on the road, back on tour, burying himself in work and never enjoying a minute of it.

He was tired of being that guy.

Dalton began moving inside her again, his cock still hard, still eager to be right there in her. Katie's eyes closed briefly, her head tilting back.

"I want to make love to you for the rest of my life," he said, his voice raspy with emotion. He pushed in deep, pulling out slowly, her pussy gripping him tightly. "I want to have plenty of babies with you. I want to spend the rest of my life making you happy, helping you take care of your sister."

Katie's arms came up around his neck, holding him tight as he continued to rock against her.

"One chance, Katie. One chance. That's all I'm asking for. I…" Dalton sucked in a breath and pulled back to meet her eyes again. "I need you, Katie. I love you."

Tears formed in her eyes but she didn't look away. He considered that a good sign.

She nodded and Dalton pressed his lips to hers, his hips beginning to move faster, thrusting harder, unable to resist the velvet grip of her pussy. She was so tight, so hot. He'd missed her. He'd missed this.

"Come for me, Katie," he whispered.

Katie's head tilted back, the narrow column of her throat exposed to him. Unable to resist, he pressed his lips there once before pulling back and driving into her. Her legs came up to cradle his hips, holding him tightly.

"That's it, baby. Love me, Katie."

"Dalton," Katie ground out his name as her body tightened, her pussy milking him once again.

When she came down, he stopped moving. He wasn't going to come again. Not yet. But that hadn't been about him. That was all for her.

Rolling off her so that he didn't crush her, Dalton dropped to his back and stared up at the ceiling.

"I'll give us one more chance, Dalton," Katie said softly, causing him to turn his head to see her looking at him. "But we have to agree to something."

"Name it," he replied.

"No more lies. You'll have to accept me for who I really am, Dalton. You can't expect to change me 'cause that's not gonna happen."

Dalton nodded. He would agree to wrangle the moon for her if that was what she wanted. He had known from the first time he laid eyes on her that Katie was going to be his. She was it for him.

Even after she'd driven him away, when he'd been with other women, the only person he saw was Katie. Always Katie.

As much as he'd denied it all this time, Dalton knew without a doubt that he would never be able to stay away from her.

CHAPTER TWENTY-FOUR

Starting over.

That was a new concept for Katie and she wasn't quite sure how she felt about the idea. She wasn't opposed to it, she just wasn't sure what to think of it yet.

She feared that Dalton was making promises she wasn't sure he could keep. And for what reason? Because he felt sorry for her? Because he was worried about Lexi? Or was it because he didn't want her to shut him out of the baby's life?

Katie could've easily assured him that the last one wasn't going to happen. The baby deserved to know its father, and Dalton deserved to be in the loop. That was the last thing she would ever want to do – keep the two of them apart.

As for the other questions… She didn't know the answers, but she knew that the chemistry between them was unmistakable. There was no denying it, even if she wanted to. She'd spent the last few months thinking of him, wishing she could've done things differently. But those had been selfish thoughts at times. She loved Dalton. She wanted to be with him, but in the same sense, she wanted to spare him the hassle of what her day to day entailed.

Dalton was the only man who owned her heart. Hell, he owned her soul if she really thought about it. But her heart… that was the fragile piece she was worried about. Without even trying, he'd shattered it so easily, and Katie wasn't sure her heart had been repaired enough to endure something like that again.

Although, she had to remind herself that the blame ultimately lie at her feet. She'd been the one to make the decision. He had just gone along with it, never fighting for her.

And that's what she feared most. Didn't matter that she'd pushed him away, he had turned around and walked without looking back. That was something she had a hard time dealing with. It hadn't been an easy thing to deal with.

She knew without a doubt that Lexi wouldn't be able to handle it if things fell apart between them.

So why was she relenting? Why was she giving in to this man when she knew she should just turn around and walk away from him? He could still be a father to their baby, even if they weren't together.

But walking away again wasn't that easy.

Her heart wouldn't let her.

"No more lies," Dalton finally agreed to her ultimatum. He rolled to his side and pressed his palm against her belly, his eyes meeting hers.

Katie turned to her side, pressing her face against his neck, inhaling his sexy, masculine scent. They were silent for a few moments before she pulled back and looked directly into his brilliant brown eyes. "I missed you, too, Dalton."

The edges of his lips tipped up slowly until a full-blown smile registered on his incredibly handsome face. The mischievous twinkle in his eyes sent a tremor through her. This man was dangerous. To her sanity, for sure.

As though they'd just made the final decision for the rest of their lives, Dalton began to right his clothes before standing up and holding out his hand for her. Katie got to her feet and slipped her panties off her ankles. He'd ruined another pair and the thought made her smile.

"So what now?" she asked, handing the panties to Dalton when he held out his hand.

As he tucked them into the pocket of his jeans, he smiled at her. "Now, we go check on Lexi. Make sure she'd doing all right with Austin. I'd like to work on getting her on a horse."

Katie's eyebrows rose. She wasn't sure that was even possible. Dalton seemed to know what she was thinking because he said, "She'll get there. Eventually. You should see her, Katie. She loves the horses."

Katie nodded, agreeing. The way Lexi had lit up that morning when she talked about the horses, and about Dalton, it was evident, she'd found something else to obsess over. And as much as she liked to see Lexi smile, Katie knew it might not turn out the way anyone wanted it to. But that was something she'd have to deal with if and when they got to that point.

"So, dinner? My house?" Dalton asked.

"Sounds like a plan."

After they had climbed down from the hayloft, Katie had spent the next couple of hours following Dalton and Lexi around the stables and the arena while he introduced her little sister to the horses, explaining how they took care of them. He had informed her that it was the same spiel they'd given on Friday, when the day care center brought her, but Dalton wanted to give Lexi a more personal experience.

Needless to say, Lexi had been on cloud nine.

So when Katie informed Lexi that they would be going to Dalton's for dinner that night, she wasn't met with much resistance.

Thank God for small miracles.

Now that it was six o'clock, Katie was pulling down the dirt drive that led to Dalton's house. The one he'd built months ago and recently moved into. Until today, she hadn't been back there since the morning she had snuck out of his bed, a little more than four months ago. Hadn't had a reason to come to the ranch since then either.

As they pulled up to the house, Katie's eyes widened.

It was impressive. Even more so than the last time she was there. The landscaping had been completed on the front of the house, making it look more like a home and less like a construction zone.

Compared to Cooper's old farm house that had been undergoing renovations for the last year, the place Dalton now called home was brand new, although it still had the same country charm as Cooper's place.

The house was white with a deep porch that wrapped around it. Back when she'd come there before, the porch had been empty, now there were several rocking chairs and a few boxes that held brightly colored flowers. There still wasn't a concrete drive, however, there were now stepping-stones that led from the dirt driveway to the house, so Katie pulled up near them and put the car in park.

"We're here," she told Lexi who was sitting silently in the back seat.

"Is this Mr. Dalton's house?" Lexi asked.

"It is. What do you think?"

"It's pretty," she offered before Katie grabbed her purse and slid out of the car.

She opened Lexi's door and waited for her sister to climb out. Expecting Lexi to take her hand, she was completely shocked when her sister bolted for the front porch. That was when Katie looked up to see Dalton standing there, leaning against the porch rail and smiling at them both.

"Hello, ladies," he greeted with that sexy drawl.

"Mr. Dalton!" Lexi exclaimed, running up onto the porch to stand beside him.

"Miss Lexi," he said in turn. "How are you tonight?"

"Good."

Katie approached slowly, a butterfly circus erupting in her belly as she did. Seeing Dalton, being this close to him again made her heart pound and her palms sweat. She had missed him so much. Missed seeing his gorgeous smile.

"Come on in," he instructed, motioning to them both before turning toward the door.

Katie watched as Lexi latched on to Dalton's hand, the little girl looking up at him as though he were some sort of miracle.

And maybe he was.

Katie followed the pair into the house, taking everything in. She could smell food, a delicious aroma that had her stomach growling, a reminder that she hadn't eaten that day. Then again, for the last few months, she hadn't been eating much. Only enough to ensure the baby was getting the nourishment it needed. Some sort of self-punishment, she assumed.

Not that she questioned it. Too much guilt had been resting firmly in her shoulders.

Glancing around, Katie admired the house now that it was complete. The floors were a gleaming dark hardwood, the cream-colored walls bare, still lacking any sort of decoration. She knew he'd been on tour, unable to completely move in, but considering how nice the outside looked, she assumed the inside would've been more complete. She'd been wrong. That or he just wasn't into decorating.

The furniture looked expensive and new. An oversized table that sat eight stood alone in the formal dining area, a single couch and a small end table resided in what Katie assumed was the living room.

She continued through the house, following Dalton's voice until she reached the kitchen. It was opened to the family room, and not much had changed in there either. Although there was considerably more furniture. No longer was there just a lone recliner and a television. There were now two brown leather couches that matched the recliner, filling the space. Unlike the recliner, the couches were a little more worn, probably having made the trek from Dalton's previous house. Clearly, Dalton spent time in that room.

"Mr. Dalton said I could set the table," Lexi declared as she rounded the bar with three plates and silverware in her hands. Her sister didn't slow on her way to the small breakfast nook. With a clatter, she put everything in its place before returning to the kitchen.

"Can I get you something to drink?" Dalton offered when Katie moved closer to the bar.

"Water?" she asked. She was trying to lay off the caffeine as much as possible. It wasn't an easy feat, but she was managing.

"Yes, ma'am."

Katie watched Dalton navigate the kitchen. He alternated between stirring something on the stove and putting ice in three glasses, then pouring tea in two of them and using the dispenser in the refrigerator door to add water to one.

"Would you mind taking the glasses to the table?" Dalton asked Lexi who beamed up at him, clearly excited about the task.

He was good with kids. That she noticed immediately.

Dalton didn't treat Lexi as though she was breakable, and Katie appreciated that. So many people looked at Lexi as though she might shatter into a million pieces from a look. What they didn't know was that Lexi was strong. Stronger than anyone gave her credit for.

Having been through more shit in her eight years than most people had their entire lives, Lexi continued to move forward, never looking back. Katie admired her sister. Sometimes she wished she was as resilient.

"You okay?" Dalton asked as he passed her, carrying a pan to the table.

Katie nodded, realizing she'd gotten lost in her own head.

Time to snap out of it. Time to enjoy the moment, she told herself.

Tonight was supposed to be a fresh start. She knew she should be thankful, but there was still a small amount of fear that resided in the far recesses of her mind, spurred on by her heart. She wanted to believe that everything would work out for them, but thanks to her past and the decisions she'd made, Katie was weary.

But, as she turned to look at Dalton, watching him interact with Lexi, she made a promise to herself.

It was time to stop punishing herself. She was a survivor. And it was time that she let go. Time to move forward.

CHAPTER TWENTY-FIVE

"So, what grade are you in, Lexi?" Dalton asked when the three of them were seated at his kitchen table.

"Third," she said as Katie piled spaghetti on her plate. He had noticed that once he had set the dishes on the table, Katie had gone back to the kitchen and searched until she found the cabinet that held the plates. She retrieved another one and now he knew why. After placing Lexi's spaghetti on one plate, she put the meatballs on another, careful not to include too much sauce.

He hadn't thought about the fact that the little girl may not want her food touching, but now as he watched her, he realized that was exactly the case.

"What do you like most about third grade?" he asked, reaching for the spoon once Katie put food on her own plate.

"Going home," she admitted truthfully.

Dalton fought the urge to laugh. He knew she was serious, but he couldn't help himself. Somehow he managed to hide his smile, nodding.

"What are we gonna do tonight?" Lexi asked as everyone ate.

"Whatever you want," Dalton answered, glancing over at Katie. She'd been quiet since she walked in the door and he wondered what was on her mind. She looked nervous.

"Can we play a game?" Lexi asked, glancing back and forth between the two of them.

"Sure," Katie agreed half-heartedly.

"Or could we watch a movie?" Lexi questioned.

"If you want," Dalton told her. "It's your night, kiddo. If you wanna watch a movie, we'll watch a movie."

"Okay," Lexi stated, turning her attention back to her food.

The three of them ate in silence for a few minutes. Dalton had no idea what to say, and he felt like an idiot. This had been his idea after all. He should've been carrying the conversation, but he was having a hard time. He didn't know what to ask. Didn't know what to say.

Katie was a stranger to him once again. For all the effort they'd put into getting to know one another in the beginning – regardless of how stand-offish she had been – it seemed as though they were back at square one. Or maybe that was his fear talking. They'd made love in the hayloft, which put them as close as two people could possibly be.

And it wasn't that Katie looked like she didn't want to be there. She just looked timid, as though she was afraid of saying too much. He needed to reassure her, to let her know that this was where they belonged. He wanted her there more than he wanted anything else.

Which meant he needed to show her. And then, he got the feeling they would be able to move forward.

Lexi was the first to finish her food, surprisingly eating everything on both plates. She sat quietly, her hands folded in her lap. Dalton wished she would've tossed out a few questions, helped to fill the silence, but he didn't get that lucky. When Katie was finished, he helped clear the table, but she managed to beat him to the sink, insisting on doing the dishes. He tried to talk her out of it, disclosing that he would be happy to do them later, but she refused to stop.

Dalton had no choice but to join Lexi in the den.

"Do you have Frozen?" she asked.

"Frozen?" he asked, confused.

"The movie."

Dalton grinned. It would take him a little while to get used to being around a kid, but truth was, he liked Lexi. Enjoyed having her around. Especially when she smiled. She was so darn cute, with her long black hair and big gray eyes. She looked so much like Katie, it was eerie. They easily could've passed for mother and daughter, except for the fact that Katie didn't look old enough to have an eight year old. Yet she did. Even if she hadn't given birth to Lexi, Dalton knew she'd raised the little girl. And he hadn't been lying when he told Katie she'd done a good job. A fantastic job actually.

Lexi was a great kid and he found himself wanting to watch Disney movies with her just because she asked.

"Let's see what we've got," he told her, grabbing the remote and flopping onto the couch when she took a seat in his favorite recliner. After turning the television on, he hit the necessary buttons to get to the Netflix menu. It didn't take long to find a movie she wanted to watch, although they hadn't found Frozen before she insisted on watching something else.

Katie joined them a few minutes later, taking a seat on the opposite end of the couch from where he was. Dalton watched her for a moment and she must've felt his eyes on her because she glanced his way. When he had her attention, he patted the cushion beside him. She slowly eased her way down until she was sitting beside him.

Without hesitating, he placed his arm along the back of the couch, his hand resting on her shoulder. They might've been having a hard time communicating, but touching her felt right. The feel of her pressed up against his side was more than he anticipated and it wasn't long before she was leaning her head against his chest and he was embracing her, holding her to him.

They finished watching the first movie and Lexi asked for another, so he once again flipped through the menu until she made her selection. He thought she was going to last all night, but the next thing he knew, Lexi was sound asleep in the recliner, her little eyes closed, her mouth slightly open, a soft snore coming from her nose.

Dalton looked down at Katie, expecting to see that she was asleep, but then she moved.

"You doing okay?" he asked.

"Honestly?" she countered.

"Yeah."

"I'm doing better than I thought I would."

"You wanna talk?" he asked, hoping she wouldn't decline.

"Sure."

When Katie got up, Dalton rose to his feet and took her hand, leading her toward his bedroom. It wasn't that he was expecting anything, but he didn't want to wake Lexi and for the time being, he still wanted to hold Katie.

Leading her to the bed, he watched as her eyes widened. "I promise, I'm not trying anything," he assured her, smiling. After their romp in the hayloft, he couldn't promise to keep his hands off her all night, but for now, he really did just want to hold her.

Katie nodded and then joined him on the bed. Dalton reclined on the pillows and pulled Katie up against his side. When she was resting her head on his chest, he exhaled deeply.

"She's a good kid," Dalton told Katie.

"She's got her moments," she replied with a smile in her voice.

"You've done a great job taking care of her."

"Haven't had much of a choice."

Dalton considered that for a moment. "Why'd your mother leave?"

"Guess she got tired of playing mom."

"What about your dad?"

"Oh, he hauled ass the minute Lexi was born. Took me a while, but I finally learned that he hadn't wanted kids. My mother thought having another would force him to stick around. She was wrong."

"So she just left?"

"The day I turned eighteen. Not quite the birthday present I had expected, but I came home from school to find she was gone. I was surprised to see that she'd left the furniture, but all of her personal things were missing."

Dalton squeezed her tightly, willing her to continue.

"So you just picked up where she left off?" he asked.

"I guess you could say that. Although I had been taking care of Lexi for a couple of years by then. I took her to day care, picked her up in the evening. My mother wasn't much of a mother, even when she was around."

"Why don't you share that with people you know?" Dalton knew the question might piss her off, but he needed to know.

Katie sighed before answering. "I don't want her to go through it again. I don't want people to walk in and out of her life. She doesn't deserve that."

"But you have friends who care about you."

"I do. My best friend Sarah lives with us. She helps take care of Lexi when I work. She's the only one I trust."

Katie's admission hit him like a sucker punch. He realized then that he wanted her to trust him. More than anything. More than he wanted to roll her onto her back and climb over her, sliding deep inside her, he wanted Katie to trust him.

But he wanted to make love to her, too. He wanted to rekindle that connection they'd made all those months ago, the connection that had been there in the barn earlier. The need to be close to her overwhelmed him.

Turning so that he could look at her, Dalton took her chin between his finger and thumb. "I want you to trust me, Katie. I know it might take a while, but I promise I won't be that guy. I won't walk away from you."

"But you did," she said, her eyes filling with tears.

"You kinda gave me no choice," he told her, keeping his fingers on her chin, insisting that she look at him. "I tried to get in touch with you, but you didn't want to talk."

"It would've been too hard," she admitted. "I needed... I just didn't want you to get hurt."

"We both got hurt, Katie."

She nodded, her eyes still meeting his.

"It was the hardest thing I've ever done," she told him. "Forcing you out of my life made raising Lexi seem like a cakewalk, Dalton. I didn't want to, but I didn't know what else to do."

"I know," he whispered. "We both could've done things differently."

"Part of me wished you would come after me. That you would fight for me." Katie swallowed hard. "It wasn't why I left. I wasn't trying to force you to do that. I really was trying to protect you. I've just... never had anyone fight for me before."

"It's one of the only things I've regretted in my life. Not forcing you to listen to me, to give us another chance... I live with that decision every day. But you've given me a second chance now. I refuse to let you down again."

"I love you, Dalton."

Katie's soft admission had his heart pounding painfully against his ribs. She'd said it earlier, but he wasn't sure he'd ever get used to hearing it. Those were the most precious words he'd ever heard.

"I love you, too, darlin'," he told her. "I hadn't planned to fall in love with you so quickly, but it happened. And I want to spend the rest of my life loving you." It was a revelation he'd made a long time ago. The only logical reason for his obsession with her. He loved her and he knew that because what he felt for her was unlike anything he'd ever felt for a woman before.

They were finally getting past those walls she had erected around herself and he wasn't going to take that for granted.

Leaning down, Dalton pressed his lips to hers. He'd intended to pull away, but when Katie's hand slid behind his neck, holding him to her, he gave in to the kiss. Sliding his tongue past her sweet, warm lips, he melded his tongue to hers. And when she pulled him closer, he eased over her, pressing his knee between her legs.

"Katie," he whispered, pulling back slightly. "You don't know what you do to me."

"I've got an idea," she said softly, a smile tipping the corners of her pretty pink lips.

"Are you sure this is what you want?" he asked her. "What happened earlier, that could be considered spontaneous. But this... If I make love to you tonight, I want you to stay in my bed. I want to wake up to you in my arms, Katie."

"I want the same thing."

He stared into her beautiful gray eyes, trying to understand what she was telling him, hoping he wasn't mistaken.

"Don't make me wait, Dalton. Love me."

Unable to resist her plea, Dalton sealed his lips over hers, coaxing her lips open with his tongue. When she let him in, the hunger ignited, taking him by surprise and he found he couldn't hold back any longer. He'd dreamed of this for months, held out hope that he'd be here again.

Not that he'd ever expected it, but he had hoped.

Now that he was here, Dalton realized he wasn't nearly as strong as he'd thought he was. Staying away from her had been painfully difficult. And now that she was in his arms again, he knew that he would never let her go again. He couldn't resist her.

Nor did he want to.

CHAPTER TWENTY-SIX

Katie knew she wasn't thinking with her brain. She was giving in to a carnal desire that had consumed her since the first time she'd been with this man. Wanting him, needing him... it was all she'd thought about for so long and now she was here.

In his arms.

In his bed.

She loved him. She'd told him as much and the words he'd spoken back had been what her heart longed to hear. And she didn't want to lose this moment. She wanted to push out the rest of the world, pretend that all of her problems weren't waiting just outside his bedroom door.

So that was what she decided to do.

Sliding her hands over his back, Katie tugged on his T-shirt, forcing it up until Dalton helped her to remove it by reaching behind his head and gripping the cotton, pulling it over his head. He knelt on the bed in front of her, and she admired him for a moment. When he started to lean back down, she stopped him with her hands. "I want to look at you for a minute," she told him, surprised by her forwardness.

Dalton nodded, their gazes held for a brief moment before she allowed her eyes to trail over his body. He was all hard planes and angles, lean muscle, ripped abs. He was, in one word, perfect. Reaching up, she slid her hands over the contours of his stomach, then up the hard planes of his chest as she sat up. Returning her gaze to his, Katie knew then what she'd denied them both for so long. She loved this man. She had loved him at the beginning and she loved him now. He had the ability to crush her heart, but he also had the ability to make her whole. She needed this. She needed everything he had to give her. Right here. Right now. She wanted to be with him, to be complete the way she'd been for the brief time they'd been together.

"Make love to me, Dalton," she whispered before pressing her lips to his chest.

She could feel the heat of his breath against her head as he wrapped his arms around her, his hands sliding down her back.

She kissed a trail up his smooth chest, over his collarbone, then to his neck, savoring the salty taste of his skin on her lips.

Dalton eased her shirt up until she had to pull back so he could slip it over her head. Her bra went next, his deft fingers unhooking it quickly. She allowed him to pull it from her body and then they were both naked from the waist up. It wasn't enough, but it would do for the time being.

Katie eased back down, pulling him to her as she trailed her hands along his body, easing between them so she could free the button on his jeans. It was then that Dalton pulled away. He glanced behind them and Katie knew what he was looking at. Lexi was just down the hall, sleeping in the recliner. If she woke up, she'd surely come to find them.

"Let me close the door," he said and Katie nodded in agreement.

She watched as he stalked across the room, the muscles in his broad back flexing as he moved. The man was so beautiful; it nearly hurt to look at him. He disappeared from the room, leaving her to wonder where he'd went.

He came back a moment later, smiling at her.

"Where'd you go?" she asked.

"Checking on Lexi. She's out like a light."

Katie's heart swelled at his thoughtfulness. He had checked on her sister, making sure she was okay. After all, she was in a strange place. It meant more to her than Dalton could possibly realize.

Expecting him to rejoin her, Katie held her breath when he stopped at the foot of the bed after closing and locking the door. She waited, wondering what he would do next.

When he reached for the zipper on his jeans, her mouth watered with the need to taste him. And when he lowered his jeans and boxers down his legs, she found herself admiring all of him. The first time they'd been together had been in the backseat of his truck, both of them fully clothed. Earlier that day had been spur of the moment, both of them completely clothed as well. She felt as though the few times she'd seen him completely naked hadn't been nearly enough. She was right, because now, as he stood before her, she knew she would never get enough of him.

"I noticed you changed clothes," he told her, nodding his head toward her skirt.

"I showered," she informed him. "I seemed to be missing pieces of my clothes when I got home. Thought it was only appropriate."

Dalton reached for her, pulling her skirt over her hips and then sliding the material over her legs, taking her panties with them. He smiled and she knew he was thinking about the fact that she'd replaced her panties after he'd torn them from her body earlier. The memory sent a frisson of heat sizzling through her veins.

And then they were both naked, staring back at one another. The heat she saw in his gaze as his eyes traveled the length of her body had her insides stirring, her pussy spasming.

His hands began a slow perusal of her body, as though he was seeing her for the first time. In many ways he was. She looked different than before, she knew. Her breasts were fuller, her belly more rounded. Yet, she still saw heat in his gaze.

She needed him.

Katie held her breath when he leaned down and pressed his lips to the inside of her knee, his tongue sliding up her thigh then to the juncture between her legs. Oh, God. She was going to implode. His mouth was hot, the stubble along his jaw sensually scraping her sensitive skin. And when he nudged her legs wider, situating himself between her thighs, Katie wasn't sure she would survive what he would do next.

"Dalton," she whispered his name, a moan escaping when his tongue caressed her delicate flesh. "Oh, God, it's too much."

He didn't seem to care that she was writhing on the bed beneath him. He began circling her clit with his tongue, his thumb brushing her entrance, slowly dipping inside.

"You're so wet, darlin'. I can't wait to bury my cock into your warm, wet heat."

"Please," Katie begged. "I need you inside me."

"Just one more minute," he told her, flicking her clit with his tongue between words. "But first I'm gonna make you come with my mouth."

The dark, sultry sound of his voice sent another bolt of sensation coursing through her. She loved when he talked to her, loved the sound of his voice, the sinful words that he spoke.

It wasn't long before he accomplished the goal he'd been set out for. Her orgasm started in her core, radiating out through every nerve ending until she could hardly breathe from the sheer intensity of it.

And then he was hovering over her, guiding himself into her. He was gentle, but the urgency was still there.

"Aww, damn, baby," he growled when he was fully seated within her. "So tight."

Katie wiggled her hips, trying to increase the friction. He felt so good. The warmth of his body, the gentle scrape of his leg hair against her calves, every sensation overpowered her thoughts until there was nothing left but pleasure.

"I love you, Katie," Dalton said, reaching behind her head and grabbing the headboard as he thrust into her, slowly sliding out. Their bodies were slick with sweat and his chest brushed her nipples, making her crazy with the overwhelming ecstasy of it all.

He continued to rock into her.

Cupping his face with both hands, she stared up at him. "Fuck me, Dalton."

His eyes flared briefly, but then he thrust into her harder than before, his pace increasing, the friction adding another layer of sensation to the overload on her circuits until she couldn't take any more. It was too much, it wasn't enough.

"Dalton. Oh, my…" Katie bit her tongue to keep from screaming as her head thrashed back against the pillow, her orgasm racing through her, more powerful than the first one moments ago.

Dalton continued to fuck her, continued to drive into her over and over and Katie held on, another orgasm building.

"Katie, baby. Oh, love," Dalton crooned. "I'm gonna come. Oh, fuck."

Katie felt him pulsing deep inside her, the gentle pressure of his pelvis against her clit sending her over the edge and into oblivion one more time.

As Dalton spooned behind her a few minutes later, Katie gave in to sleep, linking her fingers with his as his hand hovered over her belly.

"I love you, Dalton."

"I love you, too, darlin'. Forever and always."

∞ ∞ ∞ ∞ ∞

Dalton lay in his bed, unable to sleep as he held Katie close to him. He'd only left her side once and that was to clean up. He had used a warm washcloth to clean Katie as she slept and surprisingly she never stirred. After pulling on a pair of shorts, Dalton had made his way to the den to check on Lexi. She was still sleeping soundly right there in the recliner. He pulled a blanket over her and she rolled onto her side, curling into a ball.

His first thought was that he needed to get her a bed. But then he realized she probably didn't do well with change, so he needed to talk to Katie.

As he lay next to Katie, his arms wrapped around her, he knew he had to tell her. He was ready. Ready to move forward, ready to take this to the next level. He wanted them to move in with him.

More importantly, he wanted to marry Katie.

He could practically hear her rebuttal already. She would come up with some excuse. Maybe she would tell him that Lexi wouldn't be open to moving. Or maybe she'd tell him that she wasn't ready.

He wanted to be ready for anything she could throw at him, so he stared into the darkness, thinking of all the reasons he wanted her there.

It boiled down to the fact that he loved her. Hell, he'd just met Lexi a few days ago, but he already loved the little girl. She had made an impression on his heart much the same way Katie had when he first met her. He wanted to protect them, to take care of them.

And the baby, too.

His heart swelled when he thought about the fact that they were going to have a baby. They were going to be parents.

Unable to hold everything in, Dalton tapped on Katie's shoulder, whispering her name against her ear. "Wake up, darlin'."

"Is everything okay?" she asked as she rolled onto her back, looking over at him.

"Everything's perfect."

Katie smiled, her eyes slowly coming open. "Why aren't you asleep?"

"Just thinkin'," he told her.

"About?"

"Us."

Another smile, this one bigger than before turned Katie's lips up. "Wanna tell me what you were thinkin' about?"

Dalton swallowed hard, steeling himself for the argument he was expecting when he told her what he'd been thinking about.

"Katie," he began, swallowing again.

"What is it?" Her eyes widened slightly and he could tell that she was beginning to worry. So he decided to ease her mind.

"I need to tell you something."

"Okay."

Dalton took a deep breath, exhaled slowly. "When I was eighteen years old, just a few months away from graduating from high school, I got pulled over one night for speeding. What should've resulted in me getting a ticket, paying a fine and moving on with my life ultimately altered everything."

Dalton noticed she was watching him intently, her head turned on her pillow looking right at him, so he continued. "The only thing I had ever wanted in life was to be an FBI agent. I don't know what spurred it on originally, maybe a movie, maybe something I read. Don't know. But it had been my plan from the moment I was old enough to have a plan.

"That speeding ticket turned into a felony drug charge. Still, to this day, I have never bought or used an illegal drug. Never had the desire to. It would've affected my end goal. Unfortunately, the guys I was hanging with at the time didn't have any fancy plans to be in law enforcement and the weed they stashed in my car was proof.

"I went down for marijuana possession. There was a lot of pot found in my car. I knew exactly who had done it, but I never gave him up. Instead, I accepted my punishment, knowing I would have to deal with the felony I would carry with me for the rest of my life. When my music career started to launch, the press got hold of the information and had a field day with it. Took forever for that to die down, but it eventually did."

Dalton closed his eyes briefly, trying to rid himself of the memories from so long ago. "What I'm trying to tell you is that we all make mistakes, we make choices that affect our lives. We learn from them and hopefully, if we're lucky, we come out on the other side as better people. We all have secrets, Katie."

Katie's eyes glistened with what looked like unshed tears. She didn't say a word at first and Dalton wondered what she was thinking. He didn't regret telling her his story. She needed to know. It was something that would forever tarnish his good name. But it was something he'd learned to live with. And he'd put it behind him.

"I wish I was as strong as you are," Katie whispered, her hand coming to rest on his cheek. "And you're right. We live and we learn. That's all I'm tryin' to do as well."

"I love you," Dalton told her with conviction. "I don't care what you do for a living, I fell in love with you. Not your job. I'd be lyin' if I said I was okay with you going back to that life, but if it's a deal breaker, we'll learn to live with it. I only want to make you happy."

"I don't want to do it. I never want to go back to that, but I'll do what is necessary to survive. It's what I've trained myself to do. I'm in it to survive."

"You don't have to do it anymore. You don't have to survive on your own. I'm here. I want to be here." Propping his head up on his hand and staring down at her, he cupped her face with his other hand. "Marry me, Katie."

Her eyes never left his and she didn't jump out of the bed as he had thought she would. The next words that came out of her mouth surprised him.

"Tell me you love me, Dalton."

"I love you, Katie," he replied without hesitation.

"I come as a package deal," she explained, nodding toward the bedroom door.

"I know. I wouldn't want you any other way."

"Are you sure you want to do this?" she whispered.

"Positive." Dalton leaned down and pressed his lips to hers softly before pulling back. "I want to spend the rest of my life with you and Lexi. I want us to raise our baby together. I want to spend every night with you in my bed. And most importantly, I want to grow old with you, Katie. You're my everything. I've known that since the day I met you."

Katie's eyes dropped to his mouth briefly before sliding back up. Dalton held his breath, waiting for her to answer.

"Ask me again."

For a brief second, he was confused, but then it dawned on him what she was referring to.

"Will you marry me, Katie Renee Clarren? Be my wife, the mother of my children. I want to spend the rest of my life making you happy."

"Yes," she said confidently, her soft fingers coming up to brush over his cheek. "I'll marry you."

Dalton was pretty sure he was going to cry, his heart had possibly exploded from the sheer, overwhelming relief he felt.

"Under one condition," Katie added.

Swallowing past the lump that had formed in his throat, Dalton nodded, waiting for her to continue.

"We don't tell anyone for a little while. I want to let Tessa have her day. She deserves it."

"Agreed," he replied, exhaling sharply. "But will you and Lexi move in with me? I don't want to spend a minute away from you."

Katie didn't answer him right away, and Dalton's fear began to ratchet up again.

"Yes, we'll move in. It might take a few weeks. We'll have to work with Lexi, make sure she's on board."

"Understand."

Katie lifted her other hand, cupping his face in both of her hands and Dalton could tell she had something she wanted to say. She'd already agreed to move in and to marry him, so he couldn't imagine what was left, but he wanted to hear it. Whatever it was.

"What's on your mind?" he asked when she didn't start talking for long moments.

"I owe you an apology, Dalton."

Dalton's heartbeat accelerated. He wasn't sure he liked where this was going.

"I get scared easily. And I think that's what happened with you. I fell in love with you so quickly and I hadn't let you in. Didn't share my secrets. When I broke things off, I swear it was to protect you. You're the best man I've ever met. And honestly, I've dreamed of this. Dreamed that things would work out. I was the one who was wrong. You never gave me any reason not to trust you, but I turned my back. Out of fear."

"I'm here now, Katie. And I'm never going anywhere. Do you understand that?" Dalton watched as the tears formed in her eyes.

"I do," she answered. "I really do. I promise you, I'll never hurt you like that again."

"I don't need an apology, Katie. Really. I just want you in my life. That's all I need."

"Well, I'm here," she answered, a smile fixing on her lips. "We're here. Forever if you'll have us."

Dalton returned her smile. "I wouldn't have it any other way."

CHAPTER TWENTY-SEVEN

Two weeks later

Dalton felt the excitement seeping into his blood. Strange how this moment was landing right up there with the top ten most memorable moments of his life.

"What do you think, Lex?" Katie asked when Dalton pushed open the door and the little girl stepped inside.

"Yay!" Lexi squealed, clapping her hands together with glee.

"You really like it?" Dalton asked, relieved.

"It's awesome," Lexi said, running over to the bed and jumping on.

"You did good," Katie told him as she peered over her shoulder at him.

Dalton moved up to her side, wrapping his arm around her waist as he watched Lexi check out her new bedroom.

For the past two weeks, Dalton had worked with Katie and Lexi to put together the design. He had hired a local guy to come in and paint the mural on the wall, had another resident of Devil's Bend make the bed especially for Lexi. And together, he and Katie had set it all up.

Three walls had been painted light green; one had a huge mural of horses running in a pasture. The curtains were dark so that the sun could be blocked out if needed, but when left open, the sun lit up the room, making it look every bit as cheerful as Dalton had hoped.

Even with Lexi's help, he had been worried that the little girl might change her mind. But Sarah, Katie's roommate who Dalton had been introduced to when he first started this process, assured Dalton that she wasn't going to give him an argument. According to Sarah, Lexi was just as excited about their lives meshing as he was, which had made him feel marginally better.

But now, seeing Lexi's radiant smile as she admired her new bedroom put him completely at ease.

"I've got another surprise for you, momma," Dalton whispered to Katie, taking her hand. "We'll be right back, Lex. Okay?"

"Okay." Lexi didn't seem to be at all worried that they were stepping out, so Dalton tugged Katie's arm, pulling her back into the hallway and leading her down to the next room. He must've been thinking ahead when he built the house because he'd included three upstairs bedrooms in his plan, the master the only bedroom on the main floor, and in the coming months, they were actually all three going to occupied.

Sarah was actually going to move in with them for a few months, mainly to ensure that Lexi's routine wasn't disrupted too much, but also to save her a little money while she finished her degree. And Dalton felt significantly better knowing that Sarah would be there when his tour kicked off in July. They'd set up a shorter version than the last one, which would include Cooper and Cheyenne, with Brett as an opener at all the shows. He fully intended to be home when the baby was born, so they had managed to keep the tour in the south and limited it to fifteen major venues. That was something else that had been finalized in the last couple of weeks.

"Close your eyes," Dalton instructed Katie, letting her move in front of him, coming to stand by the closed bedroom door.

"They're closed," she informed him.

Dalton gripped the knob, turned it and pushed the door open, urging Katie to move two steps forward.

"Open 'em," he told her.

"Oh, Dalton. It's…" She turned to face him, cupping his face in her palms. Dalton leaned down and pressed his forehead to hers.

"You like it?"

"It's lovely," she answered.

Dalton allowed her to pull away and watched as she moved around the room, her fingers sliding over the dresser, the changing table, and then the crib.

They hadn't picked out a name yet, but they had learned at Katie's last appointment that they were having a boy. He still remembered that day so vividly.

"Hear that?" the doctor asked, smiling at them both.

"Yeah," Katie whispered.

"That's his heartbeat."

Dalton knew his eyes looked like saucers as he stared back at the doctor. Not only was he hearing their baby's heartbeat, but the doctor just said…

"Did you just say boy?" Katie asked, her voice wobbling slightly.

"I did," the doctor confirmed, using an arrow on the screen to point to a particular area that looked like nothing more than a blur of black and white to Dalton. "There's no doubt about it. It's a boy."

There was no doubt about it, the doctor had said, which was why Dalton had gotten to work having the nursery set up. He had actually cheated, going through magazines with Katie, letting her pick out the bedding and the furniture without leading on that he was going to make the purchase.

With Sarah's help distracting Katie, he'd had it all set up and completed in one day.

When Katie walked back over to him, there were tears glistening in her soft gray eyes and Dalton felt an answering emotion bubble up in his chest. "I love you, darlin'," he whispered.

"Have I mentioned how much I like it when you call me that?" she replied.

Dalton smirked. "I kinda figured it out."

"Did ya now?" Katie replied with a laugh.

"I did. Come on, let's go check on Lexi."

Dalton led Katie back to Lexi's room. Lexi was sitting on her bed watching television. Dalton glanced over to see the opening credits for Frozen coming across the screen. Lexi spared them a quick look, but her attention immediately reverted to the television.

"Hey, Lex, we're gonna be downstairs, okay?"

Lexi nodded.

Once they were back downstairs, Dalton went for the recliner, pulling Katie down beside him.

"What's on your mind?" he asked her when she remained quiet.

"I'm still just a little in shock."

"I'm gonna take that as a good thing."

Katie linked her fingers with his. "The best possible way."

"We've got Coop's weddin' coming up in a week," Dalton informed her. "I'll give them three days after that, since they're foregoing a honeymoon right now. But after that, I'm gonna make the announcement."

"I'm surprised you can wait that long," Katie teased.

"I am too. Trust me. It ain't easy." Dalton cupped Katie's jaw with his hand, turning her head to the side so he could see her face completely. "You still good with this?"

She nodded, more tears glistening in her eyes. "This is more than I ever anticipated. I've spent my entire life watching as my dreams vanished right before my eyes. Sometimes I have to pinch myself to make sure I'm really awake. I hate to say this, but it feels too good to be true at times."

Dalton kissed the tip of her nose and smiled. "I know, darlin'. I've felt the same way. But just think, while those old dreams disappeared, new ones were left in their place. Now it's time we start realizing those dreams. No more livin' in the past."

Katie nodded, glancing around the room.

Dalton looked up, following her gaze. For two weeks, Dalton hadn't been the only one working. Katie had managed to turn his sparsely furnished house into a home. There were pictures decorating the walls, flowers in vases, rugs and accessories scattered about. She had made it her mission to bring their lives together in one place and he couldn't be happier.

Then again, if he only had Katie, Lexi and the baby in his life, he could live without all the other stuff. Because in the end, they were all that mattered. They were the beating heart that kept him going.

The rest… well, the rest of those things were just accessories.

EPILOGUE

When Dalton walked in the door of The Rusty Nail, he was accosted by the familiar scents that he would always associate with his favorite place: cigarette smoke, a culmination of perfume and cologne, all varieties, plus the distinct aroma of beer. The place was busy for a Wednesday night, just as he had anticipated. Not wall to wall bodies like would be there on the weekend, but there was a crowd and tonight, like most nights, he didn't mind.

"Hey! There he is!" a voice sounded from behind the bar.

Dalton met the sturdy gaze of Jack as he stood waiting for Dalton to approach.

"Dalton!" Tessa squealed as she came toward him, squeezing past a couple of cowboys chatting near the bar.

"Hey, lady," he greeted when she threw her arms around him.

"Are they home?" she asked.

Dalton's lips tilted up into the same wide grin he'd been sporting for the last three days. "Yes, ma'am. Safe and sound."

"So what are you doin' here?" Cooper asked as he joined them.

"To celebrate. What else?"

"To celebrate?" Cooper asked incredulously.

"Fine. She kicked me out," Dalton said, laughing. "I think I was hovering just a little too much."

"Well, regardless of why you're here, I've got just the thing to celebrate this special occasion," Eric stated as his head disappeared down below the bar.

When he stood back up, he had a wooden box in hand. Lifting the lid, he spun it around so Dalton could see its contents.

Cigars.

Just what the moment warranted. Not that Dalton smoked cigars, nor did he have any plans to start now, but he wasn't going to tell Eric that.

Cooper came over and slapped Dalton on the back. "Congrats, man. That baby boy is beautiful."

"Thanks," Dalton said, his grin still plastered on his face.

Since the moment his little boy was born, Dalton wasn't sure he'd stopped smiling. Katie's labor hadn't been easy, but there hadn't been any complications and after eleven hours and twenty-one minutes, they were holding their son in their arms.

Tanner Jacob Calhoun.

"So why aren't you at home with momma and baby?" Tessa asked Dalton. She looked over her shoulder and nodded her head at Eric briefly before turning back to face him.

"I'm givin' Katie a break. She's exhausted."

"It's just the beginning, my friend," Brett added.

"And you know this how?" Cooper asked the newest member of their group. Ever since Dalton's last tour with Cheyenne and Cooper that had ended just two weeks ago, Brett Basson had become a regular fixture in Devil's Bend. And by regular, Dalton meant the guy was there every single day. He had worked out an agreement with Jack and was renting Jack's house, the one Tessa had been living in before she moved in with Cooper.

"I've got nieces and nephews, man," Brett retorted, his eyes sliding over to Jack briefly before dropping to the beer bottle he held in his hand.

Dalton studied the two men briefly. He wasn't inclined to believe that something was going on between those two yet, but he got the feeling that things were heading that way. If they thought no one had noticed the attraction they had for one another, then the light was clearly off in that closet they were hiding in. Because even Dalton saw it. And he wasn't one to notice shit like that generally.

Eric walked around the bar, six beer bottles dangling between his fingers. Everyone reached for one, including Jack who had waltzed out from behind the bar to join them as well.

"A toast," Eric announced.

Everyone lifted their bottles, but no one said anything. They were all glancing around.

"Someone's gotta make the toast," Eric announced, laughing.

"Usually when you announce a toast, it means you've got this," Cooper informed the bartender.

"Oh, shit. Sorry. I've got nothin'," Eric stated with a grin.

"I got this," Dalton said, meeting the gazes of each of his friends before he continued. "To dreams. Whether you're chasin' them, lettin' go of them or creatin' new ones, never give up."

"Here here," Cooper stated, tapping his beer bottle to Dalton's. Everyone else followed suit, clanking their bottles and tipping them back.

Dalton watched his friends, grateful. "All right, y'all. I've gotta head back. My wife's gonna need my help." Handing off his beer to Jack, Dalton hugged Cooper, clapping the guy on the back. When he stood back up, Tessa approached, throwing her arms around his neck. He leaned down to her ear and whispered, "I doubt I was the only one who noticed you didn't drink any of that beer."

Tessa released her grip on him and when he met her gaze, he saw her smile. "There's a time and place for every announcement. Katie gave me my day, I'm gonna give her hers."

Dalton nodded his understanding and then tipped his hat at his friends. "Check y'all later."

Fifteen minutes later, Dalton was walking into his house. The first person to greet him was Lexi, the second was Cowboy, one of the puppies that Lexi had recently adopted as her own.

"Dalton!" Lexi squealed, running toward him. Dalton braced himself and leaned over, wrapping his arms around her when she hugged him around the waist. "You're home. Sissy's in the livin' room."

"Is the baby awake?" Dalton asked when Lexi released him.

"Yep," she said, nodding her head emphatically. "Come on Cowboy," Lexi said to the dog. "Let's go play in my room."

Dalton watched as Lexi hopped up the stairs, the little black and brown mutt following close on her heels. When she disappeared at the top, he made his way to the living room to see his wife sitting in the recliner, their three-day-old son nestled in her arms.

"Hey, darlin'," he greeted, leaning down and kissing her upturned mouth before pressing his lips to Tanner's tiny little forehead. "How's he doin'?"

"Great," she whispered. "He just finished eating."

Dalton squatted down beside the chair, gently rubbing his hand over Tanner's downy soft head. He watched the baby sleep before meeting Katie's gaze. "Have I mentioned just how much I love you?"

"Maybe once or twice," she said with a sheepish grin. "But I don't mind hearin' it again."

Dalton smirked. God, he loved this woman.

He'd gone from being single and on the road to having a family in a matter of months. Funny how he had originally thought that a music career was what he was destined to do after his dreams of going into the FBI had vanished. But the more he thought about it, the more he realized that this was his dream all along.

"I love you, darlin'," Dalton whispered to his wife, sliding his thumb along her smooth cheek.

Katie leaned into his touch and whispered right back. "I love you, too, baby."

ACKNOWLEDGEMENTS

To my amazing husband: First and foremost, you are what motivates me each and every day. Your love and support is more than I ever could've imagined. You are the love of my life and my soul mate. I love you.

To my readers: Every day I receive the most amazing emails and letters from those of you who have read my books. I'm moved in more ways than you will ever know by your kind words and your stories. It is a blessing that I can do this, and I have every single one of you to thank for it, but to have the opportunity to interact on a more personal level is the most wonderful feeling in the world. Thank you.

Nicole-Nation: As always, you ladies keep me going every single day. The compassion and love that you show me and each other is inspiring. I love you all from the bottom of my heart.

ABOUT THE AUTHOR

New York Times and *USA Today* bestselling author Nicole Edwards lives in Austin, Texas with her husband, their three kids, and four rambunctious dogs. When she's not writing about sexy alpha males, Nicole can often be found with her Kindle in hand or making an attempt to keep the dogs happy. You can find her hanging out on Facebook and interacting with her readers - even when she's supposed to be writing.

Website: **www.NicoleEdwardsAuthor.com**

Facebook: www.facebook.com/Author.Nicole.Edwards

Twitter: www.twitter.com/NicoleEAuthor

Nicole also writes contemporary/new adult romance as Timberlyn Scott.

Website: **www.TimberlynScott.com**

By Nicole Edwards

The Alluring Indulgence Series
Kaleb
Zane
Travis
Holidays with the Walker Brothers
Ethan
Braydon
Sawyer
Brendon

The Austin Arrows Series
The SEASON: Rush
The SEASON: Kaufman

The Bad Boys of Sports Series
Bad Reputation
Bad Business

The Caine Cousins Series
Hard to Hold
Hard to Handle

The Club Destiny Series
Conviction
Temptation
Addicted
Seduction
Infatuation
Captivated
Devotion
Perception
Entrusted
Adored
Distraction

Writing as Timberlyn Scott
Unhinged
Unraveling
Chaos

Naughty Holiday Editions
2015
2016